GHOSTING IN ON THE BLIND SIDE

Josh Rogan
&
Alexandra Haines

Copyright Information:

Ghosting in on the Blind Side

Authors: Josh Rogan & Alexandra Haines

ISBN: 9798663182720

Published by Rogan-Haines

Palatino Linotype used throughout.

For further information, contact John Haines at:

john.michael.haines@outlook.com

It's January 1913. Nelson, Lancashire, England. Thirty-nine year old Eric Ramsbottom is to play his last ever game for his beloved Nelson Corinthians, the professional football club he has been with man and boy. The Corinthians have been drawn at home to play the famed and feared Manchester United in the first round of the F.A. Cup.

Around the same time, in London, almost three hundred miles away, a desperate race to find a German agent on the run spills out of the nation's capital and moves up north.

Things come to a dramatic conclusion in the Lancashire mill town of Nelson, impacting on Eric Ramsbottom, on the club, and on the town and indeed the whole country, in a way no one would ever have thought possible.

Binewood's Fine Blend
E Ramsbottom
Nelson Corinthians
The Match Day Companion
H & B Binewood & Co. Ltd

Dedication

First and foremost, this book is dedicated to the players from the true golden age of British football – when the game and not the money was king: To Lawton, Dean, Matthews, Finney, TG Jones, Lofthouse – and to all who graced the caseball era – thank you, you were giants then – you are giants now. We salute those of you who are still thankfully with us; we cherish the memories of those who have passed.

The book is also dedicated to those unique characters from the last vestiges of the British Empire; those never say die stiff upper lip types (my daughter and I call them all 'Chillingtons'). We shall not see your like again – more's the pity.

Finally, let me acknowledge the player whose antics on the pitch — namely, staying away from the pack, then at the last second sneaking up on the left of the goalkeeper whose attention, like everyone else's, was elsewhere, then latching on to a stray ball and heading or smashing it into the net — inspired the title of this book. Thank you, Martin Peters. Martin graced the English game with West Ham United, Tottenham Hotspur, Norwich City and Sheffield United, and of course was a member of the 1966 World Cup winning England team. Thank you for – Ghosting in on the Blind Side.

Josh Rogan

Merseyside, UK July 2020

Contents

Contents Continued

1

An Encore with Boots On

Saturday January 11th 1913

IT WAS THE FIRST ROUND of the 1913 FA Cup. In the home team's dressing room there was noise and laughter from most of the players, but this was a bluff as it always was in the dressing room before any game, but far more so before big games like this – Nelson Corinthians had been drawn at home to Manchester United.

Nelson Corinthians were a good, solid first division side; they had never won any honours but they always finished in the top half of the table and won more games than they lost. When on their best form they were more than a match for the big guns such as Arsenal or Liverpool, and on their travels had silenced the massive crowds at Highbury and Anfield on more than one occasion in the thirty years of their existence. Their home ground was Grindlay Park, less than a mile from Nelson town centre, in a valley below the Lancashire moors.

Jokes, cheers, jeers, and hearty boasts about what they would do to the opposing team's centre-forward were in reality efforts to hide trembling, butterflies in the stomach, and even the odd urge to throw up. But one player was neither nervous nor queasy, but nor did he join in the revelry with his team-mates.

Eric Ramsbottom was Nelson Corinthians' thirty-nine year old centre-forward. He did not look his age, was of average height with a slim build, and had a boyish face, brown eyes and sandy coloured hair. He had an almost obsessive dedication to his training which had kept him lean and fit. He ignored the camaraderie which kept his team-mates from running a mile and hiding in the nearest barn before matches, and was something which Eric was usually at the centre of. But not today. Instead, he just sat on the bench in the middle of the changing room, seemingly looking down at his feet; his mind at that moment was far, far away, but his thoughts were then disturbed by a familiar voice.

"Last game, eh?" said Derek 'Lofty' Arkwright, his long time friend and team-mate. Lofty's time at the club from boy to man was only three years shorter than Eric's; but Lofty was also five years younger than Eric and had played in defence for all that time – he was the centre-half and with a physique something akin to a brick wall.

Most teams, whether playing at grand stadiums packed to the rafters each Saturday, or who play in the quagmire to a few hundred fans stood around the touchline, always squeeze a few more years out of the boys at the back. Broad shoulders, thighs like full hams and a head seemingly made of concrete – and an innate desire to keep hospitals busy at weekends, are more important than speed and niftiness. By comparison this makes it even more unusual for any player past their early thirties to still be playing upfront, but as Eric had indeed bucked the trend this meant that he and Lofty had been together through thick and thin, over many years.

"Never mind, mate," continued Lofty, "by next week you'll be glad to be out if it; no more training in foul weather, and you can sit back, relax, and look back on a great career. Still playing up front at forty-nine! Amazing!"

"Thirty-nine," said Eric, in a small voice and still looking down.

"Oh, yeah . . . sorry," said Lofty.

Eric looked up at his good pal and team-mate, and they both burst out laughing.

"Listen, the lads are all feeling as if they could throw up for England; best go and take their minds off things. So, don't forget – I'll punt 'em. . ."

"I'll blast 'em. . ." replied Eric with a smile.

The pair had been saying this to each other since their first day together in the team many years earlier. . .

*

A younger and rather more arrogant Eric Ramsbottom, star of the team, had started the tradition off by strutting around the dressing room and singling out the new boy, one Derek 'Lofty' Arkwright, who was only sixteen but looked – and acted – much older. Eric looked at Lofty and said, "Never mind what Spratty said, just you punt the damn thing up to me, I'll blast it in the net, simple as that. Got it, sprog?"

But Eric got the shock of his life. Lofty had not got his nickname because of high business or political ambitions: he had been the tallest boy in school before leaving to become a brick layer when he was twelve and he was the biggest boy to have ever been in the Army Cadets, but was thrown out for violence before lunch time on his first day – but the Cadets' loss, as well as the building trade's, was football's gain. He stood, raised his fists, and Eric only came round five minutes before kick-off. But to the chagrin of the rest of the team, Lofty rather oddly did as he was asked: he did indeed punt the ball up to Eric as often as he could, and more often than not Eric would blast the ball into the net.

Eric and Lofty became firm friends, even before the swelling on Eric's face had fully gone down.

*

Lofty went back to gee up the lads, leaving Eric alone with his thoughts, musing over the events over the years which had brought him to this very moment. . .

2

Trouble Brewing

ERIC RAMSBOTTOM CONTINUED TO THINK OF TIMES PAST...

He had been involved with Nelson Corinthians since the age of fourteen, starting off as a boot boy, moving on to become an apprentice and then breaking into the A team as centre-forward. He went on to make the reserve team, and then finally at the age of twenty, Eric became the dazzling new star of the first team, finally achieving his life-long ambition of running out onto the pitch at Grindlay Park wearing the prized number nine shirt. It was, thought the younger arrogant Eric, just reward for having given up what was left of his youth to play more than two-hundred games for the reserves on the uneven waterlogged pitch at Solomon's Field, the reserve team's venue for their home games. He was soon to find out that the world of reserve team football was the same from Carlisle to Exeter – the pitches were simply fields, no matter the condition, with goalposts plonked at either end and that was it.

While still very young and with the arrogance literally knocked out of him by his team-mates and trainers, Eric's commitment to his club and much improved conduct on the pitch and in his private life, meant he truly deserved his star status, unlike many other gifted players...

Eric went on to play centre-forward for the first team for eighteen straight seasons, never missing a single game.

However, time marches on: his manager and trainers finally realised that Eric, as per the vernacular of the dug-out, had 'lost half a yard'; he was to the shock and horror of the fans and to most of the town, dropped from the first team.

"I'm sorry, Eric, but it had to come to an end some time, but just think – eighteen years in the first team, that's one hell of an achievement and one I don't think will ever be bettered," said Jack Spratt, the manager of Nelson Corinthians one Monday morning after heading Eric off at the gates to the ground, instead directing him to his office which was part of the lower level of the inner stadium.

"But what the hell am I going to do? All I've ever wanted to do is play football, it's all I know," replied a dejected Eric.

"Well, it's tough, I know, but still . . . thirty-eight . . . we have to think of the future, if we didn't we'd soon have no team at all. . ."

But Eric did not want to know the truth of the matter and could not accept that it was all over.

"Tell you what, I'll put the feelers out;" said Jack, "some teams want older players on short term contracts, mainly for cover and experience; you still won't be playing much longer mind, you'd be daft if you thought that, but someone may be able to squeeze a year or two out of you – what do you say?"

Eric shrugged his shoulders, picked up his bag and went off home.

A week later, he was sold to Hartney Wintney Draymen, a semi-professional team in the North-East Hampshire league.

*

Hartney Wintney Draymen originally consisted only of draymen from Flint and Gore's Fine Ales, a local brewery; but through being such a small firm and with hardly any change in personnel over the years, useful, fit and fast young men developed paunches and grey hair, and their usual standing as a good mid-to-higher table team was soon to be in tatters.

The now vastly overweight, old and unfit draymen had lost all of their games so far in the 1912/13 season.

A short while before Eric was sold on by Nelson Corinthians, the Draymen were playing at home in a traditionally grudge filled derby match against local rivals, Studley-Hitchcock FAAC.

Jebediah Flint, the MD of Flint and Gore's, which meant that he was by such virtue, chairman of the club, rose from his seat in the stand seconds after the final whistle went. The team had lost at home thirty-one nil to the Studs.

Flint looked down at the bowed figures of the entire team: most were holding their sides, some were throwing up, and the remainder were calling to the bench for tankards of beer from the equally overweight manager. On his way out, Flint nodded to his junior partner, Isaac Gore, still stuck to his reserved seat. Gore made no attempt to hide the froth under his nose. Infuriated, Flint missed the postmatch hospitality; he was going straight home to draft a proposal to be presented to the board of directors, suggesting that it was now time to buy in players from outside, something which currently was not allowed as per the terms of the club's articles.

The proposal was duly accepted and rubber stamped at the next board meeting.

*

Two days after the transfer was completed, a highly bemused and also somewhat disappointed Eric Ramsbottom sat in a third class compartment, on the train from Manchester to London. He was, however, also determined to resurrect his football career as best he could. But as the train steamed along, literally, a drama had begun to unfold back in his home town. . .

3

Boardroom Battles

Tuesday morning, 10:00 am.

THE OWNER AND CHAIRMAN OF NELSON CORINTHIANS declared the weekly boardroom meeting in session, and invited the club secretary, Eli Whittle, to announce the apologies and to introduce the first item on the agenda.

"Well, now, gentlemen, although not as much as we would have got for him in his prime, we now have two-hundred pounds in the coffers after the sale of Ramsbottom to the – erm – Hartney Wintney Draymen . . . do you say *the?* Or do you just say the actual name?"

"Get on with it, Eli," said the chairman with a groan; old Eli was known for holding up meetings over trivialities which may be interesting in a different time and place, but was not for the boardroom.

"Very well . . . so . . . what do we do? Is this purely for the players' fund? Or should this be used for improvements?"

But Eli was not to get an answer from any of the board.

A huge roar could be heard from outside.

The chairman and his entire board of directors rushed to the windows of the boardroom on the first floor; they looked down with horror upon a huge mob of angry supporters who had burst in through the gates and were converging on the stadium.

"This is for Eric!" came a yell, and the board moved back rather quickly; a brick smashed right through one of the windows, landed on the table and rolled across and came to rest on the floor near the inner wall of the board room. It had a note tied around it.

As old Eli went to pick it up another brick was thrown, this bore no message of any kind and simply smashed one of the other windows as was the intent; this was followed seconds later by a stone which hit old Eli on the head just as he was reading the note wrapped around the first brick. It simply said, *'This is for Eric.'*

"I declare this meeting closed!" declared the chairman, and may I add. . .

'Every man for himself!'"

And with that the chairman and board dashed out of the door and down the corridor only to be confronted by about fifty of the angry mob; these had forced their way past the watchman and in to the main reception area and up the stairs to the offices and boardroom of the club. They had flung the watchman's crutch out of the window of his hut and ripped up his *Daily Mirror* – right in front of his face.

The newest and youngest director, Maurice Goldstein, stood staring grim-faced at the mob; they were shouting abuse at the very men they blamed for banishing their very own local hero from the club.

But Maurice, while glaring back at the mob, addressed his fellow board members: "Fear not, gentlemen, I am a student of Freud. He says. . .

'The mob who comes face to face with the very objects of its grievance, are a mob no more; their moment has passed; it is ended. . ."

After the mob advanced rapidly on the terrified board of directors, and after Maurice Goldstein had received several hard blows to the head and chest, he again addressed his fellow board members. . .

"Run!"

The board of directors found themselves besieged by not just the team's usual stoic hard core supporters, but by, seemingly, almost the whole town. They wanted to let them know in no uncertain terms of how they felt about the disgraceful treatment meted out by the manager and board to their hero, local boy made good – Eric Ramsbottom.

Even after the local police aided by soldiers from the local barracks had arrived and had broken up the rampaging crowd who had then slunk home – or for some, been forcibly shunted off to the police cells – a certain tension had gripped the town.

There was only one thing for it. . .

*

Eric Ramsbottom alighted from the train onto platform four at Paddington Station. He was met by the chief steward for Hartney Wintney Draymen – and promptly given a ticket for the next train back to Manchester. . .

*

Jack Spratt, the team manager for Nelson Corinthians, was disgusted.

"Eric Ramsbottom's coming back! HE'S COMING BACK . . . TO NELSON CORINTHIANS!"

"Don't shout, Guv', I'm only here; and I ain't deaf! That was Arkwright's stupid joke!" said Jack, rubbing his ear, but he was absolutely outraged upon hearing this startling news from the chairman.

He tendered his resignation within a day of Eric being bought back to the club. This was reluctantly accepted; but Jack had been toying with the idea of telling the board that he was thinking of going anyway; this was due to a running joke, which over the years had become very sour indeed. . .

The first time it had happened more than fifteen years previously, he had laughed out loud along with the entire stadium. Just before kick-off as he sat on the bench in the dug-out for his first game in charge of the team, a small piece of lean, trimmed bacon landed at his feet. 'There you go, Jack! . . . And here's something for the missus!' came the shout from the wag in the crowd; the bacon was soon joined by a very fatty but equally small piece of mutton. The trouble was this had happened at every home and away game since, either as an innocent but well-worn joke if instigated by the teams' own fans – usually a well-off grocer or merchant, and particularly thoughtless in the light of the great poverty which blighted the region – or in mockery if from the opposing set of supporters. The joke, now totally devoid of humour after many years, had worn him down – he had had enough.

On several occasions over the previous season, Jack had decided to pack it in but had then changed his mind; but then the board going over his head with regard to the return of Eric Ramsbottom decided it – he was quitting. When asked in an apologetic tone if he somehow felt his position had become untenable, Jack answered, "Nah, it ain't that, Guv', but yuv made it right 'ard for me to do me job proper. . ."

4

The Revolving Door

SOLOMON GRINDLAY (who, according to the songs and chants of many comedians in the crowd at each home game was – 'born on Mindlay'), was the owner and chairman of Nelson Corinthians; he was also MD of his own company, Grindlay's General Stores.

The little beady-eyed, podgy-faced portly man with lank black v-parted hair, was sitting alone in his office; he had bowed to the pressure from many of the club's fans and a goodly portion of the townsfolk who would not normally exhibit such strong feelings over a football player, but they had indeed done so for Eric Ramsbottom. He knew he would have to find Eric a place in the team, and although it showed disdain for the manager's role by re-signing their former star player, he was nevertheless with the manager in being loath to allow Eric to reclaim the number nine shirt. It would not matter if the whole town camped in his garden all night, there would be no dropping or moving his new bright young star, Dixie Lawton, who was playing as if he could beat Eric's record of seven goals in one game. But there had to be room for Eric, but where. . . ?

Solomon Grindlay took off his little round and thin black framed glasses, stared into the middle distance, put his glasses back on, smiled, put on his hat and coat and left Grindlay Park. He was going to make a quick visit to his late brother Elijah's son, a ne'er-do-well nephew by the name of Samuel Grindlay, pariah to the family, neighbours, and a long, long time ago to his former friends.

Solomon was soon walking through his own leafy residential area. He passed his own large detached house which was down in a valley in the shadow of the Mill town; as he went by, he waved to his gardner and gave him an inane smile which he hoped would let old Ted Palfreyman know he wasn't stopping. Ted put down his hoe and scratched his head as he watched his employer climb up the rough gravelled path at the edge of the last row of the town's smarter detached and semi-detached properties. The path rose a hundred feet or so and then evened out, revealing a comparatively flat area of rough grass-land, although moss, weeds and some rather plain wild flowers readily punctuated the clumps of grass. This was Blindside Common. Ostensibly this was to provide readily accessible green land for the mill workers, but many thought in reality it was a natural *Us and Them* barrier.

Solomon Grindlay reached the eastern edge of the common which bordered what was thought of as being the worst street in Nelson, by both the poor as well as the rich – Garibaldi Street (the joke about it taking the biscuit had become very well-worn indeed). The houses here were in a desperate state of ill-repair; many windows were missing and some roofs had gaping holes which offered their impoverished incumbents no protection against the wild winters which are the norm on the Lancashire Moors. He walked up the steep cobbled street until he arrived at the worst kept terraced house, which is saying something given the general rundown nature of the area. All the windows here were missing; the one single curtain which covered less than half of the front window was filthy and the paint on the woodwork had peeled away. The front step was covered in litter.

Solomon Grindlay halted, tutted, shook his head – then refound his resolve and knocked on the door.

A few seconds later the door was opened and there stood a small but grossly overweight man in his thirties. He wore a filthy string vest, had lank, greasy black hair and wore trousers that looked as if he'd put them on many years before and had somehow forgotten to take them off again. Sammy Grindlay had a corned beef sandwich in one hand and a small bottle of stout in the other.

"Uncy Sol! Wh-what's happened?! Has Mum died?! Has she left me anything?!" hoped Sammy.

"Still the same, you drunken no good lay-about," replied Solomon. "As it happens, your mother is in fine fettle, no thanks to you. Lucky she took up with the Mayor. However, I have a proposition for you. . ."

Sammy stood there, staring at his uncle. Solomon Grindlay thought this was due purely to the shock from receiving a rare visit from his old Uncle Sol, but Sammy stood stock still, and stared . . . and stared . . . and stared. . .

"Sammy? Are you all right?" asked Solomon, now a little concerned.

"Eh? Oh, sorry, the quack says it's the booze; I'm OK now though, it just comes and goes," replied Sammy.

"Hmmm – well, then . . . shall we. . . ?" said Solomon, holding out his left arm, gesturing for the two of them to enter Samuel's homely abode and discuss Solomon's proposition. . .

*

The team's current inside-right, Jonny Allerton, was flexing his elbows as part of the next day's training session. Sammy Grindlay, the pig-ignorant thirty something nephew of Solomon had also joined in the training session, much to the squad's annoyance.

Sammy looked around and mimicked the routine of the rest of the squad and rather enthusiastically at that; in fact, rather too enthusiastically as he flexed his elbows right into Jonny Allerton's face.

"Ooh 'eck, sorry about that, Jonny," said Sammy. "Are you all right?" he added.

"Oh, dear," sighed the insincere Sammy a short while later, as Jonny Allerton was rushed to hospital with a suspected fractured cheekbone.

Sammy Grindlay – the brand new manager of Nelson Corinthians smiled – and then fingered the large white five pound note in his pocket. . .

Eric Ramsbottom was recalled to the first team. He did not complain at getting the number ten shirt rather than resuming his former role as centre-forward; inside-right was still a good position to grab goals, and if he was honest he was just glad to be back in the team at all.

"Here he is! Yeees, he's back!" yelled Lofty as Eric walked into the dressing room just before the next game, and once more put on his boots and donned his kit in the colours of his beloved

Nelson Corinthians.

The rest of the squad cheered and clapped.

"Thanks, lads," said Eric with a big broad grin on his face, but, inside – deep down inside, Eric knew that something was awry.

*

Despite the club chairman bowing to the pressure of the supporters there was still the more than small matter of Eric not being as effective as he once was; in short, he was too old, he was *past it.*

As each game came along there were private meetings between uncle and nephew – owner and manager, about what they should do about Eric, but in the end he was as usual, pencilled in.

But things were soon to change. . .

Nearing the end of one game the now thirty-nine year old Eric had huffed and puffed for most of the game. He even failed to latch on to the ball after a huge punt upfield from Derek 'Lofty' Arkwright, which placed the ball a yard ahead of Eric and with Dixie Lawton waiting in the middle. As Eric breathed hard and then came to a full stop despite the game being in full flow around him, there were murmurs of discontent from the home crowd which worsened as the visitors' right-half kicked the ball up to his own centre-forward, who lashed it into the net with his right foot.

Sammy Grindlay was not fussed in the least, he was only interested in the trappings of luxury his position as team manager had brought his way; he could now afford two extra bottles of stout per night in the Rat and Cabbage and a fish to go with his ha'p'orth of chips on his way home.

But to Solomon Grindlay, the discontent mild though it was at the minute was like music to his ears. He waited impatiently for the match to end so he could have a quiet word with his nephew. The final whistle was blown, by which time the Corinthians had finally overcome Marine, their challengers from Crosby in the first round of the Lancashire Cup. But this was no thanks to Eric; he had spent the last five minutes of the game feeling badly winded and suffering from cramp in both legs.

In the relative but highly undignified quiet of the men's urinals, with most of the crowd now on their way home, Solomon passed on his instructions to the luxury that was tolerated not afforded – his nephew, Sammy.

" . . . So, next match, we'll chance it. Start him as usual but then halfway through the second half bring him off. We'll be one man down of course but we have to test the waters, the man's a damn liability. . . "

"Got it," replied Sammy with a burp, and then another swig from his bottle of stout.

"Oh, you'll get it all right," thought Solomon to himself, as he smiled at one little part of the plan he had omitted to tell Sammy. If all went well then the club would once again be looking for a new manager, as well as finally replacing Eric Ramsbottom with Jonny Allerton.

5

Ebb and Flow

SAMMY GRINDLAY was blissfully ignorant of his uncle's devious nature, with regard to himself anyway. Worse still he knew nothing about team tactics for the great game that is football and was never going to bother to learn.

He settled into the routine of sitting in the dugout with a whole ham on the bone and a large bottle of stout, and leaving such mundane things as shouting instructions to the players to his trainer and physiotherapist. However, today, as a now even fatter Sammy tore into the huge ham and took a huge swig of stout, he would have to make his first managerial decision. . .

It was the 61st minute of the match against Liverpool; the Corinthians were already three down to the visitors but Sammy was not concerned in the least about that. The ball went out of play just by the dug-out; Sammy leapt up and approached the linesman. . .

"'Ere, Jim!"

"The name's Frank; what is it you want? I'm trying to run the line here."

"Tell the ref' we have to bring Ramsbottom off, he's – er – full of cramp."

"He looks all right to me!" replied the linesman, who signalled where the throw-in was to be made from. Seconds after the throw-in, Lofty Arkwright robbed the Liverpool player who had the ball, then shouted, 'Eric!", and pointed to the far right corner of the Liverpool half of the pitch. Eric ran twenty yards upfield, latched on to the inch-perfect pass from Lofty, went round four Liverpool players – and smashed the ball into the net.

"Yeah, OK, he's just scored, but look at those shins! You can see the flints from here – shocking!" ad-libbed the less than imaginative Sammy as Eric ran all around the pitch and then right back to the defence to thank Lofty for picking him out with such precision.

"If you say so," replied the linesman, who waited for the ball to go out of play again, and then waved his flag to get the ref's attention.

A minute or so later with the arms of the physio' needlessly placed around his shoulder, an angry and confused Eric was hauled off the pitch and out of the game.

Although it was to be short lived, Eric had chosen the right time to turn back the years; for Solomon Grindlay the total opposite was true. The crowd were outraged upon seeing Eric forcibly removed from the game; but Solomon, who knew far more about football than his opportunist and clueless manager and nephew, knew it was only a matter of time, and so it was. . .

The next six matches saw an increasingly slow and fatigued Eric Ramsbottom fail to make any impression on the game. Once again uncle and nephew tested the waters. Eric was brought off in the second half of the next game; as he left the pitch he received a few cheers and a hearty round of applause; "Polite – but ominous," thought Eric. "Bloody marvellous!" enthused Solomon, being careful to think it rather than proclaim it out loud.

Sammy just tore into his now standard leg of ham and swigged from his bottle of stout. The same happened with the next four games; although Solomon Grindlay realised it would be a lot more difficult to judge the supporters' reactions at away games due to there being just a handful of wealthier fans who could afford to travel.

But the next game was once again at Grindlay Park. Arsenal were the visitors on that day and things seemed to Eric as if things just could not get any worse. Eric felt so fatigued during the game that he signalled first to his team-mates, then to the referee and then to the bench that he was coming off of his own accord.

Solomon Grindlay smiled smugly. The time was now ripe to let Ramsbottom languish in the reserves, or retire, or die; he didn't care one iota. . .

6

More Comebacks than Frank

JONNY ALLERTON had been kept sweet through the club ordering bags of coal and a full week's groceries for his mother for the last seven weeks. As the surprised but delighted Mrs Agnes Allerton had taken delivery of the first instalment of payment in kind, the delivery man took off his cap and smiled.

"Our pleasure, Maam; and may I add, all at Grindlay's General Stores wish a speedy recovery to young Jonathan."

"Gerraway with yer, Bert, you live next door, you daft ha'p'orth!"

Bert blushed and smiled. "I know, but boss's orders; anyway. Oh, tell Henry the darts start at nine tonight, the Wakes Committee are having their meeting first. . ."

"Will do, Bert, tata," said Mrs Allerton.

*

Eric Ramsbottom's descent into footballing mediocrity had reached crisis point – for Eric – and maybe a new dawn for Solomon Grindlay and the club.

While sat alone at home in his bachelor pad (which basically meant his Mum had passed away three years earlier, and his sister Mary had gone to live in her friend's house), Eric sighed, and with his current fortunes in mind or rather lack of them, Eric Ramsbottom decided to hang up his boots. He had after all, he thought, enjoyed a long and in the main a distinguished career. He held every club record and he had even continued on into his late thirties playing for the first team, and apart from the last couple of years he had been up to the task in both body and spirit.

"Yes," Eric said to himself, "I'll go now before I make a right prat of meself."

As it was coming up to Christmas, Eric thought it rather timely to announce his retirement as he could then enjoy the festivities without worrying about over indulging. The Christmas and New Year period saw all professional teams play twice as many games as normal, with the players under the strictest of orders to watch their intake of food and drink.

Eric told Solomon Grindlay the very next day, and told him that it was with immediate effect. Solomon Grindlay was not too sure if he was happy or sad, as he had only been seconds away from setting in motion the cancellation of his contract.

First team training started at 10:00 am every week day; at 10:07 am on the Monday morning there had been no sign of Eric.

Solomon Grindlay had taken out a notepad and pen from his desk drawer; this was so he could write to Eric to inform him that regretfully, due to a very serious breach of the conditions of his contract, he had no option but to bring his twenty-five years at the club to an immediate end. But by 10:08 am Eric Ramsbottom had knocked on his door, totally bypassing the manager's office. To try and go via the correct chain of command would have been pointless anyway, as Sammy Grindlay was at home fast asleep in bed, sleeping off a hangover.

Eric informed the chairman of his decision; in return Mr Grindlay stood up, said he understood how Eric must feel and that he sympathised, and then both men shook hands.

"Close the door on your way out," said Solomon Grindlay, as he sat back down again.

As Eric went off to say a second final goodbye to his team-mates, Solomon Grindlay still had a use for the pen and paper after all.

"Dear Mr Grindlay. . ." began writing Mr Grindlay.

Although he was not to know it just yet, Sammy could, if he wished, sleep in the next day, and the day after, and the day after that. . .

Samuel Shadrack Grindlay, the ne'er-do-well pig-ignorant nephew of Solomon Grindlay, was about to be sacked.

*

Christmas 1912

Eric, determined to make a clean break from football, took himself off to the Lake District. The weather was too bad to enjoy the full range of the usual outdoor pursuits associated with the area, but a nice week in a nice hotel, good food, good company and hopefully a few laughs would take his mind off the worries over what his life outside football was going to be like. The irony here was that whether walking about the town, or relaxing in the hotel's bar or restaurant, or even on the lower slopes of a Lakeland Fell, he was instantly recognised. Eric would then patiently sign autographs, and relive his greatest moments in his beloved number nine shirt. But he enjoyed every minute.

In the middle of Eric's holiday there was a knock on his hotel bedroom door. Eric opened up and there stood a Post Office telegram boy.

"Cor! Are you Eric Ramsbottom from Nelson Corinthians?!" gushed the boy.

"I was," said Eric, who snatched the little envelope out of the boy's hand, shut the door, sat on his bed, ripped open the envelope and read the telegram:

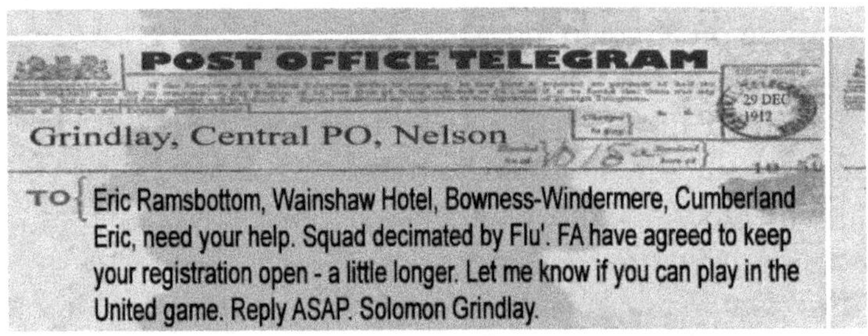

POST OFFICE TELEGRAM

29 DEC 1912

Grindlay, Central PO, Nelson

TO Eric Ramsbottom, Wainshaw Hotel, Bowness-Windermere, Cumberland
Eric, need your help. Squad decimated by Flu'. FA have agreed to keep your registration open - a little longer. Let me know if you can play in the United game. Reply ASAP. Solomon Grindlay.

"No! No, no, no!" said Eric, "Damn cheek of the man! Well tough, I'm finished with football and that's that," said Eric, firmly to himself . . . sort of.

*

A few days later. . .

"What time is the next train to Nelson please. . . ?" said Eric, to the porter at Oxenholme Station. . .

7

Team Sheet Blues

ERIC ARRIVED BACK IN NELSON on the morning of Saturday January the 4th. He wondered whether he should call in at the club, but as Nelson Corinthians had a home game in the afternoon against Sheffield Wednesday, he decided not to; the chairman had not mentioned this game, only the next week's vital FA Cup clash, so for the sake of decorum and to prevent any awkwardness, he decided not to, and instead called at Lofty's house. Eric knew that Lofty never varied his match-day routine, and that he would be sat in the front room, relaxing and reading the morning paper before leaving for the ground about 12:30 pm.

"Eric! What are you doing back here? Fall off Scafell, then?!"

"Nah, nowhere near there; stayed in Bowness, right on Lake Windermere. It was nice, but bloody freezing. I didn't think anywhere could be colder than round here in winter."

"Yeah, went round there as a kid a few times; got bored to be honest. One time I was that fed up I ate seventeen bars of that mint cake they sell up there, sick as a dog. Trouble is, me Mam was waiting for the day I got better, then I got hammered for being stupid."

"Blimey, should have ate fifty of 'em, it'd have been more merciful," joshed Eric.

"So – er – what are you doing back early; thought you were away for a month?" said Lofty.

Eric blushed. He had automatically assumed that Lofty, as well as the rest of the team would know he had been recalled for the United game. Although Lofty did not say he didn't know, Eric could tell this was the case purely due to the absence of the topic from their conversation.

"Bloody hell, Lofty, this is really awkward, thought you'd know. I'm playing next week, Grindlay sent a telegram; said the team's been hammered with the flu'. Didn't he mention it to the lads?"

"Playing in the United game?! Blimey, no, Eric, sorry, mate, not a clue. You're sort of right about the flu' though; funny, the rest of the team's OK, but all the lads upfront got it: Tad, Johnny, Dixie, Jack and Bumfluff. Front Line Fever they're callin' it. Ah – the sneaky so and so!"

"What? What is it?" asked a surprised Eric.

"I dunno whether he definitely promised you a game, but my guess is, he's just maximising his options. Sure it's the flu', but some blokes can shake it off overnight. Tad and Jonny are fine again, but Jack, Dixie and Bumfluff are still poorly, in fact Bumfluff's in Nelson General; touch and go, or at least it was."

"You're kidding!" exclaimed Eric.

"Nope, and as he's a left footer – Ha! Ha! Left footer! He is, too! Anyway, he's had the priest in. He went to give him the Last Rites, but Bumfluff came round, sat bolt upright and told him to do one; well, more than do one. He's apologised since; he's a bit better but still poorly. But the thing is, he's on the left-wing; remember Spratty's reshaping that time to confuse some of the big guns? Stuck you out on the left? Didn' work, did it?"

Lofty was actually being kind. Not only had it not worked, Eric's three games as an out and out winger had been a total disaster.

"You ain't kidding. Blimey, so I'm around just in case Dixie or Jack are still crocked?"

"Er – well, probably just cover for Dixie; Jack's inside left, can't see the boss puttin' you there either."

"Well . . . I have played there: all you do when you're just covering, is line up on the left; but once the game's underway you drift into the middle when you can, then run back over to the left again when the attack has broken down. But you're right, not the best thing in a big game. So – er – is Dixie on the mend? Or is he still bad?" asked Eric, as diplomatically and as matter of factly as he could.

Lofty smiled. "He's on the mend. But – just remembered, I think you'll be OK; have a guess why?"

"He's leaving?" secretly hoped Eric.

"Nope. Have another guess."

"Come on, Loft', just spill the beans."

"OK, he's suspended, for a month. He had a right old set-to with that full-back at Villa – er – Freddie . . . er. . ."

"Freddie Miles?" offered Eric.

"Yeah, that's him. Good player, too, but – and you've gotta laugh – Dixie had a painful corn, and Freddie stood right on it! Dixie fell to the ground, clutching his foot, then as Freddie went to tackle Tad, Dixie got up, ran over and thumped Freddie on his bonce! Next thing is, they were brawling. I pulled Dixie away, and the Villa skipper dragged Freddie off. Both of them sent off and both suspended for a month."

"Well, why didn't Grindy just say that then? Instead of all this flu' rubbish."

"Well, it ain't rubbish really, is it? Even before his corn got crushed, Jonny was already looking as white as a sheet in the Villa game. I suppose Grindy couldn't cram the lot in a telegram, so he just went with the flu'; knowing him he'll go for the three letter option over a longer word."

"So you think I'll get a game, then?"

"Ooh 'eck, Eric, that ain't for me to say, is it? But as things stand and if nothing changes, then you may well get the nod. The only other half-decent cover we've got is some hulking thug in the A team. He's bigger than me, OK with his head, but he can't really play. But it's down to old Jock, unless Grindy over-rules him. That's been happening as well lately but Jock just puts up with it. Spratty wouldn't have done; he'd have told Grindy to sling his 'ook."

"Yeah;" smiled Eric, "and then found himself slinging his own hook five minutes later!"

"S'pose you're right," said Lofty.

"I'd better go then, Loft', you'll be off shortly."

"Er – no."

"No? You're not suspended as well, are yer?"

"Nope. Grindy told old Jock to put the entire reserve team out today. He's given up on the League; can't say I blame him: we're eleventh, twenty points off the top five and eight points ahead of Notts County in twelfth. So Grindy thinks we can take a hammering today as it won't make the slightest difference; he's not risking any of the first team getting injured or sent off and such, so we can make sure the strongest team can be put out against United. Jock put up some resistance, but I think it was only for show. So, no footy for me today."

"I hope Grindy knows what he's doing. D'ya know you're not supposed to put a deliberately weakened team out?" said Eric.

"Yeah, I know, but if it's good enough for the Arsenal and that, it's good enough for us."

"Ha! Arsenal can afford the fine, I bet we can't," sneered Eric.

"Yeah, well, boardroom crap, nowt to do with us. Anyhow, got an idea. The family is off to Rhyl today, staying over; my Uncle Ted lives there. Fancy coming along?" suggested Lofty.

"Oh – er – no, mate, can't impose on a family trip like that. I'd best be off, and I'll see you when you get back."

"You'll do no such thing, Eric Ezekiel Ramsbottom!"

It was Mrs Arkwright, who had just come in from the shops and had overheard his son and his friend.

"Hello, Mrs Arkwright," said Eric with a big smile. "How's me second Ma?"

Mrs Arkwright smiled, said nothing, but held her arms out. Eric stood and hugged this very special lady.

When they broke apart, Mrs Arkwright passed on belated but deliberately subdued seasonal greetings, and then made a suggestion.

"Were you planning on seeing Mary today?"

"Yes, definitely. I was going to call in after here."

"Best get over there then, sharpish. Tell Mary to get her jarmies and spare bloomers together; she's coming, too."

At this, Lofty smiled and blushed. He hoped no one had noticed, but two knowing smiles let him know they had.

Eric knew flim-flam from the real thing. If Lofty and his mum said they wanted the company of the Ramsbottom siblings, they really did.

"OK, Mrs A. I'll go over there now. What time are we leaving?"

said Eric.

"After dinner, we're going by bus; my brother Ted's hired one for us all. Oh, almost forgot, can't leave little Bonnie out now, can we? Tell Mary to bring her along as well."

"Will do, and thanks; we'll be back shortly after dinner."

"You'll be back before dinner, soft lad, all three of you."

Eric looked at Lofty, who just grinned, and Eric grinned back.

"See you in a bit, then," said Eric.

As Eric left the Arkwright residence to make the short walk to the Wilkes household on Thraxton Avenue, an embarrassed Lofty, who was already suffering a touch of the post-holiday blues and had pestered his mother to take the decorations down early, thought that he had best maintain decorum.

"Eric!"

"Yeah?"

"Happy New Year!"

Eric turned back, forced a smile, waved, and walked on. He hadn't forgotten himself, but not only had the festive spirit, as usual, done a bunk straight after New Year proper, failing to hang around for the Three Wise Men, the sad fact was, New Year was far from his favourite time of year as his father had collapsed and died while out first-footing a few years previously.

A Rare Welsh Bit

IT WAS ONE OF THOSE CLEAR, crisp, cold but invigorating January days, and the low January sun played at pretend summer, as only low January suns can.

Everyone was wrapped up in their heaviest and warmest outdoor coats and scarves and their wooly hats. It was freezing on the bus, but this didn't stop the journey to Rhyl in the brand new Leyland S330T motor coach being an enjoyable one.

The motley gathering consisting of the extended Arkwright family, Eric and Mary Ramsbottom, Bonnie Wilkes, and several friends of Seth and Marj Arkwright, chattered, laughed and joked and even sang with great gusto as the bus trundled slowly down through Lancashire, skirting the edges of Merseyside, down into Cheshire and then over the border into Wales. It allowed Eric to dismiss, for now, thoughts of whether he was wasting his time coming back to Nelson Corinthians, and gave him some respite from the worry of what he was going to do with his life from now on.

A very tired yet red-faced coach party with numb backsides and dead legs were highly relieved when the coach finally pulled up outside the Ruthin Hotel in Rhyl, at just after 9:00 pm.

Marj Arkwright's brother, Ted Cotton, was there to greet them all. He was the high flier of the Cotton family and was the owner and manager of the Ruthin Hotel. But Ted had no airs or graces which would have prevented him from bestowing generous helpings of his good fortune on all those who knew him, and some who didn't.

"Blimey, you're late!" said Ted. "You'll have to go straight through for dinner."

"We had to make a few stops, Ted, you know how it is," replied Marj. "Ee, it's good to see yer; come 'ere!"

After Marj finally broke away from Ted, there were further rushed hugs, handshakes and belated seasonal greetings, and then Ted directed the coach party from Nelson straight into the dining room.

The meal was huge, although of course highly enjoyable: steaming hot onion soup, a turkey dinner with all the usual trimmings and more, and, due to Ted's time at sea as a lad in the Royal Navy, huge bowfuls of unusually potent rum-sodden figgydowdy, washed down with more rum as piping hot as the soup, or, for the less adventurous, tea or coffee. Even Eric enjoyed the special atmosphere generated by the establishment, which unlike both Eric and Lofty, stayed the seasonal twelve night course, thus dutifully honouring Gaspar, Melchior and Balthasar. But the coach party were so bloated that even a tree, streamers, baubles and lights could not take away that heavy stuffed feeling. The gathering afterwards in the main hotel bar was a subdued affair, and very soon the party retired to bed for the night.

Eric and Lofty were in a twin room, and after getting into bed, Eric's thoughts once again returned to the now doubtful reclaiming of the number nine shirt for one last outing.

"Do you think I've done the right thing?" asked Eric, while staring up at a spider, slowly making his way down the single vertical strand of silken thread.

"Oh, yeah, me Mam would have murdered me if you hadn't come; she'd have said I put you off or summat."

"Not coming here, clot! Coming back to the team!"

"Oh!" said Lofty with a laugh. "OK – now – don't take this the wrong way, will you? I want you to play for sure, but it doesn't actually matter, does it? You either play, or you don't, and even if you do, it really will be your last game anyway. I don't think it's worth worrying over, being honest. . ."

"D'ya know, you're dead right as usual. Funny how I couldn't see it that way – worrying about this and fretting about that; all pointless."

Eric went on to give more reasons as to why it was just as well he was quitting, but this also proved pointless as Lofty was now fast asleep.

After the Nelson coach party had had a full fried breakfast and had consumed several pots of hot steaming tea the next morning, Eric assumed it would be a case of getting togged up, picking up a flask from the kitchen and braving the elements for a constitutional along the promenade.

"Finished? Good," said Lofty. "We're off to watch our Alfie play for his Sunday League team."

"Blimey, you'd think our lives were just all about football and nowt else," said Eric, rather tongue in cheek.

"Your point being. . . ?" replied Lofty.

The two friends, as they so often did, laughed at their own inane banter.

A fleet of taxis, again courtesy of Ted, took the entire Nelson contingent out to a windswept field on the very edge of Rhyl. The pitch had originally been a common, but it had been especially flattened and was annually re-grassed; the grass usually lasted from the start of the season in August, to the end of August. The pitch today was rock hard.

It was so cold that apart from the two managers, only the Lancastrians on an overnight jolly were either brave enough or foolhardy enough to stand on the touchline for just under two hours, no shelter at all, totally exposed to the elements. But all were well wrapped up and the fun of the occasion helped take the bite out of the air.

Kimnel Bay Rangers, which had Alfred Cotton as their goalkeeper and captain, were to play Llanfair PG Athletic in the first round of the Morgan Cup; a competition for amateur Saturday morning and Sunday League teams from all along the North Wales Coast. It used to be called the Liverpool Bay Cup, but strong protests about it not being obvious it was for Welsh teams, saw the competition and trophy duly renamed after the man who had paid for the solid silver cup some ten years earlier, so the Morgan Cup it was.

While the teams were getting changed just further along the touchline to the embarrassment of the females in the company, Lofty was distracted by a whistle; it was his cousin, Alfie. Lofty went to see what he wanted while Eric looked around, saw his friend had gone, looked down the touchline, and saw Lofty talking to his young cousin. He saw his friend frown, look down, scratch his chin, smile, nod his head, and then run back towards the gathering of family and friends.

"What's up?" asked Eric, as Lofty rejoined the gathering.

"Not much, but Alfie wants to ask you something. Won't be long, folks, be back before you know it," replied Lofty, turning to his bemused family and friends.

Lofty and Eric were not back before they knew it; in fact the game kicked off and they still weren't back. Neither reappeared until a throw-in to Kimnel Bay, just by the Nelson contingent on the touchline.

"That's your Eric!" screamed Bonnie.

"That's our Lofty!" shrieked Marj Arkwright.

Indeed it was. But they were soon to find that for the next ninety minutes plus the half time break, they were now Hugh Jones, centre-half, and Bryn Elwys, centre-forward, new signings for Kimnel Bay Rangers. The gathering learned this from rushed whispers as both Eric and Lofty briefed everyone on the touchline to be rather careful when cheering them on.

"Come on . . . Hugh!" yelled the Arkwright family.

"Go on, Er-Bryn!" yelled Mary and Bonnie. "Ooer!" added Mary.

One star centre-half and one town hero in a number nine shirt a winning team does not necessarily make. Kimnel Bay Rangers were three down with twenty minutes gone. Although Lofty had done his bit in preventing at least four more otherwise certain goals, Eric had not yet played his part, but that was soon to change.

"EricBRYN!" came a yell; Eric knew who was shouting, and he knew why, and he knew where to go. He also smiled at the slip, for which even the immediate correction was rather comical.

Eric ran straight up the centre of the pitch, leaving the Llanfair PG defence wondering what he was up to; in fact their centre-half made way for him: it was either that or get mowed down. But how he wished later he had stood his ground. Just inside the penalty area, the ball landed at Eric's feet and he smashed the ball into the net. Eric tried to do the same again less than a minute after the restart, but the PG lads were not that daft, and duly sandwiched him while the referee wasn't looking.

"Bryn." This time it wasn't a shout; Lofty was right next to Eric in the centre circle. "I know it was no use for us, at home that is, but go on the wing – I don't think they can defend any sort of byline play. Trouble is, the right-winger's not up to much and can't take advantage, so we'll swap you over; I mentioned it to Alfie and he agrees it's worth a shot. If it doesn't work, then it doesn't really matter, just go back in the centre."

With a dejected right-winger swapping with Eric, the change in fortunes was dramatic. Although Eric was not an accomplished winger in the professional sense, he was still a gifted ball player. With his lack of fitness and speed negated by playing an amateur team, Eric jinked and feinted, and dribbled and ran. For the goal that would make it 3-2 to the visitors, Eric simply dashed along the byline, whipped the ball in, and who else but Lofty rose majestically to head the ball into the top right of the net. The equaliser was even better. Eric and Lofty did a series of one-twos all along the right-wing, then Eric slotted it through to the Bay's inside-right, Jack Bovey. Jack, a quick learner, ran past the opposing centre-half, but lifted his right foot, slotted the ball back to Lofty, who slipped it right again to Eric who chipped it right back to fall at the feet of Jack Bovey, who, due to the bemused goalkeeper being unsure of which way to look never mind dive, simply slotted the ball home.

It was 3-3 when the halftime whistle went, but for Kimnel Bay Rangers their jubilation was soon to turn to disappointment.

Over slices of orange and sips of hot tea on the touchline, Eric shared some worries with his good friend.

"Hey, Lofty, just thought," said Eric.

"Sorry, talking to me; your good pal, *Hughie?*"

"Ha! You can talk! Ok – Hughie! Anyway (now whispering, just in case), Hugh . . . if I get crocked here, and I do get picked next week, then the whole town will hang me if I can't then play." Eric had suggested something along these lines before the kick-off, but, rather foolishly perhaps, had still agreed to play after hearing

Lofty say he'd watch out for him all the way. But Lofty hadn't stopped the illegal sandwich, and it had made Eric think again.

Eric sighed and turned to Alfie and the rest of the team.

"Listen, lads, I'm sorry about this but I won't be able to play the second half; I. . ." But before he could continue, he saw the sea of crestfallen faces, especially Alfie's.

"I . . . er . . . well . . . it's just that . . . stuff it, I'll carry on. Lofty, just you keep any maulers, brawlers, stampers, diggers and stompers well away from me, do you hear?"

"Got it; in fact I'll stay just behind you, and belt back if I have to."

Eric's just as rapid further change of mind was just as much swung by the perceived conduct of Solomon Grindlay as the sadsack faces all around him.

The referee then signalled the restart, and from the first second of the second half, Lofty was as good as his word – almost. No one got anywhere near to Eric, not for most of the forty-five, anyway. But a somewhat wiser Llanfair PG had begun to suspect they had a couple of ringers to cope with, and duly gave up attacking and simply packed their own penalty box. They were so good at it that not even Eric could find a way through, and, amateur game or not, he was beginning to tire as he had done in the last few professional games he had played for the Cornithians.

But in the eighty-sixth minute of the game, the right-winger, duly restored to his usual byline duties, floated a pearler of a ball into the centre of the PGs penalty area. But as Eric rose to meet the ball, two defenders brazenly obstructed Lofty, while another two pulled Eric's shirt and pressed on his shoulders and dumped him unceremoniusly on the ground. But it was spotted. The whistle went. Penalty.

After hasty consultations with Alfie, it was decided that Eric should take the penalty. Eric was soon to find that being free of nerves, butterflies and all the usual pressures which go with taking a penalty, is not always a good thing.

He placed the ball on the uneven spot, walked back five paces, ran forward, and hit a lame shot right at the goalkeeper – but not so lame that the goalkeeper made a clean catch, but he did manage to thump it well clear of the goal.

But. . .

The ball dropped at Lofty's feet; he simply lashed at it, and a thunderball of a shot flew right past the stunned goalkeeper. 4-3 to the home side.

However, the celebrations both on the pitch and off were so raucous, that the home team had failed to reshape properly for the restart, and the PGs inside-right simply passed the ball to the PG centre-forward who simply lobbed the ball towards the Kimnel Bay goal. Alfie, who had ran forward to join in the celebrations, ran back frantically; he reached the goal-line, turned, jumped, and just missed the ball which plopped behind him and came to rest at the back of the net.

4-4.

Eric was then to see something which he had not seen at professional level. In the dying seconds of the game, the goalkeeper, Alfred Cotton, had joined the rest of the team in filling out the opponents' penalty area to see if he could make the one extra man count before the full-time whistle.

"Blimey, an' after what's just happened. . ." muttered Eric to himself. But he thought he would try to help make it work.

He pounced on the first loose ball, threaded it through to the left-winger, just to confuse everyone, and then ran into the middle.

"Alfie! Join me here, wait for the cross!"

Alfie did as he was told. The cross came in, Eric went up, headed the ball down, and Alfie raced through, and not too unlike Lofty, hit a rocket of a ball which almost burst the back of the net.

Before the ball could be fished out of the net, the full-time whistle went.

The final result: 5-4 to Kimnel Bay Rangers.

Mary and Bonnie ran on to the pitch to hug Hughie and Bryn, but were immediately ordered off again by the referee.

After they had ended their sojourn as two Welsh chancers, the changed but still filthy Eric and Lofty were besieged by their families and friends; they all wanted to know how they ended up playing for Kimnel Bay Rangers.

Lofty, seeing suspicious looks from the other team further down the touchline, put his finger to his lips, and directed the party back to the fleet of taxis who had just begun to arrive to take them back to the hotel.

It turned out that, rather ironically, the proper centre-half and centre-forward had both gone down with the flu', and if Eric and Lofty hadn't played, then the team would have had to have forfeited the game.

After getting cleaned up, the Nelson contingent had lunch in the dining room, and were then free for an hour or so to go for a walk, or just relax in their rooms or in the hotel bar.

Eric and Lofty opted for a short walk, asking Mary and Bonnie along. While Bonnie linked Eric in a 'he's like my brother' fashion, Mary held hands with rather an embarrassed Lofty. But the somewhat clueless men from a northern mill town were the ones nice and safe on the inside, with the two young ladies on the outside. But Mary and Bonnie did not care; they knew the two friends were good and true men; decorum in this sense mattered not.

The four friends were then greatly amused at the idea of buying and eating ice-creams on a freezing cold day, but this they did, and thoroughly enjoyed them as they strolled along the mostly deserted promenade, with only one in about ten shops or cafes of any kind, still open.

"That skipper of theirs knew, you know," suddenly said Eric.

"Of course he did," said Lofty.

"Eh?"

"That was Cousin Malcolm. But he owes Alfie one: he caught the Llanfair team playing thirteen men during one game when it got foggy towards the end, but said nowt."

"Flippin' 'eck!," said Eric, "But what about the ref? They sometimes get drafted in to cover English games; what if he recognised us?"

"Cousin Cadfael, you mean?"

"Blimey," said Eric.

9

The Ball in His Majesty's Court

Monday January the 6th 1913

ERIC COULDN'T PUT IT OFF ANY LONGER. Despite feeling that Solomon Grindlay had not given him the whole story, he nevertheless had agreed to come back, and so even if it were not to happen due to all of the front line making a full recovery, Eric felt he needed to be good to his word. But he nevertheless wanted to clear the air.

He knocked on the door of Solomon Grindlay's office.

"Come in," came the familiar voice. "Ah, Eric!" he added, as he considered his visitor as he walked into the office. "I wondered when you'd show up; getting worried. Thanks for – er – being on standby. Sit down, sit down, Eric; there, that's it. So, how's things?"

"That's just it, isn't it? The thing is, Mr Grindlay, I've promised myself that I would speak my mind today, even if it means we part on bad terms. You said, or at least seemed to imply that I would definitely be playing, but I hear that that's not actually the case, is it?"

"Now see here, Ramsbottom! (Eric noted the 'Ramsbottom'.) I didn't promise that as such, I asked could you play? I am sorry that I didn't add *if needed* or *if necessary*, but there's only so much space on a telegram and they're damned expensive things at that. I may as well be totally clear, right here and now: Surprisingly, most of those who were ill, are now fit again, apart from Bumf– er – Bullfern; very sad. No doubt Arkwright has also told you about Lawton? Damned fool. But I have to be honest and say that I hope Haskell can play – it's only right and fair, as I told – er – discussed with Mr Shanksby. Not sure if you know Haskell or not – tough lad, could do both yours and Arkwright's jobs in one go, but he's having problems with the police, some jewel robbery; he denies it of course, but we'll have to wait and see. If he takes a holiday courtesy of His Majesty, then I would need someone to step in. I'm a fair man, Mr Ramsbottom (Eric smiled at the addition of Mr), and I can overlook this tantrum, if we can come to an agreement here and now; so, a one time only offer – albeit for somewhat different reasons than we first thought. However: will you go on standby, just in case? And leave again in good grace if you don't get the nod on Saturday?"

Eric felt ashamed. He now realised that he had maximised the foibles of the club's owner and applied them in a way which was not fair, and with the end result seeming, to Eric, to be an insult to himself. He still didn't like Mr Grindlay; he did not like his manner or his methods, but here and now, on this issue alone, he was right.

"I will do that, no problem, Mr Grindlay. And if I don't play, no hard feelings."

"Thank goodness we got that out of the way! Now, training, match fitness, etc; are you honouring us with your presence all this week?"

"Yes, surely. I've got my gear and I'll run out and join the boss and the lads as soon as I've changed."

"Good, good . . . well, anything else we haven't covered?"

Eric recognised the classic dismissal. He shook hands with Mr Grindlay, and stood and turned to leave.

"Close the door on your way out," quietly muttered Eric, totally in sync' with the chairman.

A few minutes later as Eric approached the squad in the middle of their training session, Lofty, as to be expected, heralded the return of a legend, and the rest of the squad clapped and cheered.

However, the runs, the stretches, the exercises with the medicine ball and even the five-a-side game told on Eric, so much so, he knew he would have to put himself on a fitness crash-course: running, and using weights at home, even after the daily training sessions with his team-mates.

He arrived at the ground on Tuesday morning, aching all over. What made him feel a bit better was the absence of Baz Haskell; apparently he was still in contract discussions with a party interested in signing him up – the Police – who themselves had plans to send him out on an immediate two-year loan – to His Majesty's Prison Service.

Wednesday: much the same – aches and pains but no Bad Baz.

Thursday: feeling lighter, perkier, stronger, fitter. And...

Still no Baz.

Eric knew it was not really the right way to be, but he smiled, clenched and raised his right fist, and muttered, but rather too loudly—

"YES!"

Lofty looked at his pal and sniggered; the manager, trainers and the rest of the team just gave him rather an odd look.

Eric blushed and slowly lowered his right hand, but he was still smiling.

10

The Day of the Gate Rattler

Thursday January the 9th – 1913 – London

IT WAS AN OTHERWISE PERFECTLY ordinary Thursday evening. But anyone right at that moment who happened to be passing Prussia House on Carlton House Terrace in London's St. James's district, would have witnessed a sight which would have been an unusual sight on any evening – or even in broad daylight. The Prime Minister of Great Britain, Herbert Henry Asquith, was rattling the gates of the German Embassy like an angry husband trying to get in the house before the lover could jump from the window and make good his escape while carrying his pants. But with terror for half the world on the horizon, the time for Earl Gray tea and upside down cake between senior diplomats of both nations was over. This time things had to be dealt with at the very top, the Kaiser's absence from proceedings notwithstanding.

The soldier on guard duty looked to the angry gate rattler and his friends, and then across the short gravel path to the huge oak double doors of the large house that was actually the Embassy. A few seconds later a rather snooty, thin-faced, silver haired, straight-backed gentleman in a black velvet suit and black bow-tie looked across to the source of the commotion; he then looked to the guard and nodded. The soldier opened the gates and let the three gentlemen in.

Led by the round-faced rotund figure of Mr Asquith, the three men strode purposefully up the path and up to the doors, and then took off their hats as they were greeted by the man in the velvet suit.

"I take it you know who I am?" asked the Prime Minister. He had seen the man before on his many visits to the German Embassy, but the two had never spoken before now.

"Yes, of course, sir; what may I do for you?" the man replied in a tone of voice which rather made the delegation feel like tradesmen calling for their money, and was even more annoying as the man spoke perfect English with only a slight trace of a German accent.

"We are here on very urgent business; we need to see the Ambassador at once," replied the Prime Minister.

"I will see if His Excellency can receive you. . ." said the supercilious Secretary to the German Ambassador.

"You will do more than that, my man! Please take us to Prince Lichnowsky at once!" demanded the Prime Minister, a demand which brought grim faces of agreement from the two men on both flanks.

The secretary turned to the three men in turn, looked them up and down, and then with rather a snooty look on his face said, "Follow me, gentlemen. . ." and gestured for them to follow him down the hallway.

"If you would be so kind as to just wait here a moment," said the secretary as they reached a large red leather-cushioned door on the right of the wide hall, "I will inform His Excellency you are here."

The secretary knocked, opened the door without waiting for an answer, and then went in and closed the door behind him. The Prime Minster and the other two gentlemen just stood there grimly, fingering their hats in their hands.

The door opened again and the secretary stepped back out into the hallway.

"Please go in, gentlemen, the Ambassador will see you now."

The Prime Minster harrumphed and went in, but one of the other gentlemen said, "Thank you; much appreciated."

"Ah, welcome! Come in, come in! Do sit down," said the man sitting at his desk, a small slightly built man with a black moustache and thinning grey hair. This was one Prince Karl Max Lichnowsky, German Ambassador to Great Britain.

"Tea? Or perhaps a brandy to dispel the cold?" he then asked of his guests, Prime Minister Herbert Henry Asquith, the Foreign Secretary Sir Edward Grey, and Sir Vernon George Waldegrave Kell who was Head of British Intelligence. They were all now sat on large ornately carved high-backed chairs with satin covers.

"No, thank you, no. Your Excellency, we are here on a matter of such gravity, that . . . that war may exist between our two nations in a matter of days, if we cannot resolve this, *immediately,"* stated the Prime Minister, with real urgency in his voice. They may have been in the physical realm of the diplomat, but diplomacy was not on the agenda today. Total frankness and honesty was needed if war was to be averted, for this week at least.

"War? Between us?" said Prince Lichnowsky. "But we are so near to reaching an agreement, how can you say we may soon be at war?" replied the Prince.

He sounded convincing, but the world-weary and cynical gentlemen on the other side of the desk were uncertain as to whether Prince Lichnowsky was still operating within the purview of the diplomat, or if he was genuinely shocked by the Prime Minister's words. "Sir Edward, we need tarry no longer: show him the file," said Mr Asquith to Sir Edward Grey.

Sir Edward reached into his cloak and then into the wide pocket of his jacket; he pulled out a small buff coloured file and placed it on the desk in front of Prince Lichnowsky.

"What is this?" enquired the bemused Ambassador, but no one replied so he opened the file and began to peruse the contents.

"OH MEIN GOTT! WAS IST DAS?!" exclaimed the Ambassador. Prince Lichnowsky, now white faced, was looking at incontrovertible proof that one of his own junior members of staff, one Gerhard Weber, was acting as a spy.

As he continued studying what was legible and viewable of the heavily censored file, stopping only to mop his now sweating and furrowed brow, he found pictures of Weber, himself carrying a camera taking pictures of naval dockyards, of army barracks and airfields, and then worst of all several pictures of one of the men standing before him, Herbert Henry Asquith, Prime Minister of Great Britain. He quickly flicked on; there were more highly suspicious pictures of Weber skulking in hedgerows and sometimes brazenly walking around the field guns and vehicles parked up on the tarmac of an army barracks.

British Intelligence had been put on to Weber after a clumsy slip up.

Weber had been spotted looking through a gap in the perimeter fence of a naval dockyard: he was reported as having alternated between using binoculars, taking photographs and making notes. While naval security were sent to detain Weber, officers immediately passed on their suspicions to British Intelligence. Unfortunately, by the time security had reached the fence, Weber had disappeared, an amazing feat for a man with a wooden leg. Once his rage had died down upon hearing the suspected spy had escaped, Vernon Kell was of course curious as to the man's identity, and most importantly, wanted to know what his mission was. Through further presumed slip-ups by the suspect, it wasn't long before he was identified as being one Gerhard Weber, and was actually known to the British; he had not previously given cause for concern, and had seemed to fulfill his role as junior courier between Berlin and London with typical Prussian efficiency. But Kell was forming a plan: for now, surveillance rather than arrest was the way forward; although the more cynical members of the intelligence community had put this down to the fact that they didn't seem able to catch him anyway, but they were wrong: Vernon Kell did indeed have method in his perceived laxness, if not madness.

The two British agents assigned to tail him were thankfully soon back on the trail; they later reported to their superiors that Weber had the ability to fit in no matter what situation he found himself in. When he had been challenged by the duty guard at an airbase after walking right up to the prototype Avro 504 Biplane and snapping away with his camera, he had simply smiled and said, "Sorry, old bean, should have thought; but, I always think to myself, 'Ah, what might have been if it were not for that terrible night in Palestine.' Well, toodle pip," He had then affectionately patted the aircraft's engine and limped away on his wooden leg.

If the pictures were not bad enough then Weber's own hand had made things even worse.

In a notepad very recently found, only hours before in fact, the public appearances and schedules of everyone from the King down to the entire cabinet had been written out and were terrifyingly accurate. But the head of British Intelligence had taken no chances and had ensured the details of the schedules were deleted, before showing anyone from the German Embassy. What the British delegation also chose not to share with the Ambassador was that Weber had again given his tails the slip only a few hours before.

A white-faced Prince Lichnowsky now looked up to his three visitors.

"Mein Gott! I am very, very sorry to have to tell you, gentlemen that we appear to have a rogue agent on the loose. I can categorically assure you that this has not been sanctioned by my government, not with a peace agreement at stake. The question is, what do we do about Weber?"

Mr Asquith gave Vernon Kell a fleeting look; in return, Kell gave the barest of nods. If anyone knew if the Ambassador's reaction was genuine, he did. This was not noticed by the Prince.

"Your Excellency, I am glad that at least you understand the gravity of the situation, and tha. . ."

Mr Asquith trailed off as he noticed that he did not now seem to have the attention of the Ambassador, who instead just stared down at his desk, his face now ashen.

A million thoughts a second were racing through Prince Lichnowsky's mind; he loved living and working in Britain despite the dire reason for his tenure as Ambassador, which was to prevent war between the two nations – if this was at all possible. Unusually for a member of a German Royal House, he was not related to the British monarchy, but through both his diplomatic status and his familiarity with many European monarchs and their families, he nonetheless thoroughly enjoyed the trappings enjoyed by the English aristocracy – and their German cousins. All this was now in jeopardy due to some maniac of an upstart whose intent was obviously to scupper any chance of an agreement between Germany and England, concerning France, Belgium, the Balkans, Russia, and a goodly slice of far flung colonial outposts.

"Your Excellency?" said the Prime Minister. No answer. "Your Excellency?" he said again, a little louder. No answer.

"AMBASSADOR! PLEASE!" he shouted in desperation.

"Umm? Oh, I am dreadfully sorry, Prime Minister. This is dreadful news, truly dreadful. . ."

He looked up at his guests with an expression that suggested sadness, anger and fear, and with a little boy lost expression mixed in as well, all at the same time.

"We have to leave you now: we must call a meeting with our own Chiefs of Staff. I must impress upon you the need to strip this man of his diplomatic immunity, and to declare him a criminal at large, in your own country and territories, as we will do on behalf of the British Empire. At the very least – our two nations will be at one in this . . . for now," said Mr Asquith.

"I will call for my secretary to escort you out," said the Prince.

"No need, no need; no time for such piffle at such a time as this. Goodbye, Your Excellency; let us hope we can catch this man and soon, for all our sakes. . ." said the Prime Minister.

"Yes, yes, I quite agree, more than you could possibly know. . ." replied the Ambassador, but so quietly and so distractedly, his guests could not work out what he said.

11

Rats in the Kitchen

IT WAS VERY LUCKY for the Secretary to the German Ambassador that he was not called upon to escort the three guests from the Embassy.

A split-second after the Prime Minister mentioned the stripping of Weber's diplomatic status, the secretary, Otto Geff, stopped eavesdropping and ran up the staircase to his own first-floor room. After locking the door he pulled out a suitcase from the bottom of his wardrobe, placed it on his bed, lifted the lid and then turned on the short wave radio that was in there; he then carefully plugged in the antenna, the end of which was hidden in the centre of the rope pull for the curtains which allowed it to remain hidden from view when not in use. After putting on a tiny pair of headphones he then sent a message to Berlin in Morse code. He quickly took out the antenna, packed the radio away again and went back downstairs.

After ensuring that the British had left the Embassy, Otto Geff called in on Prince Lichnowsky; he asked if there was anything he needed; upon getting no reply from the white-faced Ambassador who continued to stare into the middle distance, Geff raced off down the entrance hall, into an ante room, and closed the door after him. He picked up a telephone, asked the operator for Paddington 3299 and told the person who answered the call to get out of London, and to be quick about it. He had only just put the receiver down when he heard his name being shouted.

"Geff! Hier mann. Jetzt!" came the yell from Prince Lichnowsky. Geff hurried out of the ante room and raced back down to the Ambassador's office.

After relating all that had been discussed to a supposedly shocked and horrified secretary, and after the secretary had received instructions to co-operate fully with the British government with regard to the capture of Gerhard Weber, Geff was dismissed by Prince Lichnowsky.

Geff dashed once more up to his room and again set up the short wave radio; a reply from Berlin was just coming through. The gist of this was:

'Continue to allow Lichnowsky to act as he sees fit, this will wrong foot the British. Weber will officially be disavowed, but if he survives attacks from either the British, or even German troops under Lichnowsky's command, then he is to return to Berlin to receive new orders. It will be unwise to contact us again for the time being. We will contact you by other means if need be. Over and out.'

*

Upon arriving back at 10 Downing Street, Mr Asquith gave Vernon Kell instructions to put their best man on the case, his brief would be to apprehend or kill Gerhard Weber.

*

The thin bony-faced Vernon Kell looked over his small round spectacles and across his desk to his best agent, Charles Carruthers of the elite Special Brigade. In between stifling yawns as it was now the middle of the night, he gave Charles the necessaries of his task; he had already briefed him on events thus far.

" . . . So, the thing to do next is call in at Weber's digs; he's been holed up at 8 Leinster Park in Paddington. The crap-hats have already taken a gander, so expect to find size twelve footprints and Woodbine ash all over the place. And don't take any nonsense off the proprietor, or landlady, whatever the hell she is . . . some Maltese fire-breather, you know the sort. You'll be joined by B Brigade and some of the Met' lads, Special Branch and all that Johnny. I doubt if Weber's there now, not unless he's an absolute moron, but we'd be unwise not to have one last sweep of the place, just in case there's something he's overlooked. I don't have anything more I am sorry to say, but try and get on his tail as soon as possible. But – keep it clean; apprehend him if you can, kill him if you must. Remember – we are not at war with Germany – yet. If the London papers or even some local rag stops the press and fills the front page with a picture of Gerhard Weber minus his brains, that will mean big trubs for us, and, I daresay the whole country. Do your best, Crack – er – Charles."

Charles smiled. "Will do, Boss, rest assured of that. But – he's not going to come quietly, that's for sure. If it comes to taking him down in the middle of Oxford Street during the sales, or losing him, then. . . " Charles rather wickedly made his hand into the shape of a gun, pointed it at his boss, pulled an imaginary trigger, and mimicked the sound of gunfire.

"Yes . . . well . . . if needs must. . ." replied Vernon Kell in a sombre voice.

12

Run and Hit

CHARLES CARRUTHERS took leave of his boss and went straight to the Whitehall Armoury to draw out a Lee Enfield 303. This was not his usual weapon of choice, but, horses for courses he muttered as he took charge of the rifle. This particular horse was for the particular course of a cross-country pursuit. In the event of having to abandon the surveillance only aspect of the operation, then perhaps his only chance of success would come from a single long-distance shot from a rifle; although as usual he still had his revolver tucked neatly into its shoulder holster.

Crackpot looked and acted as differently as it could ever be possible from most people's perception of a secret agent: he was only five foot five inches tall, was of slight build, looked years younger than he actually was, and had a shock of unkempt blonde hair which gave him the look of an unruly schoolboy. His original nickname was *'Crackshot'*, due to his incredible success as a sniper some years earlier in the Boar War, but this had been corrupted to *'Crackpot'* after his new Secret Service colleagues also learned of just how far he supposedly went to ensure a successful kill. It wasn't all true of course; unfortunately: all in the service believed he had on one occasion (from among the many tales of 'derring-do' spread around by all of Charles's friends), replaced an artillery shell with himself and got shot straight out of the large field gun right into the enemy lines. Crackpot had guessed that it was his good friend, Archie Bowes-White who had spread this story around, no doubt after several large glasses of port which no doubt had followed a good dinner, but as he was amused by this, Crackpot had not made any complaint in the decade or so since Archie had uttered this amazing titbit.

13

Bowler Schmowler

CRACKPOT HAD ONLY JUST LEFT Vernon Kell's office when there was a knock on the door.

"Come in," said Kell, thinking that Crackpot had forgotten something, but in walked Sir Alan Leith-Perkerson, the Deputy Head of British Intelligence.

"My God, Alan, it's not yet dawn, there was no need for you to have come in to the office as well."

"To be honest, sir, I haven't been home since yesterday . . . I am sorry to say I found the Parliamentary Sceptre in the bedroom wardrobe; if I go home in the temper I'm in, I'll be up for murder," replied Sir Alan, whose wife was an unfortunate and chronic Kleptomaniac.

"So . . . leave of absence is it. . . ?" said the bemused Vernon Kell. "If you pass me your Leave book, I'll sign it for you, and—"

"No, sir, nothing like that; I just thought you had better have this, it's just been delivered now, special night mail."

Vernon Kell now noticed his deputy was holding a large, plain brown envelope. "Special night mail? What the devil is it?" said Vernon Kell, taking the envelope from his deputy.

"I've no idea, sir, it is addressed to you, I haven't opened it and even the junior staff thought it best not to."

Vernon Kell humphed, and then rather comically shook it, then put his ear to it, decided it was safe, and then carefully sliced the envelope open at the top. He took a single piece of white foolscap out of the envelope, held it in front of him, and frowned.

"What the devil?!"

Vernon Kell turned it upside down, then held it up to the light, then placed it down on the desk, then held it up to the light again.

"Dashed gobbledegook! Is this someone's idea of a joke?!" he roared as he scanned again what appeared to be a series of little images which made no sense at all.

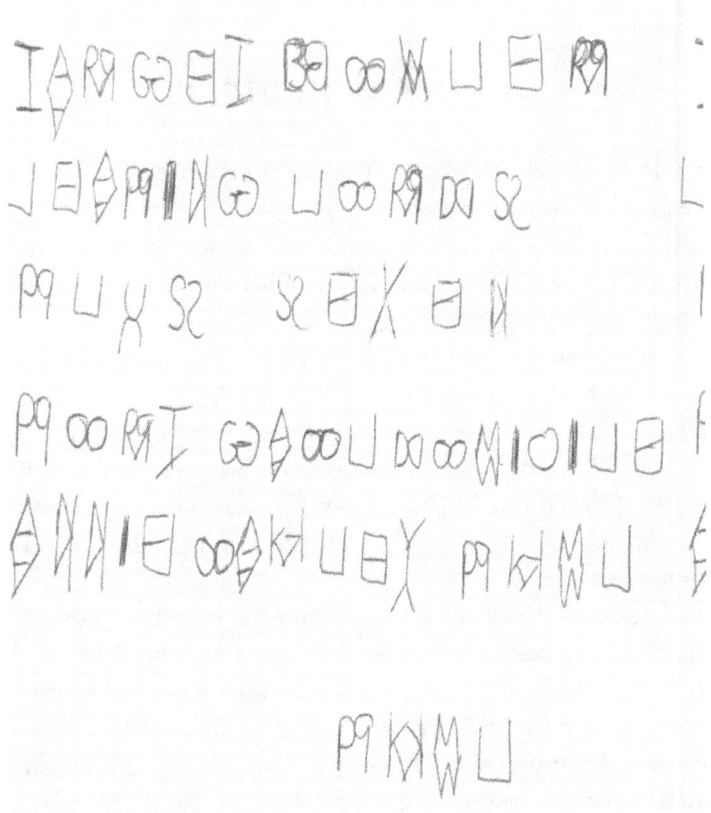

"Can I take a look, sir?" asked his deputy.

"Here, help yourself," said Vernon Kell, shoving the piece of foolscap across the desk.

With looks from Vernon Kell ranging from anger to curiosity, Sir Alan Leith-Perkerson commenced checking the piece of paper over much as his boss had done. After holding it up to the light and scanning the contents from left to right, he smiled and said, 'Aha! Got it!"

"Well?" demanded Vernon Kell, in a tone of voice which suggested that Sir Alan Leith-Perkerson was the long duly-appointed demysteryfier of mystery items found in the department's post.

"Believe it or not, Sir Vernon, it is Simple-Cypher; or at least that's what we called it in my day at Eton."

"Simple-Cypher? What the blazes is Simple-Cypher!" demanded Vernon Kell.

"Very basic schoolboy spy-game stuff, to be honest. Old Cuffley the Classics master would suddenly stop spouting on about the Sword of Damacles, say 'to hell with it' and play this game with us. As the code is so simple to break, a result was guaranteed; he'd chalk up something in Simple-Cypher on the blackboard, and the first boy to present him with the decoded message would win some minor treat – an apple or second helping of pud at dinner time. It would appear someone, perhaps an old pal of yours from school? – has written to you in Simple-Cypher. The trouble is, even the decoded writing is nonsense. Did you have a friend with a penchant for Lear, perhaps, Sir Vernon. . . ?"

"What the bloody hell are you on about?" roared Sir Vernon. "And I can't stand Lear!" he added. To Vernon Kell nonsense verse was just nonsense – and nothing else.

"Here, let me show you. . ."

Sir Alan went around Vernon Kell's side of the desk, placed the paper down on the desk top, and placed his finger under the first word.

"Simple-Cypher is just for fun, really; all it is, any and every letter is written out but doubled up, so to speak, the correctly written letter is joined to its symmetrical self, horizontally if possible, vertically if need be; but even then, many letters still stand out as their identities are hard to hide, even with its symmetrical brother tagged on – but – there's enough novelty and mystery to make it a great way to pass a rainy afternoon in a dusty classroom, rather than drool and daydream while the old man drones on about Homer."

"Can we move on, do you think?" asked Vernon Kell, trying his best and failing to feign patience with his underling.

"OK, now . . . forget the strange shapes, just look at the parts that read normally. . ."

Assuming wrongly that Vernon Kell would let his eyes follow, his deputy slowly moved his finger across the page, reading the words out one after another in a monotonic fashion - '*TARGET . . . BOWLER. . . LEAPING . . . LORDS . . . PLUS . . . SEVEN. . . PORT . . . GAOL . . . DOMICILE. . . ANNIE . . . OAKLEY . . . P–K–M–L . . . P–K–M–L. . .*'

"To hell and damnation with it, man! Just tell me what the imbecilic thing means!"

"Very well, sir, but do peruse it at your leisure when I've taken my leave, you may even find it quite amu—"

"READ THE BALLY THING OUT! IN PLAIN ENGLISH! NOW!" again roared Vernon Kell.

Sir Alan Leith Perkerson sighed, and did what was asked of him. He slowly scanned the images on the page, reading each word out loud.

"And. . . ?" demanded a seemingly unimpressed and very impatient Vernon Kell.

"I – don't know, sir, I am sorry to say . . . it may be Simple-Cypher but even the decoded words don't make sense; but let me read them out again, this time line by line rather than just the individual words. . .

'TARGET BOWLER. . .
LEAPING LORDS
PLUS SEVEN. . .
PORT GAOL DOMICILE. . .
ANNIE OAKLEY P –K –M –L. . .
P –K –M –L. . .'"

"My God! As if I haven't got bett—"

"Sir Vernon!" interjected his deputy, "I think I've got it! This isn't a stupid joke, it's someone trying to tell us something. Target Bowler! Think, sir, think! We already know of a heinous plot to kill the Prime Minister; well, who else do we know whose trademark is his hat, *AND* is believed to be in danger?"

"Mr Asquith doesn't wear a bowler, he wears a trilby, occasionally a top hat."

"Bowler schmowler, trilby schmilby," replied the momentarily enigmatic deputy.

"Eh?"

"Toppy schmoppy? Sorry, too many nights on the bourbon up the road. It's too close, sir; the fact that they've plumped for bowler either indicates flim-flam, or, as odd as it sounds, an honest mistake. Ask most foreigners what type of hat is favoured by the English upper classes, all will say bowler, none would say trilby . . . well . . . the odd one may say deerstalker due to our fictional friend, but by and large, it is the bowler which defines the British man, so in this context, it wouldn't even matter if Mr Asquith never wore a hat at all, it's simply a symbol of someone from the top drawer. For my money, bowler here means Mr Asquith."

"Bloody hell, Alan! That's it! That is it! Target Bowler; yes! YES! It must mean target Mr Asquith. Read on, Alan, see what else it's trying to tell us," urged the now captivated Vernon Kell.

But Sir Alan Leith Perkerson now looked uncertain. He may have got off to a flying start, but the flying start had just as quickly come to a dead stop.

"I – I am not sure, sir, sorry, but let's work on it. Do we know any lords prone to leaping at all?"

Vernon Kell shook his head ruefully but then stopped in mid shake, rather comically before his head had returned to its normal central position. But he slowly turned back round to face Sir Alan, and rather oddly started humming, but with the hums interspersed with words.

"Twelve drummers drumming, eleven hum-hum-hum-hum, ten hum-hum – TEN LORDS A LEAPING! No, no! Plus seven! Seventeen lords a leaping! Someone's going to blow up seventeen peers of the realm! My God, call the whole bally–"

"NO! NO, sir! It's ten plus seven all right, but I am reasonably sure it's a date in code, I think it means the seventeenth . . . well . . . maybe. . ."

"Or!" exclaimed the now inspired Vernon Kell, "It's the day the Christmas song refers to, plus seven days! Now, what day, or perhaps date to be more accurate, was the tenth day of Christmas this year?"

"The tenth day of Christmas . . . hmmm . . . I wonder. . . " mused Sir Alan.

"Wonder what?" asked Vernon Kell.

"It's not a constant, I am sorry to say; that song has at least one major secular or pagan variation which has the lords leaping on the twelfth and last day; although admittedly, most do sing the version with ten lords a leaping. But. . ."

"Yes?" interjected the ever impatient Vernon Kell.

"Assuming you are right, sir, and I think and of course, hope you are, we at least have two possible dates, which is a hell of a lot more than nothing, wouldn't you agree, sir?"

"Yes, yes, I would indeed; well done. OK, so . . . we have . . . ten or twelve leaping lords, which in reference to this year, is, or rather was (Vernon Kell counted on his fingers, humming and muttering to himself) . . . either Friday the third or Sunday the fifth of January, which, when simplified down to just numbers and the seven is added, gives us. . ."

"Either Friday the tenth of January, or Sunday the twelfth of January. But whatever we do, I wouldn't rule out Saturday the eleventh of January either."

"Why's that, then?" said Vernon Kell in an out-of-place tone, much like the straight man's lines in a way-down-the-bill Music Hall double act.

"For all we know, both the code setter and intended recipient may have known of the song's lyrical variation and used it, using the tenth and the twelfth as the pumpernickel, and the eleventh is the rather succulent beervorst in the middle. Whichever it is, it's this weekend," said a grim faced Sir Alan.

"I think I know what you mean," said Vernon Kell, but how the hell do you know all this stuff? You were never in code breaking or even code setting as far as I know – or were you?"

"No, sir, but in our profession these things are never far away, as I'm sure you will agree. (Vernon Kell gave a very uncertain nod of the head). The thing is, code can mean anything, anything at all. We must never overlook the fact that code setters can do what the hell they like, as long as the person or persons the code is to be read by, know the solution. We, the people in between if you like, can only guess. Our best chance is the application of logic, and in most cases that does the trick. But, for all we know, *Lords a Leaping* may be the secret sign to poison the Welsh, or even recruit them to open up a new front, should hostilities occur."

"But you don't think so in this instance?"

"No, sir, if I were a betting man, I would say we're on the right track. Not just because of what the message seems to tell us, but also because of the manner in which this has come to us."

"Yes, that is very puzzling indeed, what are your thoughts on this?" asked Vernon Kell.

"Obviously, someone has got that message to us, and wants to warn us of an assassination attempt. Plus, the code is only Simple-Cypher. It doesn't fit when considering purely the gravity of its message, too easy to break, too simplistic. But when you take into account the possible risks to the person or persons unknown in getting this to us, then the need for speed, in both the initial coding and then in getting it to us, would, or should I say, may – as there's no way to be certain at this juncture, have left no option but to either send it in plain English, or, make some attempt at coding, in the hope that even if others read it along the way, the message would be dismissed as a joke, or just absolutely inane gobbledegook."

"But you cracked it in an instant, who was it ever going to fool?"

"Postmen perhaps, with hundreds of other items to deal with and who shouldn't even see the contents anyway; petty thieves, who, after realising the envelope didn't contain a five pound postal order from Aunt Maude to her favourite nephew, would just throw it away. But ultimately, I just think it was a desperate attempt at rapid concealment of some sort however primitive, before getting the message to us as soon as possible."

"Hmmm . . . maybe . . . but going back to your earlier point: just who the hell has sent this to us? And of course, *why?*" suddenly said Vernon Kell, while tapping the piece of foolscap.

"Very good question, Boss. (Vernon Kell raised his eyebrows at this) . . . In my opinion, I think that someone, for want of a better phrase – *on our side,* but perhaps from a different department and seemingly deep undercover, wants to warn us. I am not certain of that; it could equally be a sympathiser, someone based in German intelligence or their military. It could also easily be heinous flim-flammery by the enemy; but – whatever and whoever – we are, in my opinion, best concentrating on deciding what the message means and what we are going to do about it. Even if it's a devilish red herring, then ironically, we still need to consider its meaning first, and worry about who sent it later."

"Yes, yes, I think you're right again. Bloody hell, they'll be putting me out to grass and have you in here if you keep this up!" said Vernon Kell with a grim smile.

Sir Alan returned the smile but then returned to the matter at hand.

"Shall we peruse the rest, sir? See how far we get?"

"May as well;" replied Vernon Kell, "you said something about a prison port or something. . . ?"

"Port – Gaol – Domicile to be exact." said Sir Alan."Tricky, we may have spoken too soon."

"Sounds like a jail in a port, doesn't it? said Vernon Kell. "Any ideas at all?"

Sir Alan frowned and shook his head.

"Not off the top of my head, no, sorry, but let's check the rest. . .

"Annie Oakley P–K–M–L . . . then there's a gap, looks intentional, and P–K–M–L is repeated, the spacing makes it seem much like any ending to most correspondence or private letters."

"Annie Oakley? Wasn't she that sharp-shooting show girl?" said Vernon Kell.

"Yes, that's right, sir, came here with Buffalo Bill some years back. Hold on! Sharp shooting you said! Bingo! I think I've got it. This is no doubt to do with the assassin. PKML must be the assassin!"

"My God, you're on fire today, old chap! Yes, that makes sense!" exclaimed Vernon Kell.

"Yes, well, you may as well call the fire brigade out, not a clue as to who PKML is, or why that's mentioned twice," said Sir Alan.

"Aha! Don't call the desk movers yet old man! I think I've got it!

Well, you've already guessed it I think. As PKML has also signed the note off, I think this message is from the assassin, letting accomplices know who the assassin is – himself!" said the triumphal Vernon Kell.

"Or herself," suggested Sir Alan.

"Ha!" retorted the chauvinistic head of British Intelligence. "And – if the sender is indeed an ally, then it would seem time or other considerations, has resulted in the message being passed on *'as is'*, as it were, and not a summary of same composed later by the sender. So . . . we have the possible dates, and we have the target, and we have the initials, we hope, of the proposed shooter. What we now need to do is work out that jail rubbish, and who on earth PKML is."

"Before we get too far down this road, Sir Vernon, what about our man Carruthers, and Weber. . . ?"

"Hmmm, yes. . ." replied Vernon Kell, who then went into a mistimed reverie, leaving his deputy hanging for further instructions.

"Sir. . . ?" said Sir Alan after a minute or so.

"Hmmm . . . oh, yes, Charles and our German chappy . . . don't worry about that side of things, Alan, I'll get onto it. For now, please have that letter copied and sent to all the heads with top secret clearance, and then call a meeting, for . . . this afternoon, 2:00 pm. And . . . blimey, here's Doris. Good lord! It's gone eight! I am sorry, old friend; you must be very tired. Best get yourself off home for a kip and a bite. I doubt we can get much further on this this morning. Send Doris in before you go, I want to write to the German Ambassador."

Vernon Kell said nothing further but looked at Sir Alan and smiled, which let the deputy know he could now take leave of his senior.

A few moments later, Doris, who amongst other things was his personal secretary, was sat at a small desk over to the right of Vernon Kell's; the pale winter sun shone in through the window, illuminating her Underwood No. 5 Type Writer. She sat poised to take the dictation from Vernon Kell.

"To Prince Karl Max Lichnowsk—BLOODY HELL! Alan, get

back in here now!" yelled Vernon Kell. A shriek seconds later followed by the sound of someone falling off their chair could be heard coming from the office next door.

"Is *Bloody hell!* all in capitals, Sir Alan?" asked the stoic Doris.

After getting no answer and after realising that *Bloody hell!* was not part of her boss's dictation; she also realised that he had just as quickly forgotten she was supposed to be taking a letter at all. Dependable Doris diplomatically slipped away and returned to her more routine duties in her own office.

After hearing the desperate yells for his immediate return, Sir Alan Leith-Perkerson had turned on his heels and had gone straight back into his boss's office. After getting the order to cancel the meeting of department heads moments after the orders had gone out, all he could do then was sit there, more than a little confused as Vernon Kell garbled excitedly about the coded message, the German Ambassador and something about needing to see Carruthers immediately. He then issued a rather distracted farewell. Sir Alan watched his boss hurry off. He sat there on his own for a moment; he realised that his promised morning of rest and leisure had not actually been recanted, and so shrugged his shoulders, put on his hat and coat, and left for home.

14

Flat Out

CRACKPOT, aided by a considerable combined force of police and secret service agents, descended on Weber's apartment in Paddington. Under Crackpot's direction, every inch of Weber's rooms on the first floor was checked and rechecked. This was to the chagrin of many of the force who had already done this. Crackpot also incurred the wrath of the landlady, who still hadn't got the place straight again after it had been taken apart only hours earlier.

"I have already told that other policeman! The gentleman only stays here a few days a week, and even then, not every week! You – you – you – *stupid English bobbies!* You are ruining my business! Gaargh!" raged the Maltese spinster and London landlady of twenty years standing, Jenta Cottlemid.

Crackpot realised Weber had made a run for it. He was almost sure it would be the case, as was his boss, Vernon Kell, but bitter experience had taught him not to dismiss the possibility of there being stupid secret agents or criminals. Only the previous year Charles had made a mad dash to Aberdeen while the pro-Palestinian bomber had had a lie in, enjoyed a full fried breakfast at the corner café, and then spent the afternoon at his aunt's house three streets away from Whitehall, where he was then arrested by the local police.

Although Crackpot knew that Weber had had a good head start, he stayed cool, calm and collected. Using a combination of the surveillance photographs and descriptions he had been given by staff from the German Embassy, he had earlier wired every major train station and port office to ask them to look out for:

'. . . a man with a wooden leg, ginger hair and an unmatching huge silvery-grey handlebar moustache. If you see this man or someone

who fits this description, do not confront him but contact the local police station or telephone Whitehall 1001.'

Hours later after a fruitless search, Crackpot stood scratching his chin in the hallway of the private apartments which had unwittingly harboured an enemy of the state. He was trying hard to concentrate, to think what to do next, but the constant comings and goings of the combined law enforcement officers, and the noise now generated by a row between the landlady and a constable who had commandeered the use of the apartment's only telephone, was interrupting his chain of thought.

"I want to telephone my brother Oscar in Pimlico! And you, you lumbering oaf, you say I *cannot* do this?!"

"That is correct, Madam, it is a matter of national importance; we need the line kept clear for important calls. I am very sorry."

"Sorry? *SORRY?!* To hell with you; to hell with the lot of you!" Jenta stormed back down the hallway and into the kitchen, slamming the door behind her.

If Crackpot thought calm would once again return to *Leinster Park Apartments for Professional Gentlemen,* he was very much mistaken.

"M-M-Mr Carruthers?" came a wheezing gasping voice from a lumbering mass of overcoat and helmet, as it staggered through the half-open front door.

"Yes?" replied Crackpot, very distractedly and without even looking up. He was 'miles away'.

"P-Paddington Station!" garbled the red-faced PC, sweating badly despite the bitter cold. He stumbled farther up the hallway.

"What's that?" said Crackpot, shaken from his reverie and turning to look at the overweight flatfoot, now stooping, holding his sides and wheezing even more. Crackpot frowned as the PC took a deep breath, coughed, straightened himself up as drool dripped down his front, and who then spoke again.

"Th-the man you are – phwaar, hang on a mo – the man you are looking for . . . he was spotted g-g-g-going into Paddington Station. The sarge and some of the lads are racing down there right now . . . I was told to run here t-to tell y-you. . ."

Crackpot thought for moment while once again looking down and scratching his chin. Eventually he looked up again and spoke to the policeman.

"Thank you, Constable, that is very helpful indeed. Er – go inside and sit down, get your breath back . . . there's a chappy."

The constable raised his eyebrows at this, but with the hot clammy sweat on his face and neck rapidly cooling, and with a waft of warmth and the smell of burning coal drifting out through the partition door and along the hallway, he succombed and walked into the living room where he sat down and lit a cigarette.

Crackpot, finally able to think clearly, quickly came to a decision. He picked up the telephone and dialled zero.

"Hello, operator, please put me through to—"

15

The Spinster hardens In Leinster Gardens

"WHITEHALL 1001, PERHAPS?" came a voice from the front door vestibule.

"Never mind, operator, thank you," Crackpot put the telephone back on the hook and turned to the door and looked at his boss, Vernon Kell.

"Hello, Boss, this is a surprise; lucky really, the boys and I were just about to—"

"And that's why I came, the boys are going nowhere — but you are."

"I – I don't understand. . . " said a baffled Crackpot.

"Can't afford it, old chap, the Secretary's on a crackdown. The last race around the country apparently put a serious dent in the department coffers, so I'm here to try and prevent that happening again . . . plus – there's been a change."

"No more *larkin'* about, then?" said Crackpot in rather an affected manner.

"Hmmm . . . you could say that," replied the only too knowing Vernon Kell. "Now to business: under no circumstances is Weber to be liquidated; I don't even want him arrested – just yet. I—"

"But you said—" interjected a confused Crackpot, forgetting his place, but this was countered by his boss.

"I know what I said, now I've changed my mind. Surveillance only is the wiser option – for now. I want to know where he goes and who he meets . . . we can't do that if he drops down dead at Paddington Ticket Office or if we drag him in before making his next contact. I've pulled the blue boys back, they're not happy but – there it is. Right then, get going."

Vernon Kell stared intently at Crackpot for a moment, then looked down the hallway and nodded to the senior police officer, who only a second earlier had rather unwisely knocked on the kitchen door to ask for tea for his men.

"Te? *TE?!* Busli sormi!" came the reply from the other side of the closed door.

"What's that mean?" asked the constable of his commander; '*Wait here and I'll bring it out to you,*' do you think?" said the constable.

"Er – yes, that's right. You wait here, and then bring it through to the lads; she's a smashin' lass that one, really hospitable," said the police commander, smiling with it as he walked off. He spoke fluent Maltese.

The equally bilingual Vernon Kell also smiled, turned back, nodded to Crackpot, and left. After one last scratch of his chin, Crackpot was also out of the door.

"Taxi!" yelled Crackpot.

16

That Friday Feeling

ERIC FELT HE COULD TAKE ON THE WORLD as he sauntered in to the ground on the morning of Friday the 10th of January: he took deep lung-bursting breaths, suddenly commenced running on the spot, and then actually made a short dash as he neared the pitch. He of course wasn't a boxer or a fighter of any sort, but he didn't think that mattered. 'Bring 'em all on!' he muttered to himself while grinning a satisfied grin. It was a satisfied grin which would soon be wiped off his face. . .

"Ullo, lads."

It was Barry 'Baz' Horatio Haskell, six foot seven inches, seemingly both ways.

"Baz! Glad you're back," diplomatically stated the skipper, one Derek Lofty Arkwright, while feeling very much for his crestfallen friend.

Eric sighed, his shoulders visibly dropped, and he was just on the point of flinging a medicine ball as far as he could, when he heard Baz talking to the manager and trainers:

"I ain't stayin'; the filf are chargin' me an' Grindy's sacked me, so I'm off for good. See yers all, then," he said, looking over Jock Shanksby's shoulders to the shocked first team squad.

And with that, Baz went off to pick up his meagre belongings from his locker, and go off home, which may not be his home for much longer.

The lads couldn't help it, they really couldn't. They didn't like Bad Baz Haskell, and none thought he could play football. Forgetting that being out of sight did not necessarily equate with being out of earshot, no sooner had Baz gone down the tunnel on his way to the locker room, than a big cheer went up and bounced around the enclosed ground.

"Yer in! You lucky old sod!" enthused Lofty, slapping his best mate on the back.

"Ow!" said Eric, while wearing a great big grin.

17

The Train now Standing Still

SUCH WAS THE CHANGING face of – or rather on the streets of London, that the nearest Hansom cab had no chance. As the cabbie hailed by Crackpot (unfortunately on the other side of the road), tried to turn the horse and carriage around, a 1911 Unic Landaulette motorised taxi, banged, coughed and spluttered to a halt right outside the apartment block.

Crackpot, in too much of a rush to worry about maintaining decorum, did not look the ruthless motorised gift horse in the mouth, and duly jumped in the back of the taxi. He flung his long narrow fishing bag down on the seat, and slammed the door. "Paddington Station! And quick about it!" he yelled.

The taxi driver promptly did an about turn and drove off in the same direction that the Hansom had originally been facing, adding insult to injury for the poor cabbie.

Although Crackpot had been in a modern taxi many times, the age of the Hansom though coming to an end, was not yet totally a thing of the past – nor was the synonymous yet annoying habit of passengers, in taxis new or old, banging on the interior of the cab to let the cabbie know to 'get a move on', but. . .

"You bang on the back of my bleedin' seat again and out you go," said taxi driver Bert Tressel. "All the bleedin' same, you chinless wonders; well, *Guv'nor,*you can *show me a shiny shillin',* you can *show me a guinea . . .* or you can show me the bleedin' Crown Jewels – but – we get there when we bleedin' well get there and not before."

Crackpot blushed, and smiled, and mused on the fact that times were certainly changing. He then went to say that the laws of physics only allow anyone to get somewhere – when they do indeed get there, but thought better of it and remained silent.

The taxi made its way through the narrow side streets of

Paddington, most of which had names ending in Gardens or Mews. Only a few minutes later the taxi reached the end of Chilworth Street, turned right onto Eastbourne Terrace, round onto Praed Street and pulled up outside the main entrance to Paddington Station.

"Keep the change," said Crackpot after getting out and passing a pound note through the window.

"Cheers – er – Guv'," replied the driver, changing to know-your-place mode, and feeling a tad ashamed to boot as he had just been given a tip which was almost fifteen times the actual fare.

"Am I in time, I wonder?" muttered Crackpot to himself as he hoisted his bag onto his shoulder and walked through the archway, and onto the brilliantly lit concourse, the light courtesy of a grand glass-panelled roof reminiscent of the famed Crystal Palace.

To the sides of the concourse were an array of shops and amenities, mostly for the well-heeled, but the hoi polloi weren't forgotten either. Crackpot walked past everything from expensive hairdressing salons to pie shops, before reaching the gate to Platform 1. He had no idea where Weber would be or where he was trying to escape to, so Platform 1 was just a good place to start his surveillance and perhaps pursuit, as anywhere else.

Paddington Station was known for being busy, all day and most of the evening, but Crackpot noticed that although the station seemed to be especially packed, the passengers did not seem to be in the usual hurry to find and board their trains. The reasons for this soon became clear as his thoughts were then distracted by two rather posh gentlemen in flannel suits and trilbys, posher than Crackpot that is. They were looking forlornly through the locked gate at a train that should have left ten minutes earlier, but which stood empty and still, and with the engine not even building up steam ready for its journey.

"The country's gone to the dogs, the dogs I say! Not a train moving! *None!* We'll bally well miss our connection! By gad! We may even miss the match tomorrow!" said one to the other.

"Dogs. Yes. Quite right, quite right," replied the other, rather distractedly.

Crackpot stopped, scratched his chin, and thought.

Not a train moving! None!

A certain realisation dawned on Crackpot; he smiled as a vision filled his mind of Vernon Kell imposing the will of His Majesty's Intelligence Service upon a giant of the transport industry, the Great Western Railway Company. More specifically, it meant that the beleagured station master in his little cubby-hole high above Platform 2, had been brow beaten into temporarily halting all rail services.

Crackpot took the opportuntity of checking as much of the station as he could, confident that at least Weber was not going anywhere by train just yet. If on the other hand Weber had already left the station, then Crackpot would take the philosophical view that he, Charles Marlborough Carruthers, was just one man.

With the ever increasing number of passengers crowding the concourse, it took Crackpot more than thirty minutes to make what at best was a cursory check of the general area, the ticket office, the amenities, and the platform entrances – even straining to take a look down the platforms themselves in case Weber had either talked his way in, or had somehow sneaked in past a guard. He knew he daren't brandish his warrant card and go beyond one of the gates himself, as to leave an almost central point of surveillance as unsatisfactory as it was, would be asking for trouble. He also wondered when someone from 'upstairs' would give the station master clearance to recommence shunting the nation from town to town again.

Hours went by; the station concourse became even more crowded, people were becoming more irritated, and the general atmosphere was rather tense and somewhat ugly.

Crackpot sighed. He seemed to be wasting his time, but his sense of duty prevailed. He made one more check of the area, until. . .

18

Train Whistle Blowin'

"PLATFORM 5! THE DELAYED 1400 TO MANCHESTER LONDON ROAD – calling at: Reading, Oxford, Banbury, Snow Hill, Wolverhampton Lower Level, Wellington, Market Drayton, Crewe, Stockport – terminating at Manchester London Road! – is now leaving from Platform 5! Through here please! The delayed 1400 to Manchester London Road! — I thank you!" The announcer finished off with the affected tone and flourish of a fairground barker; he lowered his speaking trumpet and grinned and bowed as some of those waiting chuckled.

Crackpot jumped with the shock. All around him railway staff were hastily unlocking platform gates while their colleagues blasted out information, some through speaking trumpets while those without shouted at the tops of their voices. Others hastily updated chalk boards informing the now heaving mass packing the concourse, that the clearing of the considerable backlog of delayed services could now commence.

This gave Crackpot somewhat of a problem. The heaving mass was now being dissipated all over the concourse, as many services which normally left on one platform were now leaving from another, and this was just the backlog. Many passengers who had arrived for trains that had not yet officially been delayed, desperately tried to find if they, too, would be subject to any eventual delays or platform changes. The thing that *'put the tin hat on it'*, as one wag was uttering as he walked by, was the numerous cancellations. This meant that all those whose service had been cancelled, would have to vie for space on the next available train to their destination.

Crackpot fought his way through the throngs moving in every direction, which now also included passengers from arrivals, which had finally been allowed in to the station after being queued on tracks stretching halfway across Central London. But just fighting to move along was doing Crackpot no good at all, as it prevented him from doing his job, which at that moment was to locate and track Gerhard Weber.

But. . .

"Excuse me, old chap. . ."

Clunk, step, clunk step. . .

Crackpot looked to his right to see – *a man with a wooden leg, ginger hair and an unmatching huge silvery-grey handlebar moustache* – walk quickly past him, across the concourse, brandish his ticket, and walk through the gate onto Platform 5.

"OK, Boss, you win, surveillance only," said Crackpot to himself. He went to dash off to the ticket office, but then stopped, smiled and muttered, 'Good Lord, Charles, you're on His Majesty's business,' and instead turned, walked up to the gate, proffered his ID, announced with a very grave face that he was on government business, and was allowed through. He very slowly walked alongside the train on Platform 5 while making sure that Weber was still in his sights, which he was. Crackpot was also aware that he may have to indulge in a little and perhaps childish theatrics, as he knew never to assume one is superior to one's quarry, and always to suspect that one has been 'rumbled'.

When Weber reached the second to last carriage, he hopped on board. Crackpot smiled. Weber, perhaps in need of refreshment, had gone straight into the dining car, or more pertinently to Crackpot, a public area where surveillance could be maintained rather than having to somehow check on which carriage Weber was in. Weber of course, could always move to any other part of the train later, but at least it was a favourable start for Crackpot. What Crackpot had not seen when Weber boarded the train, was that he was smiling, too. . .

"Manchester it is, then, boyo, but if it was me, me ole mucker, I'd have got the express from Saint Pancras," muttered Crackpot to himself as he climbed aboard, but straight into an empty first class carriage rather than the dining car. He then rather comically delayed ten seconds, standing stock still; he then quickly pushed down the window and looked out along the platform. No Weber.

He ran to other side of the carriage, pushed down the window. No Weber. 'Third time lucky?' he said to himself. He went back to the first window. . .

No Weber.

Crackpot thought for a moment. There were no signs at all that Weber knew he was being tailed, but neither was there anything concrete which proved that he didn't. Accepting the status quo, he decided to check on Weber from the opposite end of the dining car.

Although it was always open for light snacks and drinks, the dining car was not really busy, it never was until dinner, or until one of the other ubiquitous main British meal times; it all depended on the departure time and the length of journey as to which main meal, if any, would be served.

The Manchester train, now delayed by just over an hour, finally began to chug and puff out of Paddington, trundle and roll slowly along the station tracks, over several local junctions, and then onto the mainline proper.

Crackpot was at one end of the carriage and was able to see Weber quite clearly, sitting diagonally opposite at the other end. He was also facing the same way, which gave at least a small advantage to Crackpot in the hide and seek stakes, but only while the carriage remained quiet.

Reading – Oxford – Banbury – it was tea time. Whether the dining car staff had stuck rigidly to their own scheduled times despite the disruptions, or whether they thought a compensatory cup of tea and a bun would be nice while the last of the winter sun went down, Crackpot knew not, but there was only a handful of takers and so the surveillance on Weber remained straightforward. Crackpot checked every minute or so to ensure the back of Weber's head was where he wanted it to be.

Snow Hill – Wolverhampton: some travellers left the dining car but more thirsty and peckish passengers arrived; this went on until it was almost dinner, and then the carriage quickly filled. But several hungry travellers were irate at not getting a seat at the first sitting.

"Dash it! Most likely no damn rugger! *And now no bally dinner!"*

said an outraged Calders.

"Yes, quite, old man," replied Charticott.

This also meant that a dinner of skate and claret, which drew some disapproving looks from a number of the well-heeled diners, was rather spoiled. Craning one's neck every minute or so to see over other diners' heads so as to keep a constant eye on another traveller, does rather spoil one's evening meal.

More time slipped ever slowly by. Although thankfully it was a direct service, the known downside to this was that most GWR services from London to Manchester were usually a five and a half hour journey, unlike the speedier LNWR services from Saint Pancras and other London stations. But worse still, a knock-on effect of the delays at Paddington was that a goodly slice of the national rail network timetable had been put back; at many junctions as the train trundled northwards, the train frequently came to a full stop for anything from five minutes up to around half an hour. What really worried Crackpot was the rest of the journey. There were five more official stops during which he could easily lose his prey; or Weber could chance it while stuck at a junction; or if he was really up for it, jump while the train was thundering along at full speed. On top of this, Crackpot was already exhausted. He had got the call to arms in the middle of the night, but this was just as he was turning in after a two day stake out of a boarding house in Limehouse, in which a gang of gold smugglers were suspected to be holed up. He thought further on this, sighed very deeply, then came to a decision. . .

*

" . . . I can't promise you any reward or payment for this, but you would be doing your country a great service," said Crackpot, ten minutes later to the guard, after supplying him with the abridged version of current events, and asking for his help in keeping an eye on Gerhard Weber.

"Trooper Harris doesn't let the side down, Guv'. I met Kitchener once, you know, we had just fought at Maf—"

"Thank you," interjected Crackpot. "Let me know if he makes a move, or does anything suspicious. I'll be in compartment eighteen."

"Of course, Guv', I won't let you down."

Crackpot nodded and took the gamble of his life. He left the guard's van, walked along to his first class compartment which luckily he had to himself (second and third class were heaving), and although it wasn't a sleeper he pushed down the seat dividers on one side of the compartment and stretched out. Within minutes he was snoring.

The hours went by. Although to Crackpot it seemed as if he had just nodded off, he was suddenly shaken awake by the guard.

Crackpot stood straight up and in a split-second had the guard up against the window, and was only a split second away from breaking his neck.

"It's me, Guv'nor!" croaked the guard. "You asked for my help!"

Crackpot came to his senses, took his arms away from the guard's throat and back, and then couldn't apologise enough.

"I am dreadfully sorry, old chap, it was a reflex action; are you OK?"

"I'm fine, Guv', no need to worry, shoulda woke yer more gentle," replied the guard, while stroking his sore neck. "Any'ow, we're just coming up to Manchester London Road, and more importantly, yer man's only just stirring now himself. Minutes after you left, he drifted off to sleep in the diner; blimey, he drooled all over some old duchess! . . . Priceless!"

"Thank you, and once again, dreadfully sorry for – well . . . sorry. . ." Crackpot dug in his pockets, pulled out a ten shilling note, thrust it in the guard's hand, and left to take up the chase once more.

19

Constabulary Duties

THE TRAIN FINALLY PULLED INTO MANCHESTER LONDON ROAD STATION.

"Bloody midnight!" yelled Crackpot as he stepped down onto Platform 1. He didn't mean to yell, but he was still angry and ashamed of himself at almost despatching someone who had readily agreed to help him; and, unfortunately he still felt tired. It was now very late and cloak and dagger shenanikins all over Manchester possibly beckoned.

"I know, old chap; damn disgrace. I've missed my connection now, stuck in this hole for the night," said a bemonacled buffoon who was hoping to make it to Liverpool, but had missed the last train by twenty minutes. Official connections are supposed to wait, but the truth was – and is – they often do not.

Crackpot tried to give a sympathetic smile, but it made him seem as if he had some sort of nervous tick. He marched smartly on, straight along the platform, up the staircase and out onto London Road. His plan this time was to get ahead of Weber, keep out of sight, let him pass, and then revert to bringing up the rear. He found an ideal niche in the front wall of the Haybrook Hotel, which was to the right of the station exit on the other side of the road. It wasn't so much that this section of the dirty purple brick wall itself was out of view, but the road which gave the station its name was unusually wide, and at night it was so dark in that spot it would need someone deliberately looking for you there, to have any chance of spotting you.

Crackpot, leaning back against the brickwork, felt the heat rising from a vent in the floor, far too welcoming when one is possibly going to be traipsing round a large city on a freezing cold night. He dearly wished that Weber would simply come hobbling out of the station and straight into the hotel. It was Crackpot's lucky night. That is exactly what happened.

But Crackpot's relief was short lived. He then thought again of how he could possibly rest while trying to maintain surveillance. Yet again he would need help; on the train he had had no option but to draft in emergency help from a civilian; this time he would, hopefully at least, be able to acquire assistance from someone with a warrant card. He followed Weber into the hotel lobby, but immediately sat out of sight as Weber checked in. He also tried to listen to what was being said, but most of it was inaudible, but just as Weber was given his keys, Crackpot heard quite clearly but in German, "Ja? Gut gut. Danke," Still none the wiser, Crackpot let Weber be escorted to his second floor room by a bellboy, waited for the lift doors to close, and then went to the reception himself.

Without giving too much away, he explained the need for someone from the hotel to fetch a policeman as quickly as possible, but for it to be kept low-key; but then he also booked himself in and then sat down in the lobby and picked up the evening newspaper.

"What the Devil?!" exclaimed Crackpot, less than ten minutes later, as a police van with bells ringing loudly, screeched to a halt outside the hotel and in raced at least ten burly Manchester policemen, brandishing truncheons and some blowing whistles.

"Stop where you are!" and similar, was being yelled at anyone and everyone, almost frightening to death the very aged Lady Fallowfield, who had only just returned from the Manchester Opera House, and who was sat waiting for her almost as aged companion to pick up the room keys from reception.

"The Navy's in, lads! No wonder there's been a riot!" yelled one of the constables.

The blue brigade began rounding up a group of stunned hotel guests – namely – the Wythenshawe Operatic Company, who had chosen the wrong night to stay in costume for the benefit of the staff and guests of the hotel.

"But Officer! We're the cast of HMS Pinafore!" came the protest from a small, harmless looking man, rigged out as an admiral in all his best finery. He and his operatic troop were all being frog marched out to the police van.

"A likely story!" came the cynical retort from the policeman, "Now get in there! The lot of you!"

Crackpot rushed over to the centre of the lobby where a sergeant, six foot plus and with a wide chest and bulging biceps, stood grim-faced, waving his truncheon.

"What the bloody hell?! I asked for one policeman and I stressed the need to keep it low-key!" yelled Crackpot, who wasn't managing the low-key part so well himself, but perhaps he had good reason.

"Sit down, there's a laddie . . . or you go in the van, too."

"I BEG YOUR PARDON?! Control your men, now! Cra – er – Carruthers, Special Branch!" demanded Crackpot, proffering his tailored warrant card.

The burly copper was surprised, but soon refound his authority.

"Be that as it may, we still have to do our job."

"Do your job?! *DO YOUR JOB?!* My God, man, the trouble's not in here, it's one man, on the second floor!"

"But we were told there was a riot!"

"I beg your pardon, Sergeant, I said there was a need to keep it *quiet,"* retorted the disgruntled bell boy as he rushed by rubbing his arm; he had just managed to wrestle free from the iron grip of one of Manchester's finest.

The sergeant knew he had made an horrendous gaff and went bright red.

"I am dreadfully sorry, sir, trifle deaf; I do beg your pardon," he replied, but to Crackpot only. He then glanced at the bell boy purely to give him a look of thunder.

Crackpot moved on.

"Right, I want one of your men to stay and keep – er – help me keep tabs on one of the guests here. It's best if you take the rest of your men and lea—"

"I'll have you know I am Rear Admiral Hunt-Tavistock!" said the totally unoperatic Rear Admiral Hunt-Tavistock, who had been dragged from the restaurant to the right of the lobby while about to take a spoonful of blueberry sorbet. This had not reached the mouth of the late diner who tipped well, but had badly stained his white naval dinner jacket rather well.

"At least yer honest, not like yer pals. Now get in there and join 'em!" yelled the PC, as he dragged the outraged rear admiral out of the hotel and over to the police van.

Crackpot was going to intervene, as he definitely would have done on a less exhausting night, but instead he simply reached out, pulled the nearest police constable to him, and said to the sergeant, "He'll do."

The stunned PC looked with utter confusion at his boss.

"Special duties, Higgs; go with the man, he's from the Smoke."

Higgs' mood lifted immediately, and his eyes lit up.

"Do you know the King?"

"Shut up. Over there in the corner."

Crackpot took his charge to the far end of the lobby, away from the chaos, and explained what he wanted of him. At the same time, Sergeant Arrowsmith went outside to inform his men that someone had got the words riot and quiet mixed up.

"Someone?!" muttered one of the PCs as the sergeant's back was turned.

A few minutes later, calm had returned to the lobby of the hotel. Lady Fallowfield was being comforted by her aide, aided further by a large glass of cognac, at the same time as a great many shocked, outraged and even tearful guests staggered back into the lobby after finally being released by the police.

Crackpot looked around, nodded to the PC who was stood against the wall of the lobby as if on sentry duty, and then retired for what he hoped would be an uneventful and restful remainder of the night. The trouble was, it was so restful that hours later, Crackpot found himself being shouted and nudged, pushed and pulled, and finally pinched to make him stir.

"Eh? What the–" yelled Crackpot, jumping up and almost repeating his reflex action after a similar alarm call from the train guard, but he rather comically fell out of bed before he could do so.

The few seconds it took to free himself from the bed covers while he was on the floor were enough to bring him to his senses.

"What is it, man!" he yelled at the young bobby.

"You told me to tell you if our man makes a move; you'll have to hurry, sir! He's checking out!"

"Blast!" yelled Crackpot. He looked at his watch: just gone 9:00 am. He had slept in his clothes, which was, thought Crackpot, quite fortunate. He dragged on his coat, fumbled for his wallet, handed the constable a one pound note, put his wallet back in his pocket, picked up his fishing bag, and ran out, just about managing a nod without turning back, as "Thank you very kindly, sir!" boomed around the corridor.

With a muffled apology he pushed an elderly couple out of the way at the lift door, got in, pushed GF, and stood right in the doorway with his hand held up like a traffic policeman, preventing the stunned and aggrieved couple and now three nuns from getting in with him. The lift went down to the ground, and Crackpot dashed into the lobby. But his haste had all been in vain, in a way; Weber was in the telephone booth at the end of the lobby, with the door wide open, and not even bothering to keep his conversation private – or perhaps secret from Crackpot's point of view.

Crackpot managed a smile at something he had already noticed but didn't know why it had seemed odd. Until now. He now realised that Weber did not conform to the modern style of simply wearing trousers over a prosthetic leg, and perhaps with a wooden foot extension so a shoe could be worn; instead, he simply went pirate style, and, even though he knew he shouldn't be amused by it, he couldn't help but smile as he saw the wooden leg being used to jam the door of the booth open.

"He's been in there ages!" came rather an unsuccessful whisper from the young spotty chap at Reception. He had been advised by the young policeman to report anything unusual concerning their mysterious German guest.

"Ja? Ja ja! Der Dumpkoff?! Ja! Endgyltig. Auf Wiedersehen!" boomed Weber from the booth.

"Hmmm . . . just in time, or was he waiting? No matter, Long John, lead me to the treasure, Arrr!" mused and muttered Crackpot. He turned to face the receptionist as Weber hung up, left the booth and promptly walked out of the hotel. Crackpot could do nothing more than leave it a second, and then recommence his pursuit. Expecting to take up the delayed traipse around a large slice of Manchester, Crackpot looked right, expecting to see Weber ambling along to the shopping area, but he was not to be seen. He then looked left and was surprised to see Weber stood at the bus stop just a few yards down from the hotel on the left. A horse-drawn double-decker omnibus pulled up; Weber boarded and went upstairs to the top deck. Crackpot also boarded and he too dashed up the staircase; with his coat pulled up and his face down, he walked past Weber and sat at the first seat after the top of the staircase on the right.

"Fares, please!" came the shout from the conductor as he came up the stairs. He started at the very front of the now packed top deck. When he got to Weber, Crackpot heard him mutter, and then smiled at the conductor's reply.

"'Ere! If you mean Belle, you know, ding ding! Belle – Vue, then it's thruppence. If you really mean Belly View, then you should have walked up the road to one of them funny places."

Weber simply held out a handful of coins for the conductor to take what he needed. After issuing Weber's ticket, the conductor walked on.

"Huh! Belly View! Bloody foreigners! — Fares please!"

"Where we off to now, me ole China?" muttered Crackpot.

20

Spelling out the Danger

MEANWHILE. . .

Vernon Kell was once again sat at his desk, and once more sitting opposite him was his deputy, Sir Alan Leith-Perkerson. It was early Saturday morning. Sir Alan, although knowing it came with the job, was never happy when being called in to the office at weekends, but when his boss had a bee in his bonnet, all he could do was put away his fork, spade and dibber, tell his wife to remember to water the orchids, put on his suit and overcoat and make the thankfully short trek back to Whitehall.

"I'm sorry, old chap, nothing but briefings and meetings here there and everywhere," said Vernon Kell, who could tell his friend and colleague was exhausted and was not overly delighted to be away from his exotic plants, tropical fish and the Saturday crossword.

"Sir?" replied Sir Alan.

"As soon as this damn business is over, take a week off, and we won't put it on your leave slip. However, the matter at hand. . .

" . . . I didn't want to believe it myself," continued Vernon Kell, pointing at the piece of foolscap once again on his desk and upon which was written the coded message. "But – there it is, in black and white – literally. PKML – *Prince Karl Max Lichnowsky.* If it was just two letters to work out, then, yes, we could say it was just coincidence; three letters, fifty-fifty let's say; but, four letters which match his title and name exactly, and in the light of what we do know for sure compared with what we suspect, then, I am sorry to say, somehow, in some way, the very person sent here to supposedly help ease the tension is trying to pull the wool over our eyes. . ."

"But sir!" protested Sir Alan Leith-Perkerson, "I know the Prince better than any of us! He's as straight as a die, and is so at home here he wouldn't want to jeopardise any of that! I am not sure of this at all, and I beg of you not to do anything rash. Please do remember that even if he was part of some terrible plot, his diplomatic status prevents his arrest."

"True . . . but no harm in the old tea and biscuits routine, German tea that is. I think a mid-morning stroll over to Carlton House Terrace is in order, straight after my meeting with the PM; he's remained at Number 10 for the weekend due to the situation."

"Ah, sorry, that won't do any good. I happen to know Prince Lichnowsky is leaving for Holdsworth House straight after breakfast. Lord and Lady Harrop are having some kind of bash; he won't be back in London until tomorrow night."

"Damn and blast! I wanted to avoid this, but there's no other option now: tell Doris to contact—"

Sir Alan Leith-Perkerson groaned.

"Oh for Heaven's sake, Sir Vernon," he interjected, "not C Brigade and Gentle Jack and all that?"

Vernon Kell rather oddly gave an inane grin, and nodded.

Sir Alan went to protest one more time, but as they had now been in a heated discussion for forty-five minutes without Vernon Kell budging an inch towards the views of his deputy, he just sighed, and slumped back in his chair, exasperated. But after a minute or so of stony silence, he addressed his boss one more time.

"May I ask, sir, in the unlikely event the Ambassador is deemed to be involved in a plot to assassinate the Prime Minister, what on earth do we do then?"

"If, after talking with Prince Lichnowsky, I think there's a case to answer, then, although as you say we cannot arrest him, we can, after letting him return to the German Embassy, at least deport him at a later date, international law at least allows that," replied Vernon Kell.

"Very well . . . C Brigade it is, but don't blame me if the PM carpets you over this, you've pulled this stunt once too often. . . " said Sir Alan.

*

Seven foot one inch Jack Hulty with a fifty-six inch chest wasn't the brightest member of the secret service, but his appearance, demeanour and physique came in very useful in certain circumstances; this rather oddly included the task of calling on various VIPs to issue cordial invitations for them to imbibe with one or more senior officials of His Majesty's Government. On these occasions, Jack had never yet failed His Majesty's Secret Intelligence Service.

*

It was 8:30 am precisely. Upon arriving at Prussia House, 'Gentle Jack' bypassed the usual protocol and decorum when visiting foreign embassies. On the instant the front door was opened, he walked right up to the footman and gave him a hearty slap on the back. Then came the equally hearty salutation.

"'Ow yer doin', me ole mucker, Karlikins abaht?"

For some strange reason, Jack did not appear to have heard that the Ambassador had made prior arrangements, preferring instead to proceed onwards along the hallway, after reassuring the astounded (and shaking) footman:

"Don' worry yerself; in 'ere is it?"

Seconds later, he was stood in front of the desk behind which sat the stunned and perspiring Prince Karl Max Lichnowsky. Jack proceeded to state his business while the Ambassador looked on, aghast, holding tightly onto his white napkin while the yolk from a soft boiled egg dribbled down his chin and onto his sparklingly clean white shirt.

" . . . Mr Kell? Today? Now? I am sorry, but—" went to protest the German Ambassador after receiving the hearty invite. But it was to no avail.

" . . . Yus, Guv', he'd like to see yer, right away, fink there's upsaad dahn cake or summat; any'ow, he won' take no fer a' answer, so best ge' yer best whistle 'n' flute on and come wiv me, sharpish."

The German Ambassador to Great Britain looked to his aide, who in turn shrugged and then decided to stare down at an interesting picture of a camel on the Persian carpet.

The Ambassador mopped his brow, and the egg yolk with his

handkerchief, stood, and indicated to Gentle Jack to lead the way, waving away other staff members who appeared in the doorway and who had tried to intervene. They walked out of the office, down the wide corridor, out through the double doors, up the gravelled path, out of the gates, and up to a large imported American Cadillac, in which sat the almost equally beefy C Brigade of His Majesty's Intelligence Service. They gave wide smiles as Prince Lichnowsky reluctantly climbed into the back of the car; the Ambassador noticed quite a number of blackened teeth, cracked teeth, and the occasional gap where the black or cracked tooth which used to be there, had obviously been declared being beyond all useful purpose.

Prince Karl Max Lichnowsky was finally unnerved.

"Y-you can't arrest me! I am the German Ambassador to Great Britain! I have diplomatic immunity!"

"Arres' yer?!" exclaimed Jack. "Don' be soft, we's just takin' yer fer a birra grub wiv the boss, all nice 'n' friendly like. O' course, if you don' wanna come wiv us. . ."

The Ambassador went to explain that he really should be on his way to Holdsworth House, but then noticed Gentle Jack doing his best to adopt a friendly smile, but upon seeing Jack's face up close, the Ambassador yelped, jumped, mopped his brow again, and said, "No, sorry, my mistake. Yes, let us – er – go and see Sir Vernon. W-was I supposed to bring a whistle with me? Or a flute? Or-or both, perhaps?"

Loud guffaws from all of C Brigade within the confines of the staff car gave the Ambassador earache. The car drove off and no one spoke again for the rest of the journey, which was thankfully short.

*

Prince Karl Max Lichnowsky sat opposite Vernon Kell in the Head of British Intelligence's office. Through musing on the possibility of the Ambassador being left alone with Gentle Jack, Kell had had second thoughts; he had feigned a bad migraine and had left the PM's briefing only minutes after it had started. He wanted to ensure he was back for the Ambassador's arrival. To the right side of the Ambassador sat Sir Alan, and to the rear of the room stood the impassive Gentle Jack, not taking any notice of the proceedings, instead, just filing down his fingernails with a nail file.

" . . . This is intolerable!" protested the Ambassador, his tea and biscuits left untouched. "Brought here by force, and–"

"By force, did you say, Your Excellency? Were you threatened in any way by my men? Did they manhandle you at all?" said Vernon Kell.

"No, but–" said the Ambassador, looking nervously to the rear of the room.

"But what, Your Excellency? I was merely ensuring your security, looking after you, you know how it is these days. . ."

"But that giant of a man there! He-he-he. . ." The Ambassador mentally struggled to do so, but could not actually think of anything tangible which had happened which constituted any wrong doing, and knew that even if he was able to, it was doubtful he was going to utter it there and then. As he gave another nervous glance to the rear of the room, Vernon Kell pressed home his advantage.

"I have also been informed that Mr Hulty did enquire if you did actually want to accept the invitation? Was that not so? If that's the case, then I do humbl—"

"No, no, you are quite right," said the Ambassador, who now knew he had been outmanoeuvred from the moment Gentle Jack had arrived at the embassy. "But," said the Ambassador, at last finding some composure and resolve from deep within, "do not treat me like a fool any longer, you of all people, too. Why have you really had me brou— why was I invited here today. . . ?"

"Mr Hulty, thank you for getting His Excellency to us safe and sound, you may go," said Vernon Kell, dismissing the most terrifying bodyguard that Prince Lichnowsky was ever likely to set eyes on ever again.

Once the door was closed, Vernon Kell reluctantly laid out his suspicions, and even showed the Ambassador the message in Simple-Cypher.

Prince Karl Max Lichnowsky went white as he read the message, both in its original form, and in plain English as provided by Sir Alan Leith-Perkerson. Sir Alan, with the agreement of his boss, also went on to explain the rest of the message, now also duly decoded, or so both men believed. The Port–Gaol–Domicile part of the message, supposedly referred to Walton House, the country home of the Prime Minister; the name of this abode had become known during the frantic arranging of additional security for Mr Asquith starting that very day, and which was to continue right through to and including Tuesday January the 14th. Once the country house had been referred to, both verbally and in written form, Sir Alan knew at once that the Port-Gaol reference must mean Walton Jail in Liverpool, Britain's major port. Domicile, which, when considered on its own, then became glaringly obvious as being a sort of cryptic synonym for a house or a residence with a link to the PM, thus – *Walton House.*

"You think I sent the original coded message? *AND* you think I am an assassin?! This is an outrage! Mein Gott, Sir Vernon, if our two nations do end up at war with each other, it will be you and these crazy accusations which will have lit the fuse! And all because of some stupid prank by a dumbkoff who can't even translate properly!"

But Vernon Kell remained resolute.

"And that, Ambassador, is exactly what an assassin whose cover was blown would say, would he not? Come on, Your Excellency, trying to say it's a prank and saying the grammar's not up to scratch, you are a better man than that. Now then, Ambassador . . . we all know we can't actually touch you, but co-operate, tell us who else is involved besides Weber and yourself, and we can even work out something for you to say or do, which would enable you to save face – what do you say?"

"I DID NOT WRITE THAT DAMNED LETTER! IF I HAD DONE SO, THEN I CAN ASSURE YOU THAT THE SPELLING WOULD HAVE BEEN CORRECT! WHO ON EARTH SPELLS JAIL – *G – A – O - L ?"*

"We do," came the comic reply, made so by it being uttered at exactly the same time by Vernon Kell and his deputy.

"WELL I DON'T!" insisted the enraged and now purple-faced Ambassador.

Sir Alan Leith-Perkerson's face adopted a quizzical look. He went to say something but a gesture from his boss to remain quiet stopped him.

"You are making me repeat myself, Your Excellency. Of course you are going to deny the very thing we know you have done, that much at least stands to reason. But it's no use; *we know;* you *know* that we know; we know that you *KNOW* we know. The game's up, old friend. . . "

Prince Karl Max Lichnowsky stood, his face alternating from whitest white and back again to deepest purple. He was so outraged it had taken him beyond further verbal protests. He just continued to stand, snorting through his nose.

Vernon Kell stared intently at the Ambassador, but then his face softened and he spoke once more.

"Fortunately, Your Excellency, for you that is, I cannot hold you, this was after all, a convivial chat over tea and biscuits, was it not? You are free to go, for the moment. . . "

"And what is that supposed to mean?!" demanded the Ambassador.

"As our Pinkerton friends say, don't leave town; although we cannot arrest you, we are, I believe, entitled to ask you to co-operate further, should this be deemed necessary." Vernon Kell said this not only to irk, but also out of desperation, as in his calmer state it had dawned on him that he may be fighting a losing battle, even if his suspicions were to be proved correct.

The Ambassador raged away in German, and stormed out of the building.

After he was well on his way, late, to Holdsworth House, Sir Alan Leith-Perkerson spoke once more.

"Was that really worth it, sir? What has it proved? What use has it been?"

"Well, I didn't expect him to break down and spill the beans, but sometimes you have no option but to let suspects know that they are indeed suspects. It can panic them; make them do rash things; show their hand. . . "

"It can also enrage someone who has done nothing but good, thus far anyway, and force them to become the person you are making them out to be. Self-fulfilling demonisation I would call it! Have you thought of that, *Sir Vernon?"* said an exasperated Sir Alan Leith-Perkerson.

"Yes! I've thought of that, too! *Sir Alan—"*

"But you didn't even listen to him when he said he doesn't spell Gaol with a G! That could be important, and you just totally dismissed it!"

"Not you as well, Alan. My God, man, Gaol with a G or a J! It doesn't matter, just on the hoof flim-flam to try and weasel out of it!"

"But—"

"Enough! Please leave me for now, I need to work out what to do about Charles and our friend Weber, it looks like we're fighting this threat on more than one front."

"Very well, sir, I shall be in my office if you need me."

Vernon Kell was now 'miles away', staring at the middle distance; he eventually gave a rather cryptic reply.

" . . . Or are we. . ."

"I'm sorry, Sir Vernon. . . ?"

"Nothing, nothing," replied Vernon Kell coming back to the here and now, "I will call you if I need you. . . "

21

Are there Waves in the Water?

STOPPING every few hundred yards to let so many passengers on and so many off, the omnibus left London Road and drove straight onto Downing Street, this in turn became Ardwick Green South, called so due to the road bordering a large common on the south side, complementing Ardwick Green North on the far side. This took the omnibus out of the cotton-rich city centre, and into to the sadly-slum district of Gorton. The omnibus gently rocked as it was pulled along. The easy rhythm and the sickly smelly warmth from on-board paraffin heaters soon saw Crackpot's eyelids drooping – he also lolloped to his right with his mouth wide open and drooled down the front of a large Irish lady, large in all areas and wearing a low-necked dress. He didn't know she was Irish, until. . .

"What the Fe–"

"Belle Vue! Everyone to alight here please! Belle Vue!" came the shout from the conductor.

Crackpot sat bolt upright with his eyes doing an expert imitation of a barn owl.

With the Irish lady indulging in a little socio-ecumenism by way of demonstrating her skills in Anglo-Saxon, Crackpot, almost in panic, turned and looked to the rear of the upper carriage of the bus. He just managed to see Weber out of the corner of his eye making his next move: Weber stood and hastily made his way down the staircase, hopped off the bus at the back, and walked up and onto the gravelled area leading to the entrance of the gardens-cum-funfair-cum-zoo.

Crackpot stood and left the still irate Mrs O'Hoolihan or whoever, mopping her bosom with a handkerchief, and who had still not yet moved on from the letter F in the Anglo Saxon alphabet.

Crackpot ran down the stairs, jumped off the bus, and quickly found Weber in his sights, just feet away; he was stood to one side of the crowds approaching the entrance to a place Crackpot knew not where. As Weber, thankfully facing the entrance, lit a cigar, Crackpot glanced up and saw the handsome gold painted sign, which read:

Belle Vue Zoological Gardens

The omnibus had come to the end of its journey – a special hourly service from Manchester city centre, out to the world famous zoo and gardens. Rather ironically, the horse drawn service, the very last of its kind in the Manchester area, had been retained rather than discontinued for this route, which had long ago been the unfortunate fate of all other such services on all other routes. But the Manchester Carriage company believed the novelty of travelling to Belle Vue by true horse power would help fight off very stiff competition from electric trams, the new fangled motorised bus services and of course the ever expanding rail network – although this harbinger of doom for equinic powered conveyance had been on Belle Vue's doorstep since 1840, in the form of the especially sited Longsight Railway Station.

Over the years from its grand opening in 1836, the proprietors of Belle Vue Zoological Gardens had tagged on a whole host of other popular attractions, including two boating lakes, a funfair, bandstands, ballrooms, a natural history museum sited on an island in the middle of one of the lakes; a scenic railway which wound its way right around the perimeter of the gardens; hotels, tea-rooms, beer gardens; and even a race course. If the famed natural scientist Charles Darwin had ever been inclined to make a visit, there is a good chance he would have ended up wearing a Kiss-Me-Quick-hat while perusing the *Racing Times* at the same time as eating a bar of rock.

Although Crackpot had never previously heard of the place, if Weber was going in there for some as yet unknown reason, so was he. But right at that moment he had to move aside as Weber had done, but then turned and faced the road. He then lit a cigarette in typical Vaudeville style; this is when the atrocious bird call imitator or perhaps the Romanian juggler – in reality the ubiquitous Al Kowalski from the Bronx, gets a sign from the wings that there's an extra minute to fill – with anything that comes to mind.

A large family walked up to the admission kiosk built in to the brick archway punctuating the otherwise constant, uniform, neatly trimmed hedging which ran right around the attraction's perimeter. These were followed by Weber.

Crackpot, who had casually turned back several times, now saw Weber move smartly up to the rear of the happy, noisy brood waiting for Dad to pay up and get them in. Crackpot decided to wait until Weber was no longer the rearguard; it wasn't long before one courting couple, two old dears and what could only be a grandmother, mother and daughter, had also joined the queue. Crackpot walked over, stood behind the granite-faced member of the trio with a huge handbag, and rooted out some change for the admission. If he was too obvious or was either careless or impatient at this point, then he knew the game would be up. But neither could he risk losing sight of Weber, even in the relatively compact Belle Vue Gardens and Zoo, or what ever the hell its proper name was, thought Crackpot.

After seeing the weary father of seven lead his cash-eating offspring deeper into the establishment, Crackpot knew that seconds later, Weber would also be beyond the archway. These were soon followed by the sweethearts and the pensioners, but Crackpot then heard something to make him groan and panic inside, just a little. . .

"I'm sorry, madam, that was last week, a special – this week it is full price. Now do you want to come in – or not?"

The mother, ignoring her daughter, talked over the tearful Geraldine stamping her foot, and said to her own mother, *"Shall we?* Or is it too expensive?"

Crackpot had had enough.

"Excuse me, you may or may not want to get in, as for me, I most certainly do." He then pushed past, but accidentally stood on granite-grannie's foot as he did so.

"Ow!" said Gran."

"How very rude!" added the mother.

"Mu-um! I want to thee the cwockadillos!" said spoilt Geraldine.

Crackpot then flung the correct admission down on the counter, turned, took one step forward, and due to his anger and impatience hurt his ribs on the turnstile which he was just too quick for.

"Ooh, that hurt," said Crackpot, dashing through and immediately scanning the area for his quarry.

The ticket man turned away from the kiosk window and looked to the right and down at Crackpot. "Serves him right," he said, but only once he knew Crackpot was out of earshot. He then turned back to the window.

"Now, madam, we are very busy today; are you – oh, right. . ." In his distraction he had not seen the unhappy mother brandishing the full admission for all three generations. "Here you are, then. . ." he said, as he issued the tickets.

Although still bitterly cold, the wind which had raged all of the previous day and most of the night, had gone. For all those who were suitably wrapped up, they found a stroll around the gardens or viewing the swans in one of the lakes, a highly enjoyable affair, made even more enjoyable when it was followed by a hot sugared brandy in one of the licensed establishments dotted around the grounds. But Crackpot sighed as he walked past one such hostelry, and once more took up his tailing of an enemy of the state.

He could see Weber, slowly ambling along the path which went right around the boating lake which had been built on the western side of the grounds, and which had in its centre a man-made island upon which was the attraction's natural history museum.

Weber stopped, looked out across the lake at a bevy of Mute swans, and then lit a cigar. As he took the first drag, he turned to his left and seemed to glance down towards Crackpot, who in turn was thankful that there did not seem to be any hint of recognition and so assumed that his tailing of Weber was still untainted.

Weber turned back to his swan gazing at the same time as a plump middle aged betweeded lady, carpet bag to match and with large black glasses, arrived to feed the ducks. Weber glanced at the woman, and said to himself, 'governess'. This was based purely on the stereotypical image of British governesses and perhaps nannies, but he plumped for governess, as in his mind a nanny would look a lot kinder and friendlier; although he could never know it for sure himself, he was spot on.

Crackpot strained his eyes. He rather comically did this whenever he was out of earshot of a conversation he would much rather hear every word of, but screwing up his eyes up had not, to date, increased his hearing power and it looked very much as if this sad truth was going to be borne out today. But Crackpot suddenly realised that his usual unexceptional hearing was all that he would need right at that moment.

"A lovely morning, *yes?"* said Weber, loudly, and who then paused for a second, seemingly to await an appropriate reply, but a second later, again in a loud voice, he spoke again to the bemused bundle of tartanesque itcheries,. "I see you have made the rendevous point unharmed."

The breathing mound of bespectacled tweed twitched a little, but said nothing and continued to look at the swans.

"Are the ducks all in a row and has the eagle left his nest?" continued the now conspiratorial sounding Weber, although still in a loud voice.

The woman was now beginning to get annoyed and a little concerned, but she summoned the courage to turn and face Weber.

"I beg your pardon?"

"Well – what about the waves? Are there waves in the water?"

"What?! What are you talking about? Waves? What waves?"

"Well have you informed the *Zoo Keeper?"*

"Now look here! I don't know what you think you are—"

"Have – you – informed – the – zoo – kee-per?" repeated Weber, as if talking to a deaf person in a non-PC manner, or someone slow on the uptake – or both.

"What about the zoo keeper?!"

The lady's face was now bright red, perhaps through embarrassment and maybe fear, but also out of anger.

"Have the geese flown south for the winter?" Weber went on

quickly, still very loudly, but also with an unintentional sardonic chuckle to his voice.

"If you don't stop this right now, I am calling the police!" shouted the now scared governess, but she managed to keep the fear out of her demands to cease and desist.

Weber looked across the lake at something coming around the bend of the path towards him, and which Crackpot could not yet see as his view was obscured by several large trees. Weber nodded to himself, smiled, and spoke again, softly now, this was for the lady's ears only.

"That's it – now louder, and scream for the police; you should be able to buy me enough time to get away. When they question you, say you don't know me and that you've never had any contact with German agents."

"AARRGHH! HELP! POLICE! POLICE!" screamed the terrified and now white-faced green-garbed governess. only too willing to acquiesce to Weber's suggestion.

As the horse and cart containing elephant manure finally rounded the bend and became level with Weber and the governess, the German agent suddenly jumped up onto the front seat, threw the driver to the floor, whipped the poor horse hard, and off they dashed, the horse, the cart, and Gerhard Weber. Crackpot thought 'two can play at that game' as the cart came racing up to his position; but he was proved badly wrong when he mistimed his jump and smacked his head on the side of the cart, fell back, and Weber raced on and away. A few yards on, Weber unhitched the cart which crashed into the wall of the monkey house, depositing its load which cleared the wall and landed right on top of a chimpanzee.

Crackpot straightened up and rubbed his head. He frantically looked around, and sighed. He knew that to yell 'Stop that man! would have been pointless. All he could see were hordes of kids with harassed parents, none of whom would have been any help at all. Unluckily, there were no other carts, carriages, or horses, or any type of vehicle, organic or motorised which he could commandeer and once more take up the chase – he knew he had lost his man, as did a gleeful Weber.

Despite his mind echoing with Vernon Kell's pleas for his best man to save the day, Crackpot began to think it was not to be; on top of being despondent at losing his man he was also in a state of exhaustion which gave him a less than positive attitude; he thought he was beaten. But at least he had the consolation prize of a not too fast on her feet collaborator, so slow she actually didn't move at all; but what she lacked in guileful mobility she more than made up for in decibels. The governess screamed her innocence as Crackpot brandished his made to measure warrant card and arrested her. Crackpot was inwardly impressed by how realistic the woman's protests were, as well as her willingness to sacrifice herself to buy her collaborator some time.

Crackpot was desperate to leave the attraction and finally find a policeman to aid him. He didn't want to hurt the lady in any way, he was too much of a gentlemen, but nor could he be soft with a suspected enemy of the state and so kept a firm grip on the lady's left arm which he held up her back as they walked along. But that was not enough to stop the deafening protests.

"Unhand me, you brute! How dare you! *How dare you!'* And then with her free hand – Slap. "You will be in so much trouble when my employer finds out!" Slap. "He has friends in high places! He'll make sure you are clapped in irons and you won't see daylight again for forty years!" Slap. "You'll hang for this!" Slap Slap.

"Do make your mind up, madam," said a weary Crackpot, but still managing a grim smile while he rubbed his face which was now red and stinging badly.

But she still wasn't finished.

"Help! Help me! I'm being kidnapped! Help me, someone! Fetch the police! *MURDER!"*

One brave knight in shining armour, well, a thick travelling cloak and long heavy scarf, did try to aid the perceived damsel in distress.

He had been walking quickly due to being late for his presentation in the museum across the lake. He was almost abreast of the pair; he had heard the row and now saw that the man was holding the lady's arm up her back.

"Unhand her you vagabond! Now!"

He went to remonstrate with Crackpot, but Crackpot just about managed to hold him off, push him away and then once more proffer his warrant card with his free hand.

"Run along now, sir, you are interfering in police business. This lady has been arrested for improper behaviour, so to speak."

"But the lady is yelling *for* the police!" retorted the man, and very loudly to make himself heard over the woman's verbal outrage upon hearing the grounds for her arrest.

"Go and find a policeman, then! Bring him here," said Crackpot, outmanoeuvring the would-be rescuer.

"You'll just run away!"

"Don't be ridiculous!" snorted Crackpot. *"With all these people here?!"* Crackpot gestured with his free hand for the man to look around. The ruckus had attracted a small crowd. "I need two men to wait with me! Anyone?!"

Crackpot knew there was only a slim chance that this would be taken up by any of the adult males in the small gathering, but he really said it to convince the one person from the zoo and gardens' patrons who had tried to help – the chivalrous professor. None other came forward or raised their hand or replied, but it had had the right effect.

"I do apologise, Officer, my mistake," said the professor. "Can I assist you in any way?"

"I could still do with – er – *another policeman?"* said the hopeful Crackpot.

About two hours later, in the darkened back room of Gorton Police Station. Crackpot was stood, leaning over one side of a small table, shining the light from a table lamp into the face of the terrified governess.

"What is your name? Who is the Zoo Keeper? What did Weber want with him? What did Weber want with *you?!"* This had been Crackpot's relentless mantra for over forty-five minutes.

Despite telling Crackpot countless times that her name was Alice Abernathy and that she worked as a governess, and didn't know Weber from Adam, Crackpot just didn't believe her.

"What is your name? Who is the Zoo Keeper? What did Weber

want with him? What did Weber want with *you?!*"

"M-M-Mr Abercrombie . . . he's the z-z-zoo k-keeper, he's worked there for years; he's not a spy – and nor am I – *please . . . the light. . . it's hurting my eyes. . .*" said a tearful Mrs Alice Abernathy, governess to the children of Mrs Felicity Lowes-Byons, and her husband who was Cecil Heathcliffe Lowes-Byons - Mayor of Manchester – and long time leader of the City of Manchester Conservative party.

"This is getting nowhere," muttered Crackpot to himself. He then decided a change of tactics was needed; he left the dark room to go and tell the desk sergeant he wanted someone to go and fetch the woman's employer, who apparently would see Crackpot clapped in irons for forty years — and then hanged. He wasn't sure if his presence would help or hinder, but it was worth a try. What he could not know was that this would bring the current situation to an embarrassing head.

Cecil Heathcliffe Lowes-Byons went apoplectic when he heard what had happened to his employee – and although not common knowledge as one can imagine – his mistress. He dismissed the constable from his drawing room, picked up his telephone, and asked the operator to put him through to a very good friend of his.

"The number?" said Cecil, "Oh, yes . . . *it's Whitehall 1001. . .*"

A few seconds later. . .

"Hello, Vern, Cec here. . ."

Although it felt like an eternity to Alice Abernathy, thirty minutes later she was free once again to bore other people's children with the wonders of Latin, Homer's Odyssey and of course remembering to ignore Blucher's contribution at Waterloo. She aso hit Crackpot rather hard with her brolly as they left the station, and this went unabated in the squad car taking her home. Crackpot received one very hard clout on the head as a final parting shot as Alice Abernathy climbed out upon pulling up outside Hallgrove Manor. This was at the end of a long and winding private road, just about half a mile from the centre of Cheadle Hulme in Greater Manchester.

But upon arriving back at the station with the promise of a good meal and a kip in one of the cells, Crackpot heard the rather surprising news that Gerhard Weber had been sighted on Platform 2 Manchester Victoria Station, just sitting on a bench reading a newspaper. . .

22

Going further North

AFTER BEING GIVEN A LIFT by a constable from the police station, Crackpot rushed through the archway into Manchester Victoria, and immediately spotted his prey, sitting on the bench on the platform. He had been rumbled once, it could not be allowed to happen again. Crackpot stood by the door to the mens' conveniences, just inside the main entrance and against the wall to the left. Weber was about fifty yards away to his right. A wall which stood out from the actual entrance to the gents gave Crackpot at least some cover, and hoped that his planned game of peek-a-boo while waiting for his quarry to make a move would not result in Weber actually joining in.

A train, which had been building up steam for several minutes was now being boarded by an increasing throng of a strange mix of the poor and well-heeled: lads and lasses, families, couples, pensioners, and even several clergymen of different persuasions; many wore striped coloured scarves, and some of the younger passengers were carrying wooden rattles.

"Ah, a footy match. Wrong shaped ball methinks, but it explains a lot," Crackpot said to himself. He now knew why a regional service was so busy on a cold January morning. He dwelled no further on the matter and turned his head back and once more scanned for sight of his quarry. He saw Weber stub out his cigar, throw the newspaper into the rubbish bin at the end of the bench, and then hop up and board the train.

Crackpot left it to the very last minute.

The whistle went, the flag was waved, and Crackpot just jumped on in time, after hastily checking the destination board – the train was bound for a town called Nelson. He was in the same carriage as Weber but they were at opposite ends to each other; although he could see him clearly at the moment, he knew it may not be the case for the whole journey. All he could do was pray that when Weber made his next move, he would still be right behind.

Because the train was packed from the off, and because most passengers were going all the way to Nelson, the train simply became more and more packed. Some did alight at each station of course, but even more got on.

Crackpot's desperate commandeering of the exit door of his carriage drew some funny looks from concerned passengers and eventually, the guard, as he stepped right off at each station the train stopped at, and even leaning right out of the window as the train sped along,.

"'Ere Guv'! What's your game?! Folks's gotta get on and off 'ere!"

"Police business," came the curt reply. Without even looking around, Crackpot once again produced his warrant card for all occasions.

"Oh," is all the guard said by way of reply, and went back to his *Daily Mirror* and corned beef sandwich.

23

Milling around the Mill Town

THE TRAIN pulled into Nelson without there having been any onboard theatrics. Weber alighted, took one short casual glance over his shoulder, then along with the veritable throng of businessmen, shoppers and football fans, ambled along the platform at a leisurely pace and then hobbled up the stairs and out on to Railway Street. Crackpot, with his 'fishing tackle' slung over his shoulder, began to follow his prey. This time he was careful to maintain a safe distance so as to hopefully remain unseen by Weber in the event of his taking a chance look behind.

Neither Crackpot nor Weber had realised that the small town of Nelson, usually so dull, grey and quiet would be uncharacteristically buzzing on that particular Saturday. The reason for this was that one of the town's football teams, Nelson Corinthians, had drawn a home tie against Manchester United in the First Round of the FA Cup.

The streets were packed, which at least took some of the bite out of the icy wind for those nearer to the middle of the penguin-like moving huddles; it was freezing cold and the breath of thousands permeated the air as the crowds moved along the already gaslit streets. It wasn't actually dark yet but there was no way the gas lighters were going to miss the match. The throngs of young and old, boys and girls and men and women, made their way haphazardly along the cobbled streets to Grindlay Park, the team's home ground. Many supporters haphazardly meandered all over the cobbles themselves, resulting in angry yells from drivers and beeps from hooters from the strange mixture of cars and vans and horse drawn carts, and even the occasional angry grunty, 'Oy!', from a variety of hawkers, labourers and itinerant tinkers whose faces were contorted with the effort of pushing or even pulling huge heavily laden hand-carts.

Weber decided he may as well follow the crowd; he turned left at the top of Railway Street and then crossed Broadway, the widest and busiest street in the town. He was hooted several times and nearly knocked over as he momentarily forgot that they drove on the left in England. He also nearly tripped as his wooden leg became jammed in between two of the cobbles on the road, but by staying still and pulling hard on the leg to release it, it finally came loose and on he went, once more joining the meandering throng.

With Crackpot about twenty paces behind, although at times this lengthened a little due to his having trouble weaving in and out of the seemingly endless gaggles of spud-faced toothless grannies with bonnets, shawls, pinnies and bread baskets coming towards him, Weber simply went with the heaving mass as they turned right onto Victoria Street.

About halfway up on the right side, was Grindlay Park, Nelson Corinthians' stadium. This was one of the smallest stadiums from all of the teams in the professional league, including those in lower divisions. But it still had two largish terraces at the north and south ends of the ground. The former bordered the Leeds-Liverpool Canal, bar a short slip road with a gravel surface which ran along between the turnstiles and the high wall, preventing (hopefully) even more dips into the canal than was already the case; this was the Solomon Lane End. The latter and larger of the two ends was the Grindlay Road End.

*

Gerhard Weber was a big fan of football back home in Germany. In the last few years he had also taken to the British game. He noticed that although there seemed to be a comparative lack of skill on the ball, the game was faster and more furious. He particularly liked the early rounds of the FA Cup where veritable minnows could try and overcome bigger and (usually), better teams. Weber had become a fan of Chelsea, but he also liked Manchester United, who were the visitors in the game he was soon to watch.

Weber looked around and noticed that far fewer people were queueing for the side terraces on Victoria Road. He walked further over and joined the nearest queue, paid the penny-ha'penny admission at the turnstile and went in. Moreover, after looking at his watch, he was no longer overly concerned whether he was still being tailed – or not.

As for Crackpot, he found that twenty paces behind your quarry in a dense crowd, may as well be twenty miles.

24

A Grandstand View

THERE ARE TIMES to disguise oneself as a dustman or a bank manager, there are times to assume the identity of a plain clothes detective from Scotland Yard Special Branch, and on very rare occasions one has to own up to being a secret agent. The last option was not a good idea – not today – but nor would a dustman or bank manager seemingly holding a set of fishing rods in a bag over his shoulder, ask the chairman of a football club if there was a suitable vantage point somewhere around the stadium to be able to carry out surveillance on a known enemy of the state. This left Crackpot with only one option, as imperfect as it was.

Chief Inspector Carruthers proffered his well used of late but misleading warrant card, to the doorman in his hut at the main gates to Grindlay Park and explained his business. Alfie Snoddie, who had been badly shaken after the fracas earlier in the season and who had only remained at the club after being promised a brand new crutch, bade the chief to follow him over on to the marble porch and through the main door to the reception area. He asked the chief inspector to sit down on the leather couch while he struggled upstairs to see if Mr Grindlay was available.

A few minutes later, a puzzled Mr Grindlay came down the heavily carpeted staircase and was led to where Chief Inspector Carruthers was seated. Alfie introduced the two men to each other, doffed his cap and hobbled back to his duties.

" . . . An enemy of the country . . . right here . . . *in my stadium?"* asked a perplexed Solomon Grindlay, after the inspector had explained the reasons for his presence.

"Yes, that is correct," replied the chief inspector.

"There . . . there won't be any . . . *unpleasantness,* will there?" asked a worried Solomon.

"Not if I can help it," said the chief inspector, who knew that whatever happened during the game he had to keep the chairman as calm as possible. But he knew he could not absolutely guarantee the situation could be successfully contained or kept entirely low-key. He had considered demanding that the game be called off, but there would then possibly be the even greater problem of unrest among the large crowd leading to absolute chaos.

After more thought on exactly how he would watch, or apprehend if this became warranted, or even kill Gerhard Weber, Carruthers realised that once again he needed help for any or all of these possibilities. And if it did come to having to bring his quarry down, then he knew he simply could not risk a shot across the stadium that was, or at least soon would be packed to the rafters.

"Mr Grindlay," said Crackpot in a business like tone, "I will need the help of the local police, please contact them immediately; just say there is a troublemaker in the crowd, no more. I will need two constables, no more, no less. I will also need somewhere where I can carry out my surveillance undisturbed and which preferably allows me to survey the whole stadium."

"There's the new press box; it's not quite finished yet, there's still some painting and other bits and bobs to be done," suggested Grindlay.

"Damn! How inconvenient!" cracked Crackpot.

"Well, there's the . . . er. . ."

"I'm joking," said Crackpot, "that sounds fine; now if you would please show me the way. . ."

Crackpot followed Solomon Grindlay up the staircase, along a corridor, up a smaller, plainer uncarpeted staircase and then through a door into the brand new but as yet unfinished press box.

"Thank you; now, please do contact the police and please see that I am not disturbed, even by the painters. . ." said Crackpot with a thin smile on his otherwise grim face.

Solomon Grindlay smiled rather stupidly in return, took out his handkerchief and mopped his brow and hurried off out of the room.

Crackpot placed the bag with his rifle down upon the ledge that ran right along the bottom of the large, wide rectangular observation point. For most matches, barring the most inclement of weather, this was just an empty space with the down-sliding windows pushed down into the gap in the front wall of the press box, but at the moment they were all fully up and firmly closed. Beneath this were a dozen small wooden chairs tucked in underneath the ledge. The room was for the various sports reporters from both the local and national newspapers to be able to view the match clearly and unhindered. Exactly the thing needed right now, thought Crackpot.

"I wonder. . ." said Crackpot. He took the rifle from the bag, placed the butt tightly into his shoulder and looking over the sights pointed the gun at the windows and started to scan the crowd; seconds later he just couldn't believe his luck: Gerhard Weber of the German Embassy in London gave a grim smile, opened the top button of his cloak and reached into the inside top left pocket of his tweed jacket and took out a small thin cigar and a book of matches. He lit the cigar, left it in his mouth and leaned forward and placed both hands on the crash barrier, and then grinned broadly.

Right at that moment, Charles *'Crackpot'* Carruthers of the British Secret Service, had Weber in the sights of his Lee Enfield 303.

"Bingo!" exclaimed Crackpot. But then thoughts rather than words tickled the nerve-endings in his brain in the form of the dictat from Vernon Kell concerning the need for surveillance only.

Crackpot, although considered by many within the service to be somewhat cavalier, was only cavalier when it came to *how* he carried out his orders; there was a difference, as subtle as it may be, between how he did things and actually disobeying an order. *'If the order had been to kill,'* thought Crackpot, "Then, me boyo," he said out loud, "I'd be havin' an early tea from the chip shop and a few pints of Lancashire's best." But Crackpot lowered his rifle, sighed, and decided to wait for the police to arrive.

25

The Order of the Boot

ERIC'S MUSINGS ON THINGS PAST FADED, but as he came back to the here and now while still sat on the bench in the dressing room, he was nevertheless still deep in thought, but with more up to date concerns occupying his mind. He was not at all sure if he had done the right thing; although his deepest innermost self simply wanted to play football until he dropped, literally, rather than being hauled off the pitch due to a lacklustre performance, the spark of reality also burned deeply inside him, fighting against such unrealistic desire.

Eric nodded to himself; he now knew that this really was his last game; no matter if the rest of the club dropped dead of the bubonic plague, his playing days would in just under two hours, still be well and truly over.

Lofty came back over to Eric and sat next to him on the bench, but he didn't speak. Lofty's own prematch nerves always seemed to kick in last, well after the rest of the team so this was nothing unusual; but he also had the flu' but had deliberately concealed the worst of its effects from the manager and trainers as he was loathe to miss the game.

With his long reverie now over, Eric came back to the here and now; he saw Lofty's whiter than usual face at the ten minutes to kick-off stage and guessed the truth of the matter.

"You're – oh 'eck – bang on time."

Just as Eric was about to remonstrate with his friend, the local vicar and big fan of the Corinthians, the Reverend Heath Harrop arrived for the long established and embarrassing (to Eric) tradition of blessing Eric's right boot.

While his team mates duly smirked, the vicar duly gave his blessing; he usually whispered it so quietly that it was inaudible, but today Eric could just catch the words, 'Last time out, Lord; let him bow out with style – and put ten past the Reds. Amen.' The vicar stood and smiled, but instead of walking away as he always did with his countenance suggesting he'd just fixed it for the team, today he offered his hand to Eric; who had the good grace to stand and shake Reverend Harrop's hand warmly.

"Thanks for all you've done for me and the boys, Reverend; if the big fella's not a Corinthians fan by now, he – er – never will be," said Eric, rather uncertainly as he was not sure of how to end his appraisal of the situation.

The vicar just smiled again, turned away, and with a wave to the rest of the lads left to take up his place in the stand. Eric wasn't sure but he thought he saw tears in his eyes. Eric then turned again to his good friend Lofty.

"You're not up to this, you daft sod; why didn't you say something?" said Eric quietly to his old friend.

"Yeah, you may be right; but I thought if I got half a bottle of scotch down me and got a good kip, I'd be OK."

"But you're not, are you?" replied Eric.

"Nope; been on the bog all night, alternating each end as and when required."

"Bloody 'ell! I wonder if throwing up over the other team's centre-forward is a foul?" asked Eric.

"We'll soon find ou– pwuuurrgh," went to say Lofty, who had to dash off to the toilets to the side of the team bath.

26

The Waiting Game

CRACKPOT LOVED HIS assignments in the provinces. Although from a wealthy titled family he was, mainly through the bitter experiences of both war and civil unrest, very sympathetic to the plight and the cause of the working man and their families. To keep up appearances and to avoid any conflict with his family or employers, he guffawed away with the best of 'em at endless private clubs, country estates and embassies – but then secretly voted Labour at each General Election.

Crackpot pulled out a chair from the space under the ledge and sat down. He then leaned forward, squinted his eyes and checked to see if Weber was still there – he was but the stadium was now filling up rapidly and Crackpot knew that (Kell's revised brief notwithstanding) even if he wanted to chance it, the time had passed for a guaranteed, safe, clean kill. What concerned him now was how much longer Weber would remain in clear view.

Weber was in a part of the ground known as the Paddock, this was a small narrow area with just a few tiers of concreted steps and was patronized by mainly the quieter, more sedate fans of the club who did not want to be pushed or forced to be part of the sway of the crowd. Such roughhousing was de rigueur for fans of some of the bigger clubs and whose stadiums included huge, deep and wide terraces holding thousands of fans.

Nelson Corinthians' largest terracing was the Grindlay Road End; although not as hectic an experience as standing on Liverpool's Spion Kop – the first and largest of these huge terraces, it was still suitable only for the rougher more robust fans of the team.

Crackpot began to worry if Weber would disappear from view in the thick of the crowd, either during the game or after it and then simply wander off to wherever his plans were to take him after the game, blissfully unaware that he was indeed being tailed.

"Where are the damned flatfoots?!" a frustrated Crackpot then said out loud to himself.

Although far from happy that he could not do anything further at the moment, he sat down, lit another cigarette and settled on trying to keep an eye on Weber as well as watching a good game of football. . .

*

With a nod from the referee the stewards knocked on the dressing room doors.

"Time, Corinthians!" — "Time, visitors," came the calls to arms.

"OK, OK, OK; this is it, lads!" enthused new manager, Jock Shanksby. "Now remember – heels – fine, no one spots those anyway; but only kick a shin or do an elbow dig if you know the ref' has no chance of seeing you. Lofty? Where's Lofty? Oh, there you are; we'll need you and your mate to resume your double act today, old Jack told me all about it. Make 'em count, you two, eh?"

The white-faced Lofty with what looked like diced carrots slopping off his chin, just nodded, while Eric gave a grim smile.

"Get out there, then!"

*

Crackpot did not intend to and he was furious with himself later when he had realised what he had done, but with the sickly heat of the room aided no doubt by the windows being closed, he fell fast asleep in the chair with his head slumped over the ledge.

A huge roar from the crowd made Crackpot wake with a start.

"Wha-aa the—" said Crackpot, jumping up and knocking the chair over in the process.

"Damn!" he said to himself. "Damn damn damn!" he repeated, and worse.

The teams had just come out of the tunnel and onto the pitch; the crowd was now just a sea of pinkish faces and hats and scarves.

Most of the crowd, especially the raucous Grindlay Road End, were in the brown and cream colours of the home team. At the other end of the pitch, the Solomon Lane End had been given over to the mass of United Fans who had travelled up for the game.

The stand across the pitch played host to a hotch-potch of supporters from both teams and although Crackpot couldn't see them, this was also the case in the large, main (and more expensive) Grindlay Stand, above and below and to the sides of the new press box. Here, mixed in with the cotton-rich of Nelson and surrounding areas, were a fair number of the more affluent United fans – a well-heeled gathering of cotton and shipping merchants, stock brokers and other lucrative professions, and even the odd grocer or two who could just stretch the budget to a nice seat in the best stand for the occasional big away game.

Crackpot quickly scanned the Paddock, and there, thankfully, although not as clearly visible as he was, stood Weber, now leaning against the first barrier up on the first step. He had moved nearer to the front to get a better view of the game but was now shoulder to shoulder with the throng who had slowly but surely filled the terracing before the kick-off. Weber kept his wooden leg jammed tight against the upright of the crash barrier so as to offset any surges and swaying, although this was a rarity in the Paddock even in the most well attended games. This was due to the gap between each barrier being quite small and with a further separation of the crowd brought about by separating barriers going up and down the terracing; this boxed in small groups of supporters rather than there being a huge heaving single mass, which was mostly the case with larger end terraces.

Crackpot breathed a sigh of relief, relaxed, and in between continual glances down onto the Paddock, he also tried to take in the game – although he did wonder how much longer the police would be.

27

Under Siege

THE CROWD ROARED. THE TEAMS NOW FACED EACH OTHER.

Eric Ramsbottom, the outgoing faded star but honorary captain for his last ever game, shook hands with his opposite number. The referee produced a penny and as is the custom, asked the visitors' captain to choose heads or tails; the winner of this would decide whether their team should kick-off, or choose which end to kick into, with the option not taken then going to the losers of the coin toss.

"Tails," said legendary United centre-half and skipper, Charlie Roberts. The referee tossed the coin up and when it landed, the profile of King Edward V11 shone brightly in the pale winter sun. Eric turned to his team and gave them the thumbs up, they had won the toss.

Eric, as was to be expected, opted to attack the Solomon Lane End, thus giving the team a perceived second half advantage of attacking their opponent's goal at the end where most of the home supporters were gathered. This custom was something which was and still is much prized by all football teams, well, those who can boast a crowd large enough to make a loud enough din to both unnerve the visitors and encourage the home team.

The referee blew his whistle and the match kicked off.

As was expected by their manager, Jock Shanksby, the opening minutes saw Nelson Corinthians severely tested.

The defence was swamped continually by the fast, sharp forwards of the United team. The famed raiders of the United front line, namely Enoch West, George Anderson and Sandy Turnbull, were a real problem for not only Lofty but all of the Corinthians team, now under siege.

United almost scored in the seventh minute, but just as West took a precision through-pass along the ground from winger George Wall, Lofty made a lunging tackle across the half-frozen half-muddy penalty area, and took the ball off the feet of United's centre-forward and put it out of play. While waiting for the resulting corner kick and seeing the mauling the boys at the back were taking, Eric then shouted to the team to put into action the manager's plan to stem the tide.

The stadium was a cauldron of noise as the home fans yelled their heroes on to beat off the attackers, while the away fans roared encouragement as they saw the men in red swamp their opponents half, and for much of the time, their penalty area.

Although it was usual for the forwards to remain upfront awaiting a telling pass from the half-backs or even from deep in defence, Shanksby knew that Manchester United were the much better team. He had not told the lads this, but he did tell Eric to marshal the entire team to pack out their own defence when the heat was on. All ten out players including Eric duly trotted back and into position. The ball came floating in from the corner and was promptly taken on the chest, allowed to drop and cleared right up the field by Lofty, but this was to no one as all his team-mates were right beside him. Back came the ball again; again the defence was packed out, and again it was cleared.

The United skipper sensed that Nelson Corinthians were going to do nothing but apply spoiling tactics, and perhaps hope to get lucky on the break. But Charlie Roberts urged his team-mates on; in his mind, when coming up against a tough defence, he believed the answer was to be tougher still.

"Nothing but cloggers, the lot of 'em! Come on! Into 'em!"

The wing-halfs and behind them the full-backs answered the rallying cry of their skipper, and moved up to join the already marauding front line.

"Don't worry, lads! We can hold 'em; nowt but farts wearin' fancy after-shave!" came the (hopefully) re-assuring call-to-arms from Lofty. Although not the skipper, he felt it his duty to also keep the lads on their toes, at least in defence.

Both sets of fans sensed a sharpening of resolve on the pitch, and renewed the tribalistic calls for their team to triumph over the other. The crowd was that stirred up and vocal, that the more usual sounds of rattles were swallowed up by the deafening cacophony.

It was now a case of the marauding visitors stubbornly camping out in the Corinthians' penalty area, hopefully wearing down the home team's resistance; but the stout hearts of all the outfield players in Corinthians' colours, plus their ever alert goalkeeper shouting, encouraging, and moving and jumping, even when not being directly tested, answered Lofty's call in grand fashion.

With the full-back and half-back lines acting as sentinels, Anderson, Turnbull and West continued to hammer the Corinthians penalty area with thunderbolts, or hopeful chips from one while the other two moved forward. At times they took the Corinthians defence on man to man, and if they were able to get past, moved right up to the goal-line through a short-sharp series of one-twos, to either go on and hopefully score, or await telling crosses from either Wall or Sheldon on the wings if the ball was cleared again.

But Nelson Corinthians were ready: they tackled, slid, jumped, hoofed, cleared and headed the ball away, although usually only for it to land at the feet or bounce off the chest or head of a United player, and even then the stray ball still fell to a man in red. When it looked like the relentless pressure might tell, especially when the cleared ball got no further than the silky skilled golden trio of United half-backs, Dick Duckworth, Charlie Roberts, and the classy Alec Bell, whom Eric and Lofty knew full well could play the ball right into the danger area single-handedly, Lofty would deliberately run in front of the referee to block his view while Len Ellis and Simeon Radburn, the Corinthians left and right full-backs, pulled shirts, stamped, ankle tapped and barged the marauders off the ball or even just out the way of the incoming cross or pass. Each of the Corinthians knew full well the same would happen to them if they ever got anywhere near the United goal. As with all teams they were occasionally caught – usually by the forgotten linesmen – and reprimanded, but not today.

The ball fell to the United right-back, Oscar Linkson; he chipped it straight over the Corinthians left-half, Ivan Threlfall, who jumped, missed, and fell to the ground as the ball came down at the feet of Jack Sheldon, the United right-winger. He jinked in and out of the Corinthians defence while the marauders waited in the middle; a goal looked certain; but who but Eric came running right back, took the ball off Sheldon, slotted it beyond the left-sided attackers and out to Len Ellis, who tried to hoof it right up the field, but Charlie Roberts rose majestically to meet it, and headed it right back into the penalty area. Turnbull was on it in a flash, and lashed the ball towards the top right of the Corinthians goal. His arm was already up in celebration, but the athletic Billy Ludgate, the Corinthians goalkeeper, dived high and to his left and just managed to thump the ball away, which thankfully landed at the feet of Lofty Arkwright, and which heralded the one exciting moment of the first half for the home crowd, whose earlier vocal ferocity had been somewhat quelled.

Eric, tiring of the mass rearguard action, and with an idea formed after seeing Len's failed clearance, yelled to Lofty to tell the lads to now try and break the siege. Eric raced up the pitch. Ensuring he employed the offside trap in reverse, he slowed to allow at least one United defender to get back into position. Then, sure enough, the ball sailed up high and was coming down fast and was likely to land in the far right corner of the opponents' half. Jonny Allerton, Tad Rowson and the other forwards had also raced up with Eric; in fact they had easily overtaken the huffing puffing outgoing star. Tad groaned; it had been a constant frustration for Tad to have had to put up with the duo's constant two man route one game over the five years he had been the team's first choice right-winger; he had often thought what was the point of having wingers if they only ever tried to get the ball to Eric? As for Tom Geddings, the Corinthians left-winger, he once got so fed up of being kept out of the play that he had lost his temper in the postmatch bath and had flung a bath-brush at Eric.

However, on this occasion, the ball fell right at Tad's feet; he then went round three United players who were slow to react as they had expected to be closing in on Eric or Jonny instead. Tad raced along the byline with most of the United defence now either following or coming right at him, but he suddenly slipped the ball through to Eric who was now in the middle of the United penalty area with only the goalkeeper to beat. Eric lifted his boot – and slipped on the muddy patch by the penalty spot and the ball was cleared by the United left full-back, George Stacey. Eric jumped up, clutching a mud-dripping sod which he threw to the ground in anger. The groans from the crowd were audible, visible even, as the mass of brown and cream slumped back down almost as one from their being on the tips of their toes; this was not only to get a better view but as a reaction from their nervous expectation.

Lofty clapped his mate but the other nine players and the manager and trainers on the bench looked with thunder at their aged crock.

Nelson Corinthians were again kept penned in, but with the team once again sticking rigidly to Shanksby's instructions, a sea of feet, legs, heads (especially Lofty's), chests and even backsides were employed to prevent a United breakthrough. Corners were met with desperate jumps from all from both teams in the penalty area; but Lofty was on top of his game and managed to rise above the attackers and head the ball clear for most incoming and perhaps dangerous crosses.

Eric and Lofty between them marshalled the entire team to defend against the many free kicks conceded, all thankfully outside the box and all of which, once taken, were neutralised through a solid wall of seven of the Corinthians, who had long learned to pack together so closely that none of the opposing team could join them, at least in the middle. The Corinthians not in the wall were free to mark the most dangerous attackers, and were on hand to dash and clear any stray balls.

As valiant as Nelson Corinthians were, the truth was, the siege was so intense that Nelson Corinthians did not win a single throw-in or free kick, and were not even in the running to force any corners due to the fact they rarely left their own half.

But Nelson Corinthians' tactics, fair or foul, still served them well. The halftime whistle blew without any goals being scored at either end.

'We're still in it,' thought Eric, relieved to be able to stop and rest for ten minutes and rub his aching shins.

28

Do Shoot the Messenger

AS THE TEAMS trotted towards the tunnel in between the two teams' dug-outs, Crackpot made what seemed to be his thousandth glance over towards his quarry. He was still there, still seemingly highly contented and smoking another cigar.

"But where the hell . . ." said Crackpot out loud, "are these damned policemen?!"

Charles now had a problem to contend with. He really needed to find someone, hopefully Grindlay, and ask what on earth had happened to his help, but if he went wandering off he could not then keep an eye on Weber. But just then the door opened and in walked Solomon Grindlay, wringing his hands and once more with a rather stupid look on his face.

"I am really sorry, Chief Inspector, but we've just had to send another messenger boy straight back to the station. It appears the first one was so desperate to see the game, he simply disappeared into the crowd instead of performing his duties. A senior colleague did shout after him to come back, but his reply was, well . . . it wasn't nice. He's sacked of course, although I dare say that won't concern him in the least. I am truly sorry about this, but hopefully you won't have to wait too much longer."

"You what?!" yelled Crackpot, absolutely outraged. "I need someone to help me corner this Prussian rat, and you tell me your messenger boy is out there in the crowd somewhere, with a rattle no doubt! If I had him here right now I think I'd shoot him! Couldn't you just have telephoned the police station? I take it a big place like this has a telephone now?!"

"I-I am so sorry, Chief Inspector, but the phone line is down. It happens often I am sorry to say, it's all due to the frequent high winds over the moors."

Crackpot just sighed, and with his anger seemingly lessened, he put his hand to his chin, frowned, turned away from Solomon Grindlay and again sought out Weber.

After spotting his quarry was still where he wanted him to be – for now, he turned back around.

"Very well, Mr Grindlay . . . I am sorry I lost my temper. Let's hope these flat – er – policemen arrive soon. Thank you for keeping me informed."

"You're very welcome, sir," replied Grindlay. "I will escort the constables up here when they arrive, but for now, if you will excuse me, the Lord Mayor of Manchester is demanding a pink gin."

Crackpot just smiled but said no more. Solomon Grindlay left to find yet another messenger boy so he could send him to the nearest public house to find out how to make a pink gin.

Crackpot settled once more into his neck-straining routine of keeping an eye on the enemy as well as taking in the match.

A roar from the crowd not quite as loud as that which had woken him with a start just on kick-off, heralded the return of the teams for the second half.

With continued frequent checks on Weber, at first, Crackpot, despite being more of a rugby supporter, was soon engrossed by the game with the wrong shaped ball being played out below him.

29

West End Drama

WHILE OMINOUS THINGS BEGAN TO TAKE SHAPE in the small, icy-rain battered mill town of Nelson, equally sinister events were at play almost two-hundred miles away in Central London.

The great leveller otherwise known as a British winter saw to it that just like up north on the moors, Central London was bitterly cold and windy. Despite this, London's Brompton Road was heaving with thousands of brave shoppers hoping to bag a bargain in the January sales. One of the stores hoping to benefit from the huge influx of shoppers, was of course the world famous Harrod's department store.

Sir Timothy Sprake-Hipkiss, overtly anti-German and a senior player in negotiations concerning the future of Palestine, gave the alternative cheery salutation of a wave of his brolly to a succession of colleagues and their wives, fellow members of his private club, and the odd keen golfer friend or two as he weaved in and out of the huge crowd packing the pavement and moving both ways; he was not going to remove his hat for anyone.

"Excuse me, sir," said a cloaked dandy, as Sir Timothy was walking past.

"Yes?" came the reply.

Seconds later, the dandy withdrew the tip of his umbrella from his victim's ankle, and Sir Timothy Sprake-Hipkiss dropped to the ground, stone dead.

The wind blew cold around the assassin's soul; he pulled the front of his cloak up to his neck and pulled his wolverine hat down tighter over his ears. It was dusk, and with so many people crowding the pavement right outside Harrod's, by the time the ubiquital scream from a lush fox fur had alerted the rest of the throng, the dandy had managed to steal away up Brompton Road, unnoticed and unsuspected.

But the assassin stopped upon realising he needed some groceries. Through either stupidity, or steely nerved ice-cold arrogance, he turned back around, walked past the ever-increasing group of concerned passers-by looking down on poor Sir Timothy – and strolled into Harrod's.

*

Forty-one year old Ulster born Valentine Larkin was either the best thing that had ever happened to the British Secret Service – or he was an idiot. . .

Of the three-hundred and seventy-two arrests that had been made by the Metropolitan Police on the direct say-so of Val Larkin, three-hundred of these had been fruitless, and of these, two-hundred and ninety-three had resulted in the police having to admit to getting it totally wrong; the resulting court cases, most of which were claims for damages for wrongful arrest, had all been won by the plaintiffs and damages had been duly awarded. Relations between the London blue hats and their more clandestine colleagues had become very strained due to the embarrassment suffered by the police, which was of course made worse by the considerable dent made in the police budget through having to make financial reparation to those erroneously entrapped by Val Larkin's zealotry.

But the rub came in the form of the remainder of this huge arrest rate linked to Larkin: all of the suspects across the remaining seventy-two arrests were found guilty of a range of charges from Robbery with Violence, right up to Treason. All in all, Larkin simply played the numbers game and in his opinion came up trumps – eventually. And even his highly exasperated bosses had to admit, no other operative in so short a time had brought about the successful trying of so many suspects.

The reason why Larkin was so inclined was all to do with his upbringing. He had lived with his parents in Colm Mews, a cul-de-sac off the Shankhill Road area of Belfast. Although far from affluent, his family managed comparatively well on the modest income earned by his father, a coach driver for Belfast Corporation. Douglas Larkin was a proud Protestant; but belying this was the fact that his mother, originally from Dublin, was a devout Catholic. In the Ulster of the time this was not a good way to bring about a happy stable upbringing for any children of such mixed marriages, and as he grew up, Val found himself having to put up with bigotry from both sides, which made him conclude very early on that at best, it was no wonder most people stuck with their own, but, all things considered, there was no big fella in the sky anyway. Plus – it made him highly suspicious of everyone and everything to the point of paranoia, which, once he'd become of age, seemed to make Val Larkin an ideal candidate for the newly formed British Intelligence.

Val Larkin usually had no time for the likes of Harrod's. He did not shop there, either for trinkets, clothes or food; he didn't see any point in paying far more for something which he knew cost far less elsewhere. But today was different: he had just finished a ten hour shift staking out a large detached house in Knightsbridge. The house was believed to be a hideout for a gang of forgers. Larkin was freezing cold, his hands and feet were numb, his head pained with the stormy wind-borne battering of freezing cold rain, and his ears were bright red and very sore. For once, the warm halls of Harrod's were very appealing, at least until he had thawed out and could take on the icy winds along Brompton Road on his way back to his digs in Fulham.

After walking around the main hall of Harrod's for around fifteen minutes, he happened to notice a somewhat familiar figure mince into the shop. He watched as the man took off his Siberian style headgear. Larkin realised that the man was an acquaintance, someone he had met at various diplomatic functions at various embassies and palaces.

"Hello, Otto; getting a bargain for the boss, then?" he shouted across the busy food hall.

The man knew he was being hailed, but all he did was do a half-turn to take in whoever it was addressing him, blinked, frowned, and then turned back, and, as far as Val Larkin could work out, deliberately forced his way in to the centre of a huge crowd of well-dressed ladies on the far left of the food hall, all fighting over the half-price fresh salmon. Given the tensions that existed between Britain and Germany, and the fact that it was Val Larkin who had called to him across the crowded room, it was possibly the worst thing that Otto Geff could have done.

"Here!" shouted Larkin, perhaps unwisely. He moved swiftly across the hall, pushing anyone and everyone roughly out of his way; this included one future Grand Duke of Hesse, who picked himself up, then bent down and picked up the broken wooden replica of the mythical Argo, and went off crying to tell his mother about the nasty man.

But Geff had bluffed his would-be pursuer. He was already out and striding back up Brompton Road before Larkin realised he was chasing fresh air.

"What in the name of Eric Von Schickelgruber is he up to then?" Larkin muttered quietly in his Ulster brogue. Upon reflection, he also thought how the bevy of well-dressed ladies seemed to have deftly made room for Geff after he had hailed him.

"Hmmm . . . there is far more to this than meets the eye. . . " said Larkin to himself, as he slowly but carefully took firm hold of a slender arm covered in fox fur.

"Now, madam. . ."

Lady Geraldine Wallender-Smythe was a lucky lady. In fact, most of the ladies who had been perusing the fresh salmon could be said to have been just as lucky. They were all only seconds away from being hauled off to a make-shift interrogation room, but Larkin was disturbed by screams from right outside the main entrance of Harrod's. He put away his notepad, and went to investigate. . .

30

A Shot on Goal

AS THE TWO TEAMS RE-APPEARED FOR THE SECOND HALF, both captains mulled over their instructions, which had been hurriedly passed on during tea and slices of orange. Eric felt this had been rather redundant as he had been told, 'More of the same', by the overcautious (thought Eric), Jock Shanksby. But he was not going to be disloyal, not today of all days. However, Mr John J Benson, who was both the United manager and President of the Football League, wanted his lads to try something new, and had hurried into the changing rooms as soon as he had procured a large whisky.

"Draw the buggars out; let 'em think we've run out of puff, then, bang! Hit 'em!" he had told Charlie Roberts.

"Like we did against them nancy boys at Stamford Bridge, you mean?"

"Exactly!"

"Got it!"

The crowd gave another roar, not as loud as at the start of the match, but a roar loud enough to help dispel the biting cold from the extremities and once more act as a diverting and marshalling of the senses, which would once again be focussed upon twenty-two hairy-arsed men and a leather bag of compressed air down on the pitch. The crowd also cheered as the recently installed yet not officially sanctioned dynamo driven floodlights lit up the stadium. Director Maurice Goldstein had taken advantage of the top man's temporary absence by taking an executive decision of his own. The fact that he had had rather too much brandy at his club the night before and had wagered fifty pounds on a Corinthians victory may have had something to do with this; 'Anything that helps;' thought Maurice, 'hang the FA'.

The restart was rather comical. As the whistle went and Eric

Ramsbottom passed to Jonny Allerton to his left in the centre circle, Nelson Corinthians were so sure that it was to be more of the same, that Jonny just booted the ball up and over to the left-wing; he didn't expect Tom Geddings to meet with it, he was right, he didn't. This was followed by the whole team immediately falling back, expecting an immediate onslaught, but none came. Eric turned back round as he reached the edge of the home team's penalty area."Eh?" he said to himself, then looked to Lofty, who shrugged his shoulders. Eric thought quickly. "String yourself out at the twenty-five yard mark! But no further for now!"

Lofty nodded and relayed this on to those who may have just been out of earshot.

The United team were simply passing the ball between themselves. The referee was about to blow for time-wasting, but Charlie Roberts saw this and shouted to his lads to move forward, but slowly. After this farcical restart, the game now looked to be back on for real.

The Corinthians moved forward cautiously, but the United team had obviously been well instructed. As each United player with the ball was approached by a Corinthian player, there was no attempt to fight off the challenge and progress, the ball was simply passed to the nearest player. They were playing keep ball: moving forward when they could, just enough to stop the referee from blowing, but not enough to suggest they were resuming their marauding game of the first half.

Eric signalled to Lofty to come across to him.

"The cheeky buggars are just waiting for us to lose our shape or get angry or summat; trouble is, they are damn good at it. Pass it round: man to man marking – that will cut off the escape routes – hopefully. . ."

Lofty again nodded and did as he was asked. Less than a minute later, each United outfield player found a Corinthian player sticking to him like glue. But Eric was soon to realise that United were ready for this. Man to man marking it may have been, but the passes, even back-heels, were so quick and accurate, that although the Corinthians were now better placed to tackle, the ball still had to be there to do so. No sooner had the Corinthians stuck their feet and legs out to challenge than the ball was away again, moving right around the park courtesy of the entire United team, their goalkeeper included. Eric's fears were now realised. The lads were beginning to get rattled and a result of their tempers were becoming more rash, so much so, it was now very easy for the United team to continue their game of possession football. There were even a few instances of a United player rather cheekily playing the ball off a Corinthian so it would fly off a leg or a back and go out of play for a throw-in to Manchester United. As Nelson Corinthians became desperate, their fouling and shirt pulling and ankle tapping was now way too obvious, and United were awarded a series of free kicks; most were not in dangerous areas, but even so, United didn't seem overly concerned and simply passed the ball back through their own lines. But one was in a dangerous area, right on the edge of the box. United appealed for a penalty, but the referee and both linesmen knew it was just on the edge; a free kick it was.

After a not too urgent consultation between Charlie Roberts and Enoch West, it was agreed Charlie would take it. Nelson Corinthians' defence was packed out, red shirts mingling with the three free-range Corinthians; although the defensive wall was yet again a redoubt of cream and brown, with any red interlopers literally shoved away while the referee was busy marshalling the free kick. As the traditional jostling and shirt-pulling commenced, the whistle went, Charlie Roberts unleashed a rocket of a free kick — which sailed way over the goal and into the crowd. While most of the crowd cheered and the rest groaned, a frustrated Charlie and his team-mates realised that a casual approach has its drawbacks. But in his frustration he stomped on the toe of Corinthians wing-half, Ivan Threlfall, thinking that both the referee's and the linesmens' vision was blocked, it wasn't. Free kick to Nelson Corinthians.

Eric ran up to take the kick, but rather oddly Lofty had rushed over to Colin Banford, whispered something, and Colin raced over, beat Eric to the ball, and simply sent it out to Geddings, hoping a surprise attack could be mounted from the left, but Tom Geddings was immediately swamped by four United players and had the ball taken off him.

To their credit, the Corinthians gave no further quarter, although the battle was still being fought far too close for comfort for the home team. But time went on and the game remained goalless.

Both sets of fans had become a jaded pastiche of their earlier selves; oohs and aahs still punctuated the game but not as loud or as frantic. Sadly, despite Nelson Corinthians playing towards the Grindlay Road End in front of the bulk of their own supporters, their perceived advantage had not come to fruition. The whole stadium now expected both teams to play out a draw. But as is often the case in these tense situations, something unexpected happens which gives one team hope and the other team a dread fear that all is about to go wrong.

Charlie Roberts had taken possession from Stacey and moved forward into the Corinthians half, readying himself to pass to the far right to Sheldon, but as he lifted his right foot, he slipped on a small muddy indent in the semi-circle; not only that, as he fell to the ground, he knocked the ball straight to the right foot of Eric Ramsbottom. Straight away, Tad raced up on the right, and Jonny ran straight towards the United box. But Eric, seeing the United defence caught way out of position, simply lashed the ball as hard as he could towards the United goal. To be fair to Eric, it nearly worked. Although in reality it was over in a split-second, the amazing ability of the mind to seemingly slow everything down made the whole stadium seem to freeze for what felt like an age. With the exception of the United goalkeeper, both teams stood stock still and watched as the ball thundered on, but at the same time, Robert Beale sprang like a leopard over to his right; the ball was almost on the line when he pushed out his right arm as far as he could, and, almost miraculously, he palmed the ball around the outside of the goalpost with his right hand. Eric was denied a goal, but only by a whisker, and only because of one of the best saves he had ever, ever seen in his long career.

But if Eric thought he would at least get praise from his team for a great effort then he was sorely mistaken. Apart from Lofty who again clapped his old friend, the other players and those on the bench looked at Eric as if he was something nasty they had picked up on the sole of their boots during a sight-seeing tour of the sewage works. Although Jonny muttered and grumbled to himself, worst of all was Tad Rowson who shouted his displeasure to not only Eric but to all who could hear it; he knew that Eric had done well with the shot but he as well as the rest of the team knew that Jonny and perhaps even Tad himself had been best placed to ensure a goal, not as spectacular as Eric's would have been if he had have scored, but a goal nevertheless, and on the goalkeeper's left, which all but Eric seemed to know was his weaker side when it came to making desperate saves.

The only words that emanated from the bench were some strange, garbled almost French sounding words concerning the absent Dixie Lawton. This was followed by, "Did that jackass before me leave any stout do you know?"

The raised hopes of the home fans had been dashed in a matter of seconds.

A dispirited Eric, knowing it was highly unlikely that Nelson Corinthians would now score, hoped that at the very least the team could hold out for a replay. But this was rather a bitter-sweet thought; a replay would obviously give Nelson Corinthians another chance, but he doubted very much whether he would be picked if it did go to a second match.

Whether it was part of Mr Benson's gameplan, or whether the United skipper thought Nelson Corinthians were rattled enough and ready to be finished off, United stepped up the pace of the game, although once again employing the mesmerising routine of passing the ball when a Corinthians player came charging in. But they now did this at the same time as pressing dangerously forward into the Nelson Corinthians box, fully aware the game was almost done. The last ten minutes of a football game are 'the naughty minutes' when even giants fear the minnows, especially if the game is goalless or even if their lead is slender. It is best to see out this time in the other team's half, if possible.

However, the first such measured attack broke down and the ball went out for a throw-in to Nelson Corinthians, but Lofty's throw was found wanting, and was intercepted by Duckworth and was slotted back to the goalkeeper. Beale then started off a chain of passes which would involve all eleven United players without a Corinthians player getting anywhere near. He rolled the ball out to Stacey who kicked it forward to Roberts who passed back to Linkson; each desperate attempt at interception failed; Linkson sent it back to Roberts, who slotted it across to Bell, who sent the Corinthians the wrong way by facing left, but turning suddenly to the right and sending a precision low pass through to Sheldon. The home fans slow handclapped this routine, whereas the United fans cheered each time the ball found the next United player.

Sheldon looked up, saw his target, and chipped it straight over to Turnbull, now on the edge of Nelson Corinthians' penalty area. Turnbull jinked past Lofty, passed it back to West who saw Wall free on the left, passed it up to him, who now broke the pattern by losing two defenders and sending in a decent cross, which all the Corinthians defence missed and which was then headed down by Anderson into the path of Duckworth, who had come well out of position and almost made it count. But to the relief of the Corinthians and their fans, Ludgate dived at the feet of Duckworth and snatched the ball up and kicked it upfield but at an angle and over the touchline; a throw-in to United.

"Reshape, lads! Come on!" urged Eric. His battle cry had the desired effect and the eleven tired men in cream and brown shirts found their resolve once more, but this was yet again to mount a desperate rearguard action as the United marauders, having now finally stopped playing keep ball, attacked in waves.

After one such near-fatal onslaught, Eric, though deep in defence, found himself with the ball after it was parried by Ludgate, but he also found himself immediately besieged by red shirts, all around him, all harrying him; all he could do was swing at the ball the way he was facing in the hope it would clear the decks once more. Thankfully it went through the legs of the marauders and over to Simon Radburn on the right, and in turn he hoofed it forward to the right-half, Colin Desmond. Although it wasn't deliberate and wasn't anything they had rehearsed in training, out of sheer desperation, Nelson Corinthians, more by luck than judgement, emulated the United team, managing to put a string of passes together involving the whole team with the ball miraculously evading the outstretched feet, legs, raised heads and even chests of the marauding red shirts. Radburn, trying to go forward but finding himself blocked, crossed the ball right over to the far right, this was picked up by Tad Rowson who could do nothing but kick it back to the left-half, Ivan Threlfall who in turn passed back to Ellis who picked out Colin Banford, drafted in from the reserves to play inside-left. Even he could not penetrate further and kicked it back to the well out of position Tom Geddings who slotted it right to Jonny Allerton who, finding his path blocked on all sides, turned and hoofed it right back to Lofty. Rather comically, the slow handclaps and cheers now came from the opposite sets of fans. It may have looked slick to the average fan, but the truth was, eleven sets of aching legs where just kicking and hoping, and on this occasion, they had simply got away with it.

Lofty, perhaps unwisely, moved with the ball over to the left; he managed to give Bell the slip, but a crunching tackle from Duckworth saw the ball bounce between them and then off Lofty, and out for yet another United throw-in.

*

Unfortunately, Crackpot had allowed himself to become far too engrossed in the game. The frequent glances down to the paddock became occasional glances – "Come on, Ref! Their centre-half's an animal!" – then they were forgotten – "Ye-Yes! Nooo! Good effort, that man!" But then he remembered why he was there in the press box at all. "Oh my sainted aunt! Damn and blast!"

Crackpot looked down at where he had last seen Weber.

He wasn't there!

He looked again, then to the left and right of the terracing, then further up, and then down below nearer the touchline, then the same all over again – there was no sign of Gerhard Weber.

Crackpot stood up, and yelled, "And where are these damned flatfoots!"

"They are dead, my friend, quite dead," came a chilling voice, while an unseen hand pressed the muzzle of a pistol into

Crackpot's temple.

While still firmly pressing his own gun into Crackpot's head, the assailant reached in to Crackpot's coat and pulled out a Luger 9mm P08 pistol.

"Tut tut!" said the voice. "Does Mr Kell know you have forsaken the Webley? I can't say I blame you of course, but a superior gun for an inferior agent; rather a mismatch, wouldn't you agree?" said the voice, putting Crackpot's Luger in his own coat pocket.

"Now . . . I am going to take the gun away from your head; if you move, I will kill you. I may have to kill you anyway, or I might just pull the trigger for, how you crazy English say . . . the hell of it." Gerhard Weber removed the gun from Crackpot's temple and moved back by a foot, but he still had the gun pointed straight at him. "Now – sit down, my friend – that's it . . . for now – we talk. Although I knew you were following me . . . indeed that was the whole idea, I am, however, curious as to what put you on to me. Was it one of my . . . *careless clues?* Or is your secret service worthy of being called . . . *British Intelligence?* Now face me, and talk!"

Crackpot was surprised by the perfect English, but the accent although slight, was still as he expected it to be – German.

Crackpot turned to face his foe. He knew Weber was trying to assess how much the British actually knew, over and above the immediate need to chase a hairy Bavarian cripple over half of England. But Crackpot had decided not to co-operate and instead offer up the simplest summary of current events, even if this provoked the German agent into pulling the trigger of his Luger pistol.

"Not wishing to be rude, old fellow, but your unfortunate malady and general appearance made you stand out all the way from London to here. We were on to you days ago, old bean."

At this, Weber smiled and said, "This, you mean?" He put his left hand behind his back, seemed to fiddle with something that was attached or tied to his body – and then his wooden leg fell to the floor. His real and fully trousered left leg dropped to the ground without even unbalancing Weber or his showing any signs of soreness or stiffness at all.

"You've done this before," said Crackpot, but Weber chose to ignore this as he was not quite finished with his little performance.

"And this;" he added with another sardonic smile and ripped off his moustache; "and of course . . . this," he said, as his wig came off in a second.

Standing before Charles 'Crackpot' Carruthers was a much younger fresh-faced fair-haired man, not too unlike himself.

"Bloody hell," said Crackpot, rather understatedly.

"Ha! So you thought you were up with the game, eh? Time to think again, my friend. We made our plans so long ago, that not even Prince Lichnowsky knows I have a full complement of very real live legs. You, my friend, are the one who has been caught out. Let me explain. . .

"As I have already told you . . . *I wanted to be followed;* the real action is back in London, and my orders were to make myself as conspicuous as possible and set a trail all the way to . . . well, wherever. I had to make the train journeys a truly random affair to ensure it seemed as if I was panicked into escaping London, and then later on of course, acting as if I thought I was free and clear. This would at least force your precious Vernon Kell to spread his forces very thinly indeed. Where are your comrades, by the way? Having tea somewhere no doubt, complaining that the crusts have been left on the cucumber sandwiches?"

"Very . . . clever," replied Crackpot, very impressed, albeit reluctantly, but nonetheless very impressed indeed. But at the same time something else came to mind, and he almost smiled a smug smile of satisfaction but forced himself not to. In the rush he had not given a moment's thought as to why this had been a solo assignment. He knew his boss's tactics inside out; if he thinks he has his man – or woman – all bar the canteen lady are tooled up and ready to dash to the centre of the drama in an instant; if the danger level increases, then the stew is left to burn and Doris sticks a Derringer down her bloomers and she too joins the party. Vernon Kell would never let budget considerations get in the way of an operation, not if national security was at very grave risk of being compromised. He smiled again; he realised Kell's following on to Weber's apartment was really to ensure he (Crackpot), was kept on his toes, and did not have time to relax and mull things over.

"Crafty sod," thought Crackpot.

No matter what happened next, Crackpot knew he had to withhold the fact from Weber that he and his little spy cell were, hopefully, not quite as free and clear as Weber believed to be the case.

For now it was time to wing it with useless time-burning banter.

"Well buggar me. . ." said Crackpot with an affected sigh. "D'ya know . . . and I of course bitterly regret this now, but I could have shot you dead well before the ground began to fill, but—"

"But you had orders to take me alive . . . if you could. . . ?" cut in Weber. "I could not be sure of this; you too will know full well the uncertainties we have to accept in our profession, but it was a chance I had to take. Today I survived, I may not next time – such is the fickle thumb of fortune."

"Finger of fate," suggested a thinly smiling Crackpot.

"Ah, yes, that's it. I do apologise, but you see, my tutor from the academy was shunted over from her chosen profession of code breaking to English classes, which she detested. To get her revenge and no doubt for her own amusement, she misinformed us on many things, the silly nincomcrap," replied Weber.

Crackpot just smiled, this was amusement enough on its own without offering corrections.

"If I may, old boy," said Crackpot, "how did you know I was here? OK, you knew *someone* would follow you, in fact for most of the way you seemed to know I was on your tail; but how did you know I was up here, in the press box?"

Weber grinned broadly.

"You know, we are often told that although you are – or at least will be – our bitter enemies, that this is a great shame. We are told that the British are just like Germans: we both wish to make our countries great by ingenuity, industry, efficiency; that only our two countries alone stand out among the vast intellectual and industrial wasteland that is Europe, kept down by the canker of peasantry. Even the very term *Anglo-Saxon* tells us there is something between us. But now – well . . . I am not so sure. . .

"You thought by being up here that it would be just like being on top of the Statue of Liberty, let us say – looking down on the Poles, the Italians, the Jews and the Irish, slugging it out on the streets of Manhattan, and that you could watch every single flash of a switch blade without being seen in return. Well, my friend, this is not the Statue of Liberty and this is not New York. I saw you plain as day, staring at me from here. My perfect vision, honed by years of tracking both enemies and game down on the veldt helped of course – Africaan mother, German father you see; but in essence you were not as high up or as camouflaged from view as you thought you were. One chance moment, I happened to glance up . . . and I saw . . . *you.* I know *this* press box is not yet open; again by chance I heard a photographer talking on the touchline, and I know for certain that only extraordinary circumstance would see a solitary figure, with . . . *a fishing bag* . . . at a football match, being allowed in to a room that has not even been finished and then home in on the crowd far more than the game.

"Pointing a Lee Enfield 303 at me was also a very bad mistake. I do not think Wally Harris of the *Times* kisses his wife, wolfs down his toast and then checks to see if he has his pencil, notebook . . . *and a high powered rifle* packed up before leaving for Highbury.

"But as ever it was not risk free. I knew if I moved you would give chase, but I had to try and twist the furniture on you. I may be the decoy but that doesn't mean I have to die. I could not believe my luck, following those two gainsboroughs along the deserted corrid—"

"Constables," cut in Crackpot, who couldn't resist it, although he thought to also make reference to the erroneous furniture metaphor was overkill.

"Yes, yes, of course, Frau Marks, the stupid butch. Anyway, it was obvious that the local police had been alerted, and it was obvious that these two . . . constables . . . would lead me to you. And now (looking at his watch), with the task at hand to be completed by another agent back in London, I think I will take my leave of you and get some well earned rest. No need to see me to the door – you'll be dead."

Crackpot was then to benefit from a very lucky escape: just as Weber went to press the trigger of the revolver now pointing directly at his heart; the one thing the German spy had overlooked now came to the rescue. The door to the new press box was unlocked, in fact there wasn't any kind of lock or bolt inside or out fitted to it yet. But not only that, as the room was quite small and narrow it also meant that anyone standing near it. . .

*

It was nearing the end of the game.

The desperate rearguard was reformed once again, and yet again, another strong United attack was thwarted – just. However, in the dying seconds of the game the *fickle thumb of fortune* once more intervened in the life of Eric Ramsbottom.

United relaxed, only for a short time, but enough for Nelson Corinthians to try and mount a counter-attack. Lofty, now with the ball and acting more like the skipper than the skipper, urged the lads forward.

Knowing it was most probably the last chance to either score a goal or prevent it, the entire stadium cheered as loudly as in the first half, urging their heroes to 'Get in there!' or 'Keep the buggars out!'

Eric heard a familiar voice from the back and made his customary run – and then stopped. It was indeed Derek 'Lofty' Arkwright, shouting and punting the ball up-field, but rather unusually he had not shouted Eric's name. Lofty had come to realise that in this game at least (although perhaps many others over many years, too, but he forced this thought to the back of his mind), he had not always done what was best for the team but rather what was best for his friend, Eric Ramsbottom, and by extension, himself. Lofty, knowing that his long time friend and team-mate was not up with the game at all, for once let common sense prevail. He had shouted, 'Geddo!', and pointed to the far left corner, and Tom Geddings, already up-field, had positioned himself to receive the incoming pass. Eric, knowing he still had a duty to the team, saw this, smiled grimly and ran up to the United penalty area as soon as he could; sadly he was once more eclipsed by his fellow forwards as they all raced up to be part of the action.

This time, Geddings went round Oscar Linkson with ease, but as the rest of the left-sided defence and wing-halfs came at him, he knew not to push his look and sent a curling cross of pin-point accuracy towards Tad Rowson, his counterpart on the right.

Tad Rowson took the ball and immediately steamed onwards towards the United goal. He passed one player, put the ball through the legs of another and ran past him, then put the ball to the left of the next player and ran to the right and past the player to reconnect; then he turned 360 degrees on the spot, leaving his next opponent on the ground, dizzy. Tad ran on with the ball – and then received a huge kick in the groin from the United centre-half and skipper, Charlie Roberts. Tad collapsed in agony. But the rather obvious centre-half was to pay for this dearly. The whistle went, the trainer came on to look at Tad, and Charlie Roberts was duly sent off with only seconds left of the game, and with a penalty kick being awarded to Nelson Corinthians. . .

*

"Chief Inspector! Chief Inspector!" came the shout from Solomon Grindlay as the door burst open, which then slammed into Weber, who was then sent sprawling over the ledge of the press box. "My God! That's the fella I came to warn you about!"

"Get out, Grindlay – now!" shouted Crackpot, who knew the aged portly chairman would be more of a hindrance than a help. He was also in two minds as to whether he should fight for the revolver or try and get his rifle from his bag on the ledge. The sudden movement from Weber decided it and Crackpot launched himself on top of the German spy and tried to wrestle the gun from him.

While this was happening, Solomon Grindlay rushed out and along the corridor; he was in a state of great anguish about having to ask for more policemen, and no doubt having to answer the question of what had happened to the first two he had been sent. He had been informed by a steward that he had come across the bodies of the two policemen and that someone with a wooden leg was making his way along the corridor towards the new press box.

Weber now had Crackpot up against the inner wall with his left hand rather comically covering Crackpot's face, somewhat like an alien squid-like creature in a Sci-Fi film, with his right hand pressing down on Crackpot's left hand but still keeping hold of the revolver. Crackpot hit out repeatedly with his right hand, thumping Weber's temple hoping this would eventually stun him, but Weber croaked, "All — Prussia — Middleweight — Champion — nineteen — o — three," in between each punch.

Crackpot gave up the attempts to achieve a submission by way of cranial thumping syndrome and simply tried to grab Weber – and push, and kick and scratch, even pulling his hair and grabbing his groin. But no matter how much of a purchase Crackpot gained on any part of the person of Gerhard Weber or how hard he kicked out or tried to push Weber back, it was all to no avail, Weber was like an immovable rock.

To prevent his eyes being gouged, Weber was savvy enough to have his face turned away from Crackpot's free hand; he also used the side of his head as another weapon, pressing down hard on Crackpot's upper chest, throat and chin.

*

After trying to get Tad Rowson to stand and move without success, the trainer frowned and then signalled to the touchline for a stretcher; Tad's upper thigh was too badly bruised and swollen for him to continue. Eric Ramsbottom was team captain, honorary perhaps, but he was still the captain right at that moment in time. He had a decision to make. . .

Eric thought for a few moments. Going purely on up to the minute form then there was only one contender for taking the penalty kick, but he had just left the field unable to carry on. This left . . . Eric himself. Eric had taken many, many penalty kicks over the years, and had scored every time. The only other player on the pitch who had taken any at this level was Lofty, and he had missed more than half of his; rather awkwardly for Eric, Lofty ran the length of the pitch and picked up the ball.

"No, Loft', sorry me ole mate. I know I'm crocked in open play, but I can still blast a penalty past any keeper, you do know that, don't you?" said a regretful but still resolute Eric.

Lofty looked seriously at his old friend, then grinned, then nodded.

"Thanks, I thought we were heading for an argument there," said Eric.

"Just put it away. One thing to remember though, he's dodgy on your right, his left – got it? *HIS* left, not yours. . ."

"Why didn't you tell me that before?" said Eric with a smile.

With both teams duly marshalled just outside the penalty box in the case of a rebounded shot from either the goalkeeper or the posts, Eric placed the ball on the penalty spot. Both sets of fans were shouting at the top of their lungs; this was either to encourage Eric and to put the keeper off; or to encourage the keeper and put Eric off, but to Eric it was all the same and made no difference.

The referee blew his whistle to indicate that the penalty could now be taken.

Eric turned and walked back five paces as if he was going to shoot the keeper in a duel somewhere in a forest just outside Paris. He stopped, turned, ran up to the ball. . .

*

To Crackpot's great dismay he found Weber beginning to get the better of him; although Crackpot held on as tightly as he could to Weber's right hand, Weber slowly but surely showed his greater strength and stamina and began to pull the revolver around towards Crackpot. He was only a second away from finally pulling the trigger when suddenly both Weber and Crackpot found themselves being forced over to the other side of the press box and slamming into the outer wall. The revolver was now pointing straight at the nearest window and in both men's attempts to gain the upper hand, the trigger was squeezed, the revolver was fired and the window was smashed. This left a gaping hole through which the roar of the crowd filled the room. The gun went off again a split-second later, but this time the bullet whizzed cleanly through the gap. This was followed by another roar, far louder than normal.

*

. . . and fell down dead as a bullet went right into his back at an angle and straight into his heart. . .

31

Two Spies . . . and a Crutch

CRACKPOT WAS DISTRACTED by movement elsewhere in the room. Out of the corner of his eye he could see someone, he wasn't sure whom, brandishing an odd T shaped object; he then heard and felt a thud and a split-second later Weber staggered and fell to the floor, but with Crackpot underneath him.

Despite being the filling of a floor and Weber sandwich, Crackpot suddenly felt as if he could now breathe freely and felt the pressure from Weber's cast iron grip ease.

With one push from Crackpot, Weber fell limply to Crackpot's left side.

Crackpot put his hands down on the floor so he could then push himself back up but then found them covered in blood. He rather crazily patted himself all over. He looked more like a man who had lost his wallet after offering to foot the bill for dinner at the Ritz for a Bavarian trade delegation, rather than someone checking for possibly fatal wounds upon his own person.

"Here," came a voice, this time a friendly voice. Alfie Snoddie, who had only just picked himself up off the floor, handed Crackpot a handkerchief.

As Crackpot struggled to his feet and wiped his hands, he looked down on Weber, and grimaced. The left side of Weber's head was bashed in and oozing blood. Putting two and two together he then looked to the top of Alfie's crutch, now back under his arm-pit, and that too was covered in blood.

"I didn't mean to kill him, o' course," said a rather matter of fact Alfie. "I just heard old Grindy knickers shoutin' about a kerfuffle in the new press box. But I know the routine, Governor; if I ain't a' bashed him – twice – then I'm sorry to say he looked as if he 'ad you beat – I think he would 'ave killed you dead."

"There's no think about it, my man – he would have killed me stone dead if you had not turned up – no doubt at all. Thank you, you've saved my life." He held out his hand to Alfie, who smiled and shook it warmly in return.

An increasingly loud thud thud thud along the corridor outside the press box heralded the return of Solomon Grindlay, but with a very real police inspector and four constables in tow.

"Oh, my Lord! Dreadful! *And in my stadium!"* bemoaned Solomon Grindlay.

The inspector looked at Crackpot, down on Weber, then to Alfie, who was now making a roll-up, and then back to Crackpot.

"Inspector Dixon, CID Lancs Divisional. And I take it you are Chief Inspector Carruthers? From the – er – *Met'?"* asked Dixon.

"Yes, Inspector, that is correct," replied Crackpot, who now sounded as exhausted as he felt.

"You and you, Reception; you two, outside, man the door here," said Dixon, turning to his men. "Now – Mr Grindlay, and – er. . . "

"Don'' worry about me, I ain't lettin' your two flatfoots muck up the place!" said Alfie striding out as if he had just intervened in a minor fracas rather than killing a man stone dead, enemy of the state or not.

What Crackpot did not know but would find out later, was that Alfie had been in the army and had acquitted himself admirably in South Africa. However he had returned from the campaign early after suffering terrible injuries to his left leg; these were inflicted on him while saving a comrade from what would have been certain death.

"I'll need to speak to you later!" shouted Dixon as Alfie clomp clomped out of the room and after the two policemen.

" . . . Mr Grindlay, I need to speak with Chief Inspector Carruthers alone, I will call for you later when we are done; please close the door after you," said Dixon, so firmly that Grindlay recognised the dismissal loud and clear.

"Yes . . . yes, very well. . ." and he too left the press box.

"Now then, I take it you are really from Intelligence. . . ?" asked Dixon, who was well versed in the alternate identities of secret agents – but all was not over yet. The door bust open again – only seconds after it had been closed. . .

32

Taking a Dive

AT FIRST, there were groans from most of the crowd; but then the referee, the players and even the linesmen looked over to the limp form of Eric Ramsbottom sprawled on the cold hard ground. Lofty ran right up to his friend, bent down and gently shook Eric, but before he even stopped shaking him he knew that he was dead. He gently rolled Eric over and made the sign of the cross. Then came a scream from a woman in the crowd, then more shouts, more screams, yells to call the police . . . and shouts of - *'He's been murdered!"*

"Damn!" exclaimed Maurice Goldstein.

*

". . . Sir! Sir!" again spluttered PC Ferrris, one of the constables who not long before had been sent to control the reception area. "Eric Ramsbottom's dead!"

The odds of the death of a football player happening at the same time as the death of a foreign agent only yards away in a press box, with there being no connection between them, were so slim it would give the word slim a bad name if someone tried to write it off as coincidence. Crackpot ran to the smashed window and looked out onto the pitch and then down upon poor Eric; he knew the truth a split-second after the constable had burst back into the room – Eric Ramsbottom had been killed by a bullet from Weber's revolver.

Although he did not know if it had been his or Weber's finger or even both, that had squeezed the trigger during the fight to then fire the fatal shot, he dearly hoped (and perhaps rather in a cowardly fashion), it had been Weber's.

As tragic as the deaths were, Inspector Dixon, after setting in motion the controlled emptying of the stadium of the stunned crowd, concluded in his mind that it was all over; but if he thought he was about to retake control of the situation after a hearty handshake with Crackpot and arranging a lift to the station for him, then he was very sadly mistaken. . .

"I won't be a minute," mumbled Crackpot, as he hurriedly left the press box, hoping the policeman would take the hint and not follow. The astute Inspector Dixon stayed in the press box.

A few moments later, Inspector Dixon stood, scratched his chin, and stared down from the press box and across the pitch as Charles Carruthers emerged from the players tunnel and hurried across to the penalty area where poor Eric still lay, and where two ambulance men were about to place the body on a stretcher and carry him out of the ground and into a waiting ambulance. The inspector saw Carruthers talking to the two men, and although it was only a split-second view in profile due to the distance and poor angle, he knew the two men were at least mystified or perhaps even irked at what Carruthers had said to them. But a few seconds later, Carruthers turned and commenced walking back towards the tunnel. The ambulance men stood stock still for a short while, staring after this stranger with a fruity accent. But one then nudged the other, gave him a decorum-void gesture which seemed to represent the analogical and undignified emptying of waste from a wheelbarrow or hand-cart into no doubt a refuse dump, and they resumed their task of taking the body of poor Eric Ramsbottom to the mortuary.

"May I ask what you said to the ambulance men, Chief Inspector?" asked Dixon, as Crackpot walked back into the press box.

"You can ask, yes," replied the enigmatic and unsmiling Crackpot.

"I see. . . " replied Inspector Dixon; he scratched his chin – again.

"Please clear the room, Inspector, or failing that, find another private room where you and I can talk. Thank you," said the no longer enigmatic but certainly brusque Chief Inspector Carruthers.

"This will do just fine," said the thick-skinned Dixon. "Ferris?! Out! Take the others and help cover Reception. Now . . . (turning to Crackpot, but he then frowned and turned to the door which was about to be closed again), Oh, Ferris, hang on, no; in fact, get everyone to sweep the corridors and immediate area, no one is to be within a hundred yards of here for the time being."

As the policeman and the chairman left the room, Crackpot smiled. The inspector's dictat was over dramatic and actually unnecessary, and probably unachievable barring an immediate and huge logistical exercise, considering something like twenty-thousand people were still in the process of exiting the stadium, but nor was it harmful so he let it go. He waited until they were alone and addressed the inspector.

"Now then, Dixon . . . to business: after I have told you of what we have to do next, and just as importantly, what we have to say – press conferences, statements and the like – we – er – you will then have to brief your gainsbo– er – constables on certain matters of national security.

"I see. . ." said the inspector – again.

33

Suspicious Minds

Saturday Evening

SIR ALAN LEITH-PERKERSON looked out of the window of Vernon Kell's office, which looked down on the street outside. It was long since dark, and the fog almost negated the light from the street lamps. But Sir Alan frowned as the taxi taking his boss out to a remote airstrip in Surrey, fired up and went off down the street and out of sight. Upon getting the wire through telling him the terrible news about Eric Ramsbottom, Vernon Kell had decided on the spot to travel north to help his best agent with some impromptu damage limitation. Vernon Kell was one of only a very few from the service who could pilot an aeroplane. In a strange way, Kell was glad of this diversion, as his mulling over what could be done concerning the German Ambassador had not provided clarity and a way forward, but rather a severe headache.

"Damn fool, flying in this weather at this time of the year," Sir Alan said to himself, "Oh, well, that's his decision (he sighed, and looked around the office) . . . might as well call it a day."

Sir Alan Leith Perkerson went back to his own office, collected his things, put on his coat and walked down the corridor to the staircase at the far end. Coming up the stairs was Val Larkin.

"Hello, Sir Alan . . . boss in, or have I missed him?"

"Missed him – just, unfortunately. What is it, Larkin? Overtime forms? Or anything I can help with?"

"I am not sure if you can, sir, and it's probably nothing, but you know me. . ."

"Sorry?" replied a mystified Sir Alan.

"It's Sir Timothy Sprake-Hipkiss, sir. . . "

"What about him?"

"He's dead, sir."

"Dead?!"

"Yes, sir, it only happened a short while ago, he seems to have just dropped dead outside Harrod's."

"Poor chap, that's dreadful. You must have known the boss and he were close friends. Is that why you're here, to let Sir Vernon know?"

"Well, yes . . . but not because they were pals, I didn't know that. I am here because around the same time, that Geff chap from the German Embassy was acting rather shiftily in the Harrod's food hall. I have informed the Duty Officer, but I thought I would try and get it to the top, sooner . . . just in case."

At that moment, Val Larkin's reputation came to the fore.

"Oh come now, Larkin, he was old and not too well, I believe; and we know all about Geff: typical Prussian arrogance, someone to avoid at parties, but that's about it. Surely you—"

"Normally, I would agree with you, sir, but we have had the odd chat here and there at various places. I know he looks down his nose at the British, but despite that he's still personable enough, even if through duty not choice, but today . . . well. . ."

"What, man? Out with it?"

"Unless I've got this very wrong, Sir Alan, I could have sworn he saw me . . . and bolted, or rather, he bolted *because* he saw me; in fact, I think he ran off down Brompton Road. On their own, each thing seems nothing; Sir Tim may well have died of natural causes and Geff may have had a bad day with his boss and couldn't be bothered with anyone, but the two things together, minutes, perhaps seconds apart, well. . ."

Sir Alan's brain had been racing as the two incidents were related to him, and then something rather worrying popped into it.

"You may be onto something, Larkin. Now, do you know where Geff is right now?"

"No, sir, I am sorry, I don't. So you think there's something to this, then?"

"Maybe, Larkin, maybe, but with all the odd things going on at the moment, we cannot ignore it. Now, anyone at home waiting for you?"

"Not married, sir, no."

"Good . . . well, not good you are not married, I mean . . . right, nothing we can do right now, so coat off, tell Doris she's on over–er – even more overtime, and to get us some coffee. Let's see what can be done, my office. Oh, tell me . . . how do you spell gaol?"

"Jail, sir?" replied the mystified Larkin.

"Yes, gaol. I'll explain later."

"J-A-I-L, sir," said Larkin.

"Thanks," replied Sir Alan.

"Sir?"

"It doesn't matter . . . now then, where were we? Oh, yes, my office. . ."

*

Crackpot sat at a table next to the rear window in the public bar of the Amos Hills Hotel, which was opposite Nelson railway station. The room was small, dimly lit, shabby, miserable and smelt of paraffin. He was the only person in there; this was, thought Crackpot, more due to the hotel bar prices rather than the downbeat decor.

It was 8:45 pm, just on four hours since the sad demise of Eric Ramsbotton, and, Crackpot thought, far too late to start the seemingly endless round of telephone calls to arrange the bringing together of the gentlemen of the local and national press, all the relevant authorities, and of course the chairman and board of the club; far too late for Crackpot – but not for. . .

"Hello, Charles, I thought I would find you here."

Crackpot knew the voice straight away; he looked up from the *Nelson Gazzette* evening extra – and went white.

"Boss! What are you doing here?" spluttered Crackpot, standing up and almost knocking over his pint of best bitter.

Major-General Sir Vernon George Waldegrave Kell walked from the doorway towards Crackpot, ahead of the wisps of Lancashire fog which seemed to have decided to call in for a quick one themselves; he spoke as he steadied his underling's half empty glass.

"Hmmm . . . let's see: don't stray far from major transport links if you can avoid it, and try not to stand out in any way – or have you forgotten your training? Add to that your known preference when it comes to beverages, and – er – local folks, and here we are. . ."

Crackpot, who had actually asked why his boss was here and not how did he find him, was irked. He wanted to call Kell a smart arse but thought better of it, but he may as well have just blurted it out to complement his rather stunned countenance.

"Yes, true, I can be a smart arse at times; my apologies old boy, habits of a life time and all that," said Kell, an excellent reader of faces. "Plus, I asked Doris before I left in the FE2."

There were a few seconds of awkward silence, but after seeing the barman disappear down the cellar steps and after looking around the bar and was satisfied that no one was in earshot, Vernon Kell spoke again.

"What a right state of affairs this is; a German agent and a local hero both dead as a doornail, not fifty yards from each other."

"Yes, right cock-up; sorry about that, Boss." said the very regretful Charles Carruthers.

"Don't be," said Kell, with just a hint of a thin smile.

"Eh?" said Crackpot, duly confused.

"If it's any consolation, the local lab' man, a genius at anatomy as well as trigonometry, is certain Weber pulled the trigger for the second shot, not you. Trigonometry is nothing to do with triggers, by the way. Very unfortunate though; a pistol's range is not that great, but the lab' chappy says it is not unknown for a combination of gusts and maybe ricochets to send pistol shots further than normal."

The stony-faced Crackpot stared in disbelief at his boss, but then moved on.

"Well, yes, but it sort of doesn't make any difference, does it? We were scrapping and our desperate attempts to get the upper hand saw the gun go off, so I think we both had a hand in the death of Ramsbottom, no matter whose pinky actually did the deed."

Kell sighed. He wasn't heartless, but nor could he be sentimental in his position. It was also something he demanded of his operatives. There was also something else, a twist in the tale, which would mystify Crackpot if he was told, but that could not happen just yet.

"Now, look, Charles: OK, you and Weber may have brought about the death of a great footballer, but you didn't damn well mean it, and as odd as it may seem to say, I don't think Weber would be happy with his handiwork either. But the last thing I need right now is someone who is going to tear themselves apart over an accident."

Crackpot sighed and nodded but said nothing.

"OK, now . . . I take it you've made a start on arrangements for a press conference?" asked Kell.

"Yes, sir, I have. But I've done as much as I can for now, though," replied Crackpot, "Grindlay and his over-fed cronies know about it, and there's nothing can be done now until Monday. I am going to brief the local blueboy on what to say at the press conference, then stay in the background just in case. Come the afternoon and it's a first class compartment and smoked salmon on the way back to the Smoke."

"Piffle and Poppycock;" said Kell, "get that revolting brew down your neck. We're going to my hotel room, and you, my friend, are not having dinner until you have contacted everyone from the chairman of the Football Association down to the Town Clerk's deputy secretary's messenger boy's fag. We're having a press conference at the ground tomorrow, whether anyone likes it or not."

"But it's Saturday ni—" went to say Crackpot, but the stony countenance of Kell made Crackpot think better of it and he stopped dead. But he then said by way of a rejoinder, "I don't think council office messenger boys have fags; this isn't Eton."

"One less call to make then, isn't it?" retorted Kell, but this time with a smile.

Crackpot inwardly groaned, downed the rest of his cloudy brown brew, and left with his boss to go to the Goldstraw Hotel, which was a hundred yards or so along Railway Street and was a far grander affair than the Amos Hills.

*

Crackpot was on his own in his boss's hotel room, in the grandest room available in the best hotel in town, but still far from what senior public servants are used to, especially when it comes to the cuisine. Vernon Kell had muttered something, ostensibly to Crackpot but more to himself, about trying to find a decent restaurant as he left the hotel around 9:30 pm. It was approaching midnight. Crackpot had lost count of the times he had been reminded of the day – and the time – by infuriated diners who were just relishing the fish course only to be passed the telephone by their butlers. But Crackpot knew the high and mighty were always going to be miffed at such inconvenience, whether due to the highly irregular press conference to be held the next day - 'On a Sunday?! Dash it, man!' - or merely for the call telling them so, but he didn't really care about that; one missed pink gin or even a sherry-sodden dessert was, to Crackpot at least, absolutely nothing in the great order of things. Crackpot put the receiver back on the hook for the last time, let out a huge sigh and flopped back in the desk chair, just as his boss walked back into the hotel room.

"All done, I hope. . . ?" asked Kell.

"Just now, sir; we've ruined everyone's evening just by contacting them, and the less said about how they all feel about missing a stroll on the links tomorrow the better."

"Yes, well, needs must. Here you are, Carruthers, best I could do given the time. Damned provinces; can't get a decent meal anywhere."

Vernon Kell handed Crackpot a rather squashed up armpit indented package, its outer covering a badly print-smudged and greasy newspaper inside which was a stone cold portion of fish and chips. As Crackpot was famished he duly and gratefully accepted the offering.

"I hope you don't mind my saying so, sir but do we need everyone there tomorrow? If we're controlling the show, then wouldn't less people mean less risk of straying off the party line?" asked Crackpot as he quickly unwrapped his very late supper and crammed in a handful of cold chips into his mouth.

"Hmmm, you surprise me at times, Carruthers, you really do. In situations like this, then appearances are everything. As long as someone from the FA, the club, and the local constabulary are there to at least be on hand to answer questions, which will not happen of course, then all will seem normal. And here's the coup de grâce; you say everyone was a tad miffed? Good. By tomorrow afternoon, they'll be looking at their watches and not daring to delay things further by offering to add to the proceedings. Never mind Monday, old boy, with a little luck you'll be back within the sound of Bowbells by tomorrow evening."

"Good," said Crackpot, but without much conviction; he never told anyone in the service this, but he hated London: the dense, claustrophobic atmosphere of Central London was something he was always glad to get away from and not be in too much of a hurry to return to. The damned provinces were fine by him, but he was fortunate that he never stayed in one place too long, thus never knowing that one town or city was pretty much the same as any other, in the end. Crackpot stuffed more chips in his mouth, tore away a little piece of cold greasy battered cod and that went in, too. He then offered up the package of congealed fish and chips to his boss.

"Would you like some, sir?" asked Crackpot in a very thick voice.

Vernon Kell humphed, grimaced, and poured out two whiskies instead.

34

The Game's Afoot

SUNDAY MORNING. 0130 A.M. Valentine Larkin and Sir Alan Leith Perkerson were slumped in cosy armchairs, almost asleep. At least Sir Alan had had the decency to send Doris home some hours earlier, this was after eliciting from the multi skilled cook, secretary and backup operative that she spelt the word gaol with a G.

"Even Stevens either way, damn and blast," said Sir Alan Leith-Perkerson as the equally mystified Doris Parker had put on her hat and coat and dashed off home.

Apart from Sir Alan deciding to call in their own pathology staff to take over the procedures after the death of Sir Timothy Sprake-Hipkiss and to get their findings back to them as soon as possible, their brain storming session had come to nothing; no potential avenue of enquiry had presented itself; all they had was Val Larkin's oft uttered suspicion, 'Actin' right queer, so he was, so he was . . . and poor Sir Tim, dead on the floor – shockin,' in his broad Ulster brogue, and Sir Alan's brain cells whirring round inside his head at light speed, telling him that on this occasion, Larkin's suspicions could not so easily be dismissed.

Sir Alan sat upright and forced himself into full consciousness.

"Right, Larkin, come on man, sit up, let's go through things once more. Up to today, Geff usually spoke openly and freely with you, his arrogance notwithstanding?"

"Yes, as I've told you, yes. It was the fact he acted the way he did, with Sir Tim lying dead on the pavement which made me log it in."

"OK, OK . . . right, well, we know one thing, or at least I hope we do. . ."

"What that might be then, Sir Alan?"

"As bad as it is, we can no longer prevent the assassination, as far as I can tell, it appears to have happened. The target appears now not to have been Mr Asquith, but Sir Tim, and his absence seriously dents our position in the talks over Palestine, I am sure that that was the motive. But – and as terribly sorry I am about this, it does make things a little more straightforward, not easy . . . but straightforward."

"I am not with you, Sir Alan, sorry," said a confused Val Larkin.

"It's a plain and simple manhunt. We have no evidence that there are other targets in imminent danger, though of course, all senior public figures are always in some sort of danger, but, my hunch is, for now, the worst has happened, so let's find the scum that did this."

"Shouldn't we get in touch with the boss first?" suggested Larkin.

"Indeed we should – and will, but I am hanged if I am going to be piggy in the middle doing things by remote: endless phone calls and cables to and from t'up north, as it were. I'll tell him of what's happened, and strongly suggest he gets his arse back here, but up until he shows his face, I'm in charge."

"That's the spirit, sir, but . . . that's Yorkshire, not Lancashire, just thought I'd mention it," said Larkin with a cheeky smile.

"Ee bah gum, that raght, lad?"

Their ad-libbing on things comically northern was interrupted by a knock on the door.

"Come in."

The door opened, and a young man in heavy outdoor clothing edged rather nervously over to the desk.

"I'm from the department laboratory. I've got to give this to Sir Albert Leith-Parkinson."

"Close enough," said Sir Alan with a smile.

"I beg your pardon, sir?"

"I'm – er – Sir Albert, here, let me have that, and here's something for your trouble."

Sir Alan handed over a half-a-crown with a smile, which was returned by the messenger boy.

"Is there anything to go back with me, sir?"

"No, you may go, and thank you, young fella," said Sir Alan, as he watched the young man leave. "Right, let's see. . ."

Sir Alan ripped open the buff envelope, took the single piece of paper out of the envelope, but unlike the message in Simple-Cypher, the contents were perfectly ledgible. He studied it for a minute or so and then replaced the paper back in the envelope.

"Well . . . you guessed right, Larkin, well done."

"Sir?"

"Cyanide poisoning was the cause of death, and although they cannot be 100% certain, it looks like it was injected into Sir Timothy's ankle; there is a small puncture mark on his left ankle."

"Blimey, that's straight out of Arthur Conan Doyle!"

"Well, let's go and push our Moriarty off the Reichenbach Falls then, shall we?"

"I'm flippin' Watson, then!" joked Larkin.

Sir Alan stopped – thought – and then laughed out loud as he stood, donned his hat and coat, and bade Larkin to follow.

"Where are we going, sir, exactly?" asked Larkin.

"To the German Embassy, or, Carlton House Terrace to be precise; we'll have to stake the place out. We cannot enter; technically we're not even allowed to arrest anyone from there, but I'm hanged if I'm going to let Geff off the hook."

The grim-faced Deputy Head of British Intelligence and an uncharacteristically uncertain Valentine Larkin, left HQ to make the short journey to the German Embassy.

35

Three Steps to Heaven

VAL LARKIN was confused; moreover, he was more than a little concerned that the senior officer sitting next to him in the staff car, parked right outside the main gates to Prussia House on Carlton House Terrace, was breaking the law. He had to wait while his senior received a whispered verbal report from another operative at the near-side front window before he could air his worries. Sir Alan Leith-Perkerson finally nodded, and wound his window back down as the B Brigade operative went back to his own vehicle.

"I'm sorry, Sir Alan, I just don't get this. I've an inkling we're not even allowed to stake out foreign embassies; plus, aren't we a little obvious? We're bound to be seen."

"Precisely."

"Eh?"

"You may – going strictly by the letter of the law, be right. But if you, Sir Vernon, or even Mr Herbert Henry Asquith think I am just going to sit back and do nothing and allow a murderer to sit in there, drinking schnapps and chomping on Beervorst sandwiches while we're left to clean up the mess, then you all have another think coming. I can't just stand by while a perfectly innocent man is ruined, personally and professionally, not while I am sure as eggs is eggs that the guilty party is less than fifty yards away. Immunity or not, I am making it my business to see justice done."

"A perfectly innocent man? Who might that be, sir?" said Larkin, who had not been told of Sir Vernon Kell's belief that Prince Lichnowsky was the assassin.

"The old *Need to Know* caper, Larkin; sorry, but no doubt it will all come out in the wash, as they say."

"Aye, probably," replied Val Larkin. "But why are we parked in plain view with the headlamps on? If Geff comes back to the embassy, he's sure to see us."

"I want him to see us; the more Geff realises we're on to him, the greater chance there is of him doing something stupid. I at least agree with Sir Vernon on that?"

"Eh?"

"Nothing. Now, as much as I wish we could call for backup, we can't as this is all unofficial, at least at this juncture anyway, so it's just us. So – all we can do is wait, and hope our friend comes home early."

"What if he doesn't, sir?"

"B Brigade has at least been able to report he's been throwing his money away in the Crockford, but apparently, it's a set routine. He empties his wallet on Red on Roulette, bums a drink or two from a chappie from the American Embassy, and gets a cab back home, usually about now. But if we have to, we'll wait all night. When Geff does show, then he is to be prevented from entering the embassy at all costs; if we manage that then we can nab him, and question him; I will deal with any repercussions that may arise later. But if he gives us the slip and five minutes later appears at the window, grinning, and toasting us with a small glass of schnapps, then we may have lost him for good, but with a little—"

A dig in the ribs cut short Sir Alan Leith-Perkerson's diatribe on the woes of suspected criminals hiding behind their diplomatic status.

"That's him, sir. He's the front passenger in that taxi that's just pulled up."

"In the words of the great Sherlock, the game's afoot, Larkin. Flash the head-lights then leave the cab-light on. I want to see how he reacts when he knows it's us."

"If you insist, sir," sighed Larkin, far from happy at having seemingly being dragged across the accepted line by Sir Alan Leith-Perkerson.

Geff had paid his fare and was about to get out of the car when the flashing lights from a car horizontally opposite distracted him. He leaned over the driver's seat so he could get as close as he could to the windscreen, screwed up his eyes, and looked across. The lights stopped flashing, the internal car light came on, Geff rubbed his eyes to dismiss the dazzle, and then when he looked again, his face dropped. There, in the road outside the German Embassy less than twenty feet away, were none other than the Deputy Head of British Intelligence and the paranoid operative, Valentine Larkin, sitting in a car, grinning inanely and waving. Geff forced a smile, went to wave, stopped himself, and while a million desperate thoughts raced through his brain, just stared aghast at the two extremely eccentric British Gentlemen.

"Get out," said Geff suddenly to the driver.

"Beg yer puddin'?" replied the driver, who thought he had misheard.

But Geff was not in the mood for further debate on the matter. With great speed and tremendous dexterity and strength, he pushed the driver forward with his right hand, reached across with his left, opened the front near-side door, twisted round so he could grab the driver by his shoulders, hauled him over to the left, and then unceremoniously shoved him out of the car by the seat of his trousers. The driver had not even had time to rub his aching and bleeding forehead after becoming intimate with the windscreen, before he found himself unceremoniously ejected from his own motor; he was now belly-down and legs akimbo, sprawled out on the pavement of Carlton House Terrace.

Geff clambered over into the driving seat; luckily the driver had left the engine ticking over to prevent having to restart, as he had expected Geff to have got straight out.

With another quick glance at 'those two English lunatics', Geff put his foot down. But in his panic to get away, he overdid an attempted reverse and half-lock; the car mounted the pavement and a split-second later a dull thud and a severe jolt let him know he had hit the Embassy's perimeter railings with the right side of the car, but apart from some dents and the loss of some best coach-paint and varnish, no real damage was done. After a further scrape, Geff finally drove off down the road.

"After him!" yelled Sir Alan.

Otto Geff not so much roared as stalled and stuttered and

banged and clanged away. He drove across the wide road at an angle, straight towards the Duke of York column which seperated the East and West flanks of the front facades of Carlton House Terrace. He missed this by inches, just managing to veer left of the column. But Geff did not straighten up in time, just about avoided crashing into a large elm tree, only for the car to then bounce and crash down a series of concrete steps – the Duke of York steps – these punctuated an embankment of trees and bushes which ran along the south side of Carlton House Terrace and which seperated the Terrace from the Mall, a wide thoroughfare down on the lower level. It was only pure luck that prevented the car from literally coming apart and would have meant certain death for Geff. But with a comical – in a way – bouncing up and down as he desperately tried to keep the car straight, and with his whole frame shaking and his head bobbing up and down making him go, 'YUHYUHUYUHYUHYUHYUHYUH!', Geff, and the car, reached the Mall with a tremendous thud, giving Geff an equally tremendous jolt.

Meanwhile, Sir Alan Leith-Perkerson and Valentine Larkin had been unable to take advantage of someone either not familiar with British cars, or, as it seemed so to Larkin, couldn't drive at all, at least officially, and was on day-one lesson-one, of one hell of a frantic on the job crash course. His suspicions were more or less confirmed as he watched the Unic Landaulette take a rather dramatic short-cut. Two minutes had passed and yet the supposed pursuers had not moved an inch; the engine had died as Valentine had tried to drive off at speed. He roared, pulled his hair in rage, flung the door open, scrambled out, grabbed the starting handle from the bracket above the front grille of the especially imported Cadillac Five-Person 1912 Tourer, rammed the handle in the crank-hole and frantically turned it. If he had stayed calm, then he may have been able to apply the maxim – more haste less speed. But his manic attempts were hopeless. The handle jammed, sprang back and gave his wrist a nasty wallop; it then wouldn't turn as fast as he wanted and ended up straining his hand, and on the third attempt, the handle just flew out and hit him on the head before crashing to the ground. Although yells such as 'Get this damn thing started, you Irish buffoon!' didn't help, Larkin mopped his brow with his hand, took a deep breath, picked up the handle, and more carefully but more purposefully this time, inserted the handle. Being careful to keep his thumb clear, he turned the handle and the engine fired up.

Larkin didn't even return the handle to its proper place, instead he just threw it on the road, scrambled back in the car, and drove off after Geff. Unfortunately, Larkin forgot that the western end of the terrace was a cul-de-sac, but thankfully a circular one. He went right round at speed, back along the terrace and slowed down at the Duke of York's column.

"What's it to be, sir? Go north to then veer west and hope we catch up somehow? Or take a risk and down the steps?"

"If I said it's not my car, does that give you a clue?"

Larkin said no more, backed up on the turn a few yards, and then accelerated towards the Duke of York steps. He knew that there was a high risk of failure but he thought if he didn't go too fast nor too slow, they might just make it safely down onto the Mall. Unlike Geff, the two intelligence men found their journey downwards less frantic than Geff's had been, but the downside to this was each drop down to each step made the jaw-bashing and jolts to the back more pronounced. But men and motor just about retained their integrity and they safely although noisily reached the thankfully flat plain of the Mall.

"I meant as it's not mine, we'd best be careful," muttered Sir Alan Leith-Perkerson.

"Eh?"

"Nothing, nothing, just get after him."

It had been very lucky for Geff that there were no pedestrians and not much traffic, either motorised or horse-drawn, on the side roads around the Saint James' Park area as he drove very haphazardly southwest along the Mall. To be fair to Otto Geff, he was a quick learner, and now having seemingly the time, and the space, he gradually got used to the controls and managed to safely accelerate, but to where he knew not.

But Geff's head start was already being worn away. Geff just happened to glance in the rear-view mirror, and spotted his pursuers now gaining on him.

This heralded a desperate chase through Central London. Geff put his foot flat down on the accelerator.

He sped southwest along the Mall for about a hundred yards; what traffic there now was, luckily for Geff, was oncoming on the opposite side of the road. Without reducing speed he took a left fork onto Spur road; this was almost disastrous as he lost control for a split-second on the reckless turn. Geff, sensing he was going too far to the left, veered over to the right, and almost went straight into an oncoming omnibus, but as Geff again veered left, so did the driver of the bus, and both were safe. He took a glance in his rear-view mirror – no one was on his tail; he hoped he'd lost his pursuers, but. . .

It was hard to tell who was more grim-faced, Larkin or Leith-Perkerson; Larkin sped along the Mall, spotted Geff turning onto Spur Street, hoped the German driving novice had lost it completely on the bend, but as he roared around at speed, knew that this had not been the case, as he could see the 1911 Unic Laundaulette racing along Spur Street. But they were gaining. Geff now knew this, too. . .

Otto Geff's mind was racing. He concluded that to stay on the one road for long periods would most probably result in his pursuers catching up, but to use any and every turn he could, he might just finally lose them. . .

At the next junction, indecision combined with inexperience actually ironically aided the German spy. With the kind of luck which sees the worst swordsman ever on his first duel kill some fruity French duke who'd swished his way to more than forty kills, Geff swerved right onto Buckingham Palace Road, but rather crazily changed his mind and did a full-lock on the wheel, and again rapidly using up a quota of luck which most people don't get through in a lifetime, managed to turn back around.

Despite a terrible squealing of brakes and tyres, white knuckles, sweat soaked temples and a face not usually seen outside of geriatrics with constipation in an old folks home, Geff was able to take the left fork at speed, and was soon racing along Horseferry Road.

Larkin had not been so lucky; he had almost caught up with Geff, had seen the mad full turn – but was unable to copy the either imbecilic or highly skilled manoeuvre (he soon decided on the former) and found himself ten yards along Buckingham Palace Road, and almost at a stand-still as a sudden increase in traffic both ways – a variety of motorised private and commercial vehicles, night buses and other horse drawn cabs, carts and carriages –meant he could not yet resume his pursuit.

With another glance over his shoulder, Geff hoped he had finally lost the two mad Englishman (Geff had never realised Larkin was irish, but he did wonder about his strange accent), but as he reached the end of Horseferry Road and made to turn right, the Cadillac came into view once more, and of course, the same was true from Larkin's perspective. Geff just saw the back of the Unic Laundaulette as it veered right onto Victoria Street.

Geff put his foot fully down once more, but this was rather ill-timed. Victoria Street was very busy with traffic; he overtook, dodged and weaved in and out of a couple of omnibuses – one coming each way; three Hansom cabs – two of which were on the right, and a taxi and a private car on the left. But as he approached Westminster Cathedral on his right, he was going too fast to both get through and avoid a collision with either one of two more cabs both adjacent to each other on each side of the road, all he could do was wrench the wheel fully over to the right. But as a soldier on leave and a nice lady from Central London jumped out of the way, the car mounted the pavement right outside the cathedral, banged right into the first of the steps which led up to the entrance; the car then rolled right over at an angle, went up the first step, crashed into a column on the left, rolled over to the right and up onto the second step. The car then somersaulted and Geff was flung out through the windscreen, with the shattered glass now spread all over the entrance area, some of which was now stained crimson red. The car continued to career up towards the entrance, losing more parts and panels and fittings as it did so, until finally coming to a halt just before the entrance.

Geff had landed head first with a sickening thud on the third step up to the cathedral, and with his arms and legs twisted in the most unnatural way imagineable.

Valentine Larkin and his boss were only two streets away now, still speeding, but the haste was now more to do with finding out the source of the horrendous sounds which had resonated all over Victoria and which they had guessed not only to have been as a result of a serious accident, but more specifically through Otto Geff losing control of a car he couldn't even drive properly in the first place.

They finally reached the cathedral and slowed down as they came across the tragic, chaotic scene, which had now attracted the attention of passers-by as well as some cathedral staff who had dashed out of the huge wooden doors of the cathedral upon hearing the terrible noise. They now knew it was as a result of a car accident, and was not the roof falling in.

While Valentine ran to check on Geff, Leith-Perkerson hailed a passing policeman and told him to run and bring an ambulance, then fetch his commander and to get more men as soon as possible. It was imperative the immediate area was kept clear.

Larkin bent down over Geff. "Can you hear me, Geff? Just nod if you can, shake if you can't—er . . . nod if you can."

Geff groaned and looked up at Larkin.

"Pr–pr–priest — get me a priest, please . . . dying. Get me a—"

"A priest?! And what flamin' use do you thi—"

"Larkin! That's enough! Do as the man says! . . . A Catholic, eh? At least he crashed in the right place," added Leith-Perkerson in an undertone, but without any sort of humour attached.

"But sir!"

"Do it!"

Larkin slunk off to look for a priest, muttering as he went.

Sir Alan Leith-Perkerson bent down so he was face to face with Otto Geff. Geff was coughing and spluttering, with each cough accompanied by a trickle of blood coming from the corner of his mouth. Leith-Perkerson wasn't at all sure if the priest would be in time.

"Geff, we've gone for a priest, shouldn't be too long. But this is important; can you tell me . . . how do you spell the word – *Gaol?"*

Geff coughed, leaked a little more blood, and smiled. It was such a smile that the Deputy Head of British Intelligence didn't even need a verbal answer.

"There's always something one overlooks," he managed to say, in between more coughing and more blood.

"I'm glad we cleared that up. Now, Geff, what about the coded letter which seemed to implicate the Ambass—"

"Got him, sir. None other than the head honcho."

Sir Alan-Leith Perkerson, recognising the summoned cleric, was outraged, despite the fact that he was an unapologetic confirmed atheist.

"Larkin! Show some respect, man! This is Francis Bourne, His Grace the Bishop of Westminster and the de facto Catholic Cardinal of England and Wales! Address him properly in future!"

"I beg your pardon, Your De Facto."

Despite the dire reason for being dragged from his quarters, more precisely his bed, the Cardinal couldn't resist a smile, but then he nodded gravely at Sir Alan Leith-Perkerson. He moved past the intelligence men, took out a small bottle of oil, knelt down, and started talking quietly to Otto Geff. Sir Alan Leith-Perkerson diplomatically stepped back a few feet, dragging Larkin with him.

After a couple of minutes, the Cardinal annointed the dying Geff, and made the sign of the cross.

"In nomine Patris et Filii,
et Spiritus Sancti. Amen."

Both men knew that Geff had made his last confession and had received the Last Rites, the Cardinal stood, said, 'Gentlemen,' nodded, and returned to the Cathedral.

Sir Alan once more bent down to speak to Geff. But Otto Geff was wheezing heavily and his eyes were glazed over.

"I am sorry, Geff, but if you can hear me, please answer. Who really was the assassin? Was it you? And did you send the coded message as a red herring? Is the Ambassador totally innocent in this matter?"

Despite the intense pain, Geff just about managed to lift his hand and beckon his questioner to bend down even further. With their noses almost touching, Geff then pushed Sir Alan Leith-Perkerson's head to one side and spoke in a hoarse barely audible whisper into his left ear.

Sir Alan listened intently for just on a minute. Then as he went to straighten up, Geff gave one last wheeze, and fell back, dead.

By this time, the area had been cordoned off, and an ambulance had finally arrived to take Geff away.

"Shall we, sir?" said Larkin, pointing to the staff car, parked on Victoria Street.

"Yes, I think so."

Larkin drove back to Whitehall in a far more leisurely fashion than he had when pursuing Otto Geff.

36

The not so Grassy Knoll

IT WAS SUNDAY AFTERNOON.

Vernon Kell and Charles Carruthers stood on the left side at the end of the rather cramped reception room of the Grindlay stadium. Three long tables covered in plain white table cloths had been placed together, and behind these, almost flush with the back wall, sat a rather grumpy looking array of representatives from the local constabulary, senior members of the Football Association who had travelled overnight from London, and Solomon Grindlay and the entire board of directors of the club. Stood to right of these was Inspector Keith Dixon, looking very nervous and trying desperately to clear the constant trickle of sweat from his forehead and neck. The main body of people in the room, all badly cramped up on around fifty small rickety wooden chairs were the gentlemen of the press, looking somewhat bemused, and just like those they had come to question, in rather a hurry to return to their usual Sunday routines, what could be salvaged of them, anyway.

Kell gave the slightest of nods to Dixon. The inspector gave one last wipe of his brow with his handkerchief and walked nervously to the front of the muddled delegation of various authorities. He looked with a little trepidation upon the sea of faces that made up the press in attendance; these were various hacks from a combination of local and national dailies, evening papers, Sunday papers, even a magazine; and completing the motley crew was one freelance journalist who did features for anyone or anything, just so he could eat and get a bed for the night.

"Good afternoon, gentlemen . . . now – erm – as you know, Eric Ramsbottom, the centre-forward for Nelson Corinthians, here in Nelson—"

"Funny that, thought they were based in John-O-Groats,"

interjected the unfunny although he always thought he was, Clive Harpin of the *Nelson Gazzette* sports pages.

Inspector Dixon groaned. He had had dealings with Clive Harpin on several prior occasions; but he gamely recovered.

"Any more, Harpin – out, and I mean it. As you all know, Eric Ramsbottom collapsed and died of heart failure as he was about to take a penalty in the dying seconds of the match against Manchester United. Since yesterday, rumours have quickly spread to the effect that Ramsbottom was murdered, but I can categorically assure you all, and of course, your readers, that this is not the case. A post-mortem has reveal—"

"Rubbish! It's a cover up!" shouted Harpin from the middle of the hoi-polloi, for once being the journalist of integrity he always meant himself to be; well, for two weeks in August many years before when pimply gangly Clive Harpin and his pencil, walked into the newspaper offices for the first time.

Harpin's interruption was the cue for all gathered to shout their own protests at what they clearly believed was going to be an attempt at a total whitewash.

"Heart failure?! He was shot! You know he was; everyone knows he was shot!"

"Garbage."

"Tripe!"

"What are you trying to hide?"

"Whitewash!"

"It's a scandal!"

"Heart failure my ar—" went to add Harpin.

"Out! Now! Don't say you weren't warned, Harpin; just get the gist from one of your cronies when we're done," demanded an angry Inspector Dixon. He watched Harpin stand, struggle along the narrow gap between the rows of chairs, and sullenly slink away and out through the glass door, but the inspector managed a wry smile as he saw Harpin duck behind a marble column in the foyer, leaving just his right ear in view. "The rest of you, don't make me call your editors so they have to give you the drill themselves, or the sack – I don't care. Now ask your questions in an orderly fashion, if we're lucky our respective good ladies can rescue the roast. Now, let's hear them. . ."

There were frantic yells, waves, some with notepads some without; some burst their lungs from their chairs, others stood. Dixon, well used to such organised chaos, simply shouted "Second row, third from the left. No! My left! My God, how you lot manage to even get the crossword out each day is a mystery! YES?" He finished, in an unfriendly tone.

A small unpleasant looking rotund chappie in a tweed jacket and pudding bowl haircut spoke up.

"Harris, the *Times,* Crime and Sports sections. Now, Inspector, you state Ramsbottom's death was due to heart failure? But how can you account for the many different reports of gunshots, a broken window, and blood on the fellow's shirt after collapsing in the penalty area?"

Every single one of the gathering of the great and good, faced the press with one big stony face. Both Crackpot and Kell gave the barest of nods, noticed only by Dixon, purely because he happened to be looking for a sign to continue.

"As already stated," said the resolute Dixon, "Eric Ramsbottom was not murdered, he collapsed and died of heart failure. Our own pathologist has concluded that a hitherto unnoticed heart condition combined with the stress of still playing top flight football at the age of thirty-nine brought about a seizure; there was nothing that could have been done to save the poor fellow. As for the blood on his shirt, this was not as a result of being shot, but was from a boil on his back which had burst just before the start of the second half. Unfortunately there had not been time for swabbing the area or applying ointment"

Inspector Dixon stopped there, thinking he had covered all aspects and looked around in readiness to take the next question.

"And the window, Inspector?" asked Harris of the *Times,* but with a smile.

"Oh, yes, sorry; oh, that's easily explained," replied Inspector Dixon, returning his gaze back to Wally Harris. "The window was not broken during a deadly gun battle, it had already been smashed by a builder a few days before; the replacement is due tomorrow. The sound that came from the new press box through the broken window, was not the sound of gunfire, it was the noise from a new kind of super-rattle brought to the game by club watchman Alfie Snoddie's youngest nephew, Reuben, who had not done as he was told and had wandered off around the corridors and offices of the inner stadium."

A sea of uncertain faces stopped, thought, then looked down as they scribbled away as fast as they could on their notepads, but the cacophony soon returned.

The next fifteen minutes or so saw an increasingly frustrated gathering from the nation's newspapers and journals, frown, tut and shake their head as their supposedly searching questions were answered with increasing confidence by Inspector Keith Dixon. Some of the questions were really aimed at others from the cumberbund attired dignitaries, but on each occasion, 'I'll field that one if I may,' became the adopted mantra of the police inspector.

Time went on. And perhaps somewhat akin to a music hall comedian on a bad night in front of a hostile audience, Dixon knew he was running out of material; but then came a diversion from the pack drill, although a very unwelcome one.

"Back row, first left. Your question please?"

A very scruffy, unshaven man in his forties almost leapt out of his ill-fitting grubby suit as he realised he was being prompted to ask a question.

"Oh . . . um – thank you, Inspector. Colin Maltravers; freelance. Can you confirm that Ramsbottom was insured for two-thousand pounds? And has his sister, Mary Rambottom, been able to explain why she was seen laughing and joking with her boyfriend, very shortly after her brother had been pronounced dead?"

There was a stunned silence in room, until. . .

"You what?!" yelled Inspector Dixon, who had had the harrowing experience of informing young Mary of the death of her brother, and had seen a bright, innocent laughter-filled face go white with shock and become soaked with tears a split-second later. "If you think I am going to dignify that with an answer, whoever you are, you gutt—"

"Maltravers, freelance," replied the unshaken hack.

"Out! Right now! Out out out! You! (Pointing to Crackpot and forgetting both pack drill and status.) Escort that man right out of the building; if he arrests, resist him!"

Dixon's fury had such an effect on the gathering that the forcefully exclaimed Spoonerism was at least ignored, if not missed entirely.

An awkward looking Crackpot looked to Vernon Kell; in return Kell gave one of his trademark nods noticed only by those waiting on them. As Crackpot strode toward Maltravers, who rather oddly just stood there and grinned, Dixon still had not finished his tirade.

" . . . And if I read one word, anywhere, inferring such tripe, you'll find yourself with some serious charges against you!"

Maltravers smirked and said, "Did you mean imply, perhaps? Reporters don't infer, Inspector, our readers do; we just report the fa—"

But the equally outraged people-loving spy was with his blue-hatted colleague all the way. Crackpot ran at Maltravers and landed a perfect right hook on his jaw. He caught him as he fell, and dragged him out of the room, through the foyer and ejected him from the stadium.

"Snoddie?!" Crackpot suddenly shouted.

"Yes, sir?!" came the smart reply from the watchman's hut.

"Hit him!"

"YES, SIR!"

As Crackpot went back in to the press conference, he heard several loud yells and yelps coming from the vicinity of the main gates.

Crackpot walked back in, in time to see a much calmer Inspector Dixon get the conference back on track.

"Time is short, gentlemen; one more question and that will have to do you all." said the inspector, "Yes?" he added, pointing to row four, four along.

"Thank you, Inspector. Ingle, Harcourt. *Lancashire Journal,*" said row four, four along, in even a fruitier voice than Harris of the *Times.* "Well now . . . there seems to be some irregularities concerning the procedures immedately after the shoo– er–

incident. Now I'm no medical expert, but are all local cases of fatal seizures, heart attacks and so on, dealt with at the police laboratories, rather than by the local infimary? Their mortuary is very good . . . so I've heard. . ."

To muted laughter from both the press and the attendees, Inspector Dixon commenced his answer.

"Thank you for your question, Mr Harc—"

"Ingle,"

"Er – Mr Ingle. Things may seem somewhat awry, but there are perfectly good explanations for the – er – post-incident procedures.

"Ramsbottom was indeed taken to the police laboratory in Nelson town centre, rather than the local infirmary, or their mortuary to be more precise. This was due to an outbreak of influenza, around 5:30 pm, among the County Coroner's own staff, who are all now in strict quarantine in a remote village on the Island of Anglesey.

"As you may also know, the post-mortem was completed very quickly; this was due to the entire staff from the Constabulary's Coroner's own office having to leave early on the Sunday morning for a Police Pathology department conference in Exeter. By pure coincidence, they had only been placed on the waiting list a very short time after Eric Ramsbottom's death, and were then informed almost straight away that the Blackburn sub-office had had to cancel due to an outbreak of Laryngitis; this allowed the Nelson contingent to duly attend and as a result, this made it necessary for the post-mortem to be expedited. So, gentlemen, there you have it. Thank you for coming here today. . ."

Upon their dismissal, the gentlemen of the press stood and grumbled loudly as they left to make the journey to the nearest telephone or post office, or their own offices or even the train station, to get their copy submitted to their own rags as quickly as possible. They weren't happy, they knew it was a sham – but – copy was copy.

Although each paper would use their own preferred angles, such as *Poor boy made good then dropped dead; Can the Mill town of Nelson ever recover?;* and so on — all would report the same official reasons given, in some way to some degree, for the death of a thirty-nine year old local hero.

No sooner had the press left the room, than they were quickly followed by the sea of cumberbund trying to get home in time for the sherry trifle.

37

A Night to Forget

IT WAS TIME TO PACK UP AND GO.

"Well, sir, shall we collect our things and take a cab to the station?" suggested Crackpot, forgetting what his boss's mode of transport had been for the journey north.

Kell humphed, but then smiled. "Do you like flying?" he asked.

Less than an hour later and with Kell in the cockpit and Crackpot sitting directly opposite in the observer seat, the brand new De Haviland FE2 took off from a remote airstrip on the Lancashire moors; the plane ascended and headed south. Left behind on the freezing moor was Inspector Dixon; he was furious as he wiped his oily hands on a rag after spinning the propellor for Kell – and spoiling his number one uniform into the bargain. He was going to shake his fist up at the plane but instead just muttered, 'What the hell,' and left to go home to at best a cold roast, but more probably a small plate of sardines as his wife looked stony-faced at him across the dining table.

"You look tired," shouted Kell over the open cockpit, after noticing the wan features of his best spy.

"That I am, sir; straight to bed when I get home," Crackpot shouted back. He was going to add that flying high on a cold winter's afternoon while totally exposed to the elements was not exactly helping, but the sudden roar of the engine put paid to that.

"Stuff and nonsense," replied Kell, after he had turned the plane around and headed north for Scotland. "A fresh salmon supper and a few single malts will do the trick." But there was a little method to his madness. "If the PM thinks it's off to Number 10 for a debriefing as soon as we land in London, then he's got another think coming. I could do with a break myself!"

"Eh?!" Crackpot shouted over the roar.

Kell did not struggle further to make himself heard, but some time later he did go 'Blimey!' in rather an excited fashion as the plane rapidly began to run out of fuel. Kell had forgotten to take into account the limitations of the FE2. Its 70 hp 52 kw Gnome engine with a full tank could only stay in the air for three hours or so before refuelling, and as their destination was almost four hours away, landing to refuel was not only necessary but imminent.

Using the lights of a Scottish village which Kell believed to be around ten miles north of Edinburgh, Kell brought the plane down to land with a bump in a farmer's field. He then sent a disgruntled Crackpot off in the pitch black with a kerosene lamp to look for a gate, and to see about getting fuel for the plane.

"How the hell do I know where we can get petrol from?" muttered Crackpot to himself as he squelched his way in the dark to what he hoped would be the edge of the field. Once there, he thought, he could then follow the hedge around until he came across any sort of opening. Moving with caution it wasn't long before he brushed up against the perimeter hedging; carefully he began to edge along. "Bingo!" he shouted seconds later, as his hand discerned a sudden change from cold damp twigs to freezing bare metal.

Crackpot held the lamp up, worked out what was what, opened the gate and walked on down the lane, hoping he would soon meet someone who could direct him to a petrol station. These were still in their infancy in urban areas and were rarer still in the sticks, but he had to try. Luckily, someone was coming towards him; in the pale moonlight all he could see was a huge beard with a huge overcoat, ambling along rather unsteadily.

"Evening!" shouted an overly breezy Crackpot. "Could you tell me where the nearest petrol station is please?"

The beard lifted itself clear of the huge lapels of the large trench coat.

"Ha! None round here, Sassenach. I am glad to say you have an eight mile walk to the edge of town," came the reply in a broad Scots accent. "Just keep on this lane, you'll get there – eventually."

"Thanks," said Crackpot, not entirely sure if he meant it. "Eight miles!" he added but only to himself. "Nope, no chance," he continued to no one, "but I think I know a way. . ." He did an about-turn and made his way back to the impromptu landing strip.

*

"Come on, Charles! You can do better than that!" urged the relatively warm and relatively dry and relaxed Vernon Kell from the Cockpit, as Crackpot huffed and puffed and pushed the plane down the country lane and onwards toward the petrol station.

"I thought you said it could run on vapours for a while!" came the puffed reply.

"Well, yes, but the while – and of course, the vapours – sort of ran out, sorry old chap. Now come on, push!"

Crackpot now looked every bit his nickname as he managed to free one arm and wave to an amazed passer-by.

"Nice night for it, eh?" he joked.

The reply came in the form of a thick Scottish brogue; the words of which Crackpot could not quite work out, which was, perhaps, just as well. . .

Crackpot was certain it was the slight downward slope which was allowing the plane to move rather than his own efforts, but then he looked up past the FE2 further along the lane, and groaned. He saw that the lane began to rise in the distance, but. . .

"Here we are! Well done!"

Crackpot looked to his left: he saw an old farmhouse, a gravelled off front yard – a Hibernian forerunner of the forecourt, to the front edge of which was one rusting petrol pump. Thankfully the passer-by had been joking.

Kell and his underling manoeuvred the plane right onto the forecourt; Kell jumped down and then both men looked around. They both sighed upon the realisation that unlike many rural businesses, the shop was not also the home. Everywhere was in darkness; it was closed and looked likely to remain so until the next morning.

*

"That's the Johnny!" enthused Kell after Crackpot had broken the lock and was almost done filling the tank.

"What the hell do ya think yer doin?!" – and more – came the yells, also in broad Scottish, but on this occasion it was very very clear to both men as to what had been said.

Although to stand there, smile, explain, and then pay would have been the more reasonable thing to do, it must be remembered that both men were at all times, secret agents.

"Bloody hell!" shouted Crackpot and his boss at the same time.

Kell scrambled up and into the cockpit and Crackpot span the propellor which luckily fired first time. Kell steered the plane out onto the lane and Crackpot ran and climbed up into the observer seat, but not before the proprietor, who had only been out checking for poachers as he was also the local gamekeeper, had made a detour upon hearing noises coming from his garage and had ran up and held onto Crackpot's trousers, which had then come clean away as Crackpot scrambled into his seat.

"I'll have yer, yer thievin' Sassenachs!" shouted the proprietor, as the FE2 sped down the lane getting ready for take-off.

As the plane finally took off and ascended, two barrels of shot whizzed past Crackpot's ears. "Bloody hell!" he shouted again, not just because of the near miss but also because he was now trouserless.

*

Although the novelty of a night in an exclusive Highlands hotel – after first landing on the lawn of the rear terrace and only just missing the water feature – had enlivened Crackpot's spirits, it was not to last.

In the almost empty restaurant of the Glen Burton Hotel in Aviemore, the two men had thoroughly thawed out in front of the huge log fire, but the salmon had long gone and both were on their eighth single malt. By the fifth, Crackpot had carried on in the hope it would numb his brain, rather than like Vernon Kell, because he liked it so much.

"Ha ha! So . . . there we were in the foyer of the Astoria. I walked up to the box office and asked the chappy, 'Two tickets for George Formby please.' Do you know what the cheeky blighter said?"

Crackpot gave a smile-free shake of his head.

"'Oh, no need, sir, George Formby has his own.' What do you

think of that?!"

"Do you mind if I call it a night, sir? I'm really done in," said Crackpot, side-stepping the levity.

Vernon Kell looked surprised. He had never failed before to get a laugh at the London Astoria gag.

"Er . . . yes, of course, Carruthers, I'll meet you in the dining room just before 7:00 am. Sleep well,"

"Good night, sir," said Crackpot, taking leave of Vernon Kell.

"Bloody younguns; no bloody energy," muttered Vernon Kell to himself, and believing it to be out of earshot.

"Now when *I* was a nipper. . . " said Crackpot to himself with a smile; he'd heard it all before. "Ooh 'eck!" he added, as the seat of Vernon Kell's spare trousers split wide open.

38

Odds and Loose Ends

IT WAS MONDAY MORNING. A weary Vernon Kell was back in his office musing over the weekend's events – and, due to an immediate briefing from his deputy, not just the events that he had been privy to or even part of.

"Oh my Lord! Oh my!" was all he could say.

"I understand how you feel, Sir Vernon: your good friend dead, and to be proved wr– for both us to be wrong over just whom the target was, and indeed, the shooter. And to be incommunicado while it all panned out . . . but – there we are – life goes on. . ."

Vernon Kell gave his deputy a look of absolute fury, but after a few seconds he allowed it to soften.

"But can we take Geff's word? OK, it was a death-bed confession, but he'd already received absolution seconds before; you know what these left footers are like, no sooner out of the cubby hole than they're at it again!"

Sir Alan Leith-Perkerson sighed.

"Sir Vernon, if you are asking me to prove beyond all doubt to you or indeed any other party, that all Geff said before he died was a 100% true, then I cannot oblige. All I have is my gut feeling; as far as I am concerned he was telling the truth: he did kill Sir Tim, he did send that note, he did try to frame Prince Lichnowsky, although he did say his orders came from a rogue cell in Berlin, but what's new there? If you cannot accept yourself that this is the case, then – unfortunately – it means you and I , Sir Vernon – are at an impasse on this."

"Damn it, Alan, you are bloody well right as usual. . . OK, old chap, best leave me to it, I have a rather embarrassing telephone call to make, and if it goes the way I think it will go, a journey across the park not long after. . ."

Sir Alan Leith-Perkerson stood and left his boss's office.

A few minutes later. . .

"Hello, Prime Minister," said the white-faced Vernon Kell down the telephone. "I am sorry to say that we have been chasing the wrong man. Under the circumstances, I think it would be prudent for both of us to call on the German Ambassador and offer our sincere apologies. . ."

A short time later. . .

"Ich sollte Dir eigentlich eins auf die Schnauze hauen! Wie auch immer, Nachmittagstee und Cremekuchen bei der Ritz werden als Entschuldigung genügen." ("I ought to punch you in the face! However, afternoon tea and cream cakes at the Ritz will do by way of an apology,"), raged Prince Lichnowsky at the shame-faced Mr Asquith, while standing behind his desk in his office

"Erledigt," ("Done"), replied Mr Asquith, while the very red-faced Vernon Kell, who knew a private ear-chewing due to it being the PM having to eat humble pie and not him, would follow once they were back in Whitehall, just kept his head down.

39

Farewell to Eric Ramsbottom

ERIC'S FUNERAL was on the following Wednesday; it was snowing, icy cold and windy.

With the aged ineffective Eric now forgotten, the club, the supporters and in fact the whole town, only had room in their hearts and minds for fond memories of the energetic young man who had played centre-forward for Nelson Corinthians for eighteen straight seasons without missing a game. He held all of the club's records for goals and appearances in all competitions. He had never been sent off, and if one could forget the last two seasons, which the whole town was only too willing to do, he had never had to leave the field through injury or fatigue throughout his whole career.

As the landlord had already relet Eric's house, the body of Eric Ramsbottom was in temporary repose at the local funeral parlour. Lofty's parents, who had always thought of Eric as a second son, gave swift and gracious permission to allow mourners to gather at their abode, a little terraced house on Bloxall Street near to Nelson Station. Sadly, the house was just too small to bring the coffin in the night before to allow Eric to take centre stage at his own wake, but even the suggestion of such a thing had been met with howls of disapproval from Mary Ramsbottom, who pointed out that Eric had never been a drinker. "Fair point," said old Seth Arkwright as he replaced the crate of stout back in the cupboard.

The mourners began to arrive around 9:00 am. Mary Ramsbottom could only greet so many at the door before she broke down; she was taken upstairs by Lofty's sister, Milly, to save her from further distress.

Just before 10:00 am, two horse-drawn hearses arrived with the front hearse bearing Eric. The large black shire horses, two to each carriage, were each adorned with two large black feathers and were still and silent as if they knew to show great respect to a local hero.

With Lofty and Milly supporting Mary, the three walked out of the house and climbed up the step and into the second carriage. Despite the terrible conditions the rest of the mourners slowly and sadly made their way out, buttoning up their coats, donning hats and turning their heads from the wind as they did so. They either lined up behind the carriages to form a human cortege, or turned left at the gate and began to make their own way to the church, which was on the corner of Railway Street and Broadway.

The funeral cortege moved slowly along; both sides of the main roads were packed out with mourners and curious bystanders who had braved the foul weather to say farewell to Eric. The cortege moved on – up Victoria Street and on towards Grindlay Park, turning right at Grindlay Road. Here the carriages stopped for a few moments. The stadium staff who could not get time off for the funeral, which included Alfie Snoddie, lined the road on the stadium side as a mark of respect for the team's greatest ever player. Alfie forgot himself for a moment, lifted his crutch to his head in salute, and fell over – again.

The players and staff were moved to tears by Lofty's floral tribute, the only tribute that Mary Ramsbottom, Eric's sister and all the family he had, allowed to go in the funeral carriage carrying the coffin, apart from her own. The flowers of Lofty's wreathe, laying long-ways alongside the coffin had been arranged into the words, *I'll punt 'em. . .* The fact that there was no one now to answer this was felt very keenly by the players, but of course, most of all by Lofty who was now in a worse state than Mary and had buried his head in her shoulder.

They then made a full circuit of the outside of the entire stadium; this was more to allow an easy turn-round than further tribute, but perhaps this was just as well. More fans packed the roads which surrounded Grindlay Park and many of these had to back up and move out of the way as the cortege negotiated the narrower Solomon Lane End.

The sad procession went back up Victoria Street and on towards Saint Ogbert's C of E Church. Once the lead hearse had come to a halt just by the church doors, Lofty, Tad Rowson and four more of the playing staff carefully lifted the coffin down from the carriage and took it into the church; once the coffin was placed at the front of the altar, the vicar – a very, very white-faced and tear stained Reverend Heath Harrop, did his best to provide a worthy funeral service.

Reverend Harrop was also fuming; he understood perfectly well that most football players were ordinary working lads who were just not used to speaking in public, and so was not surprised when he could not get a volunteer to offer a eulogy; but he at least thought the public figure that was Solomon Grindlay would readily oblige. "No time, sorry," he had replied when asked; Solomon Grindlay did not attend any part of the funeral. But Heath who had supported the team since its inception and had thought the world of Eric, duly paid a fitting tribute.

" . . . And all in all, he was with the club for just over twenty-five years.

"And for all of those twenty-five years of loyal service, Eric can be proud of himself as he looks down with, I am sure, great fondness for you all, for his home town and of course for his beloved Nelson Corinthians. The current campaign to allow reserve players to replace the injured or fatigued will, I am sure, be rather redundant here. I am certain we already have our own twelfth man, helping out the lads from above; perhaps even loftier than you now, eh, Lofty. . . ?"

Lofty jumped a little and blushed; it was perhaps not the best thing for Heath Harrop to have said, or perhaps it was more the timing was wrong to have surprised the latently gentle giant like this. The big man gulped and fought back the tears while the vicar moved on to further extol the virtues of Eric Ramsbottom.

" . . . Pride of the type we expect to see in people is not a sin – no, no, no; the sinful form of pride is really *excessive selfishness.* A good form of pride is when we do our very, very best for others, and by this virtue, ourselves, and when we achieve this we can be rightly proud. When we see this in others, we can be proud of *them* – as we all are of Eric.

"Now . . . do you know who Eric *really played for. . . ?"*

Those in the congregation who were neither familiar with rhetoric nor had truly caught on to where the vicar was going with this, actually went to answer before getting a dig in the elbows from their wiser better halves. But one six year old boy shouted, 'Nelson Corinthians, silly! Everyone knows that!'

"Yes! That is right, m'boy – he did indeed! Well done!" said the kindly vicar, while those gathered gave a little laugh and the boy's mother blushed and smiled.

" . . . But, more importantly, Eric carried *your* dreams, *your* hopes. For many, many years much of what he did, much of what he achieved, he did for *you,* and for me I may add. Yes, he was the Corinthians' greatest ever player but he was also yours. And yet, what a remarkably unassuming young man he was for all that: never big headed or bad tempered, on the pitch or off, and always ready with a helping hand or even just a smile as he passed you on the street. I am sure you will agree with me when I say that all who knew him well, or perhaps hardly knew him at all with their paths just crossing once, will miss the humanity of Eric Ramsbottom.

"If, to finish, I could just paraphrase my old Aunt Sheila, God rest her soul, upon the passing of my own father:

'To be born a gentleman is heritage; to die one – is an achievement. . .'

"As we leave shortly to say our final farewell to a great player, let us also remember to say farewell to the great man that was Eric Ramsbottom. . ."

The vicar, white-faced and trembling, left the altar, and the congregation broke into a highly unusual round of applause. The vicar knew it was for Eric, and was glad; the congregation knew it was for both.

*

On Wednesday, January the 15th, 1913, Eric Ramsbottom was laid to rest in Nelson Municipal Cemetery.

*

On Thursday, January the 16th, 1913, Solomon Grindlay arrived at his office in the stadium, whistling and singing to himself. The winds had dropped and today was a cold but crispy clear day, just the day for a shot of something, he thought, which was rather superfluous as he often came to the ground in baking temperatures later on in the year, declaring it to be just the weather for a shot of something. Minutes later Jock Shanksby knocked on his office door; not long after that, Solomon Grindlay was ecstatic as his manager informed him that as the entire squad were now over the flu', and as Lawton had had his suspension reduced on appeal to just two games, he could send a full strength team out for the rematch of their first round tie. The original match had been declared void.

*

On Wednesday evening, January the 22nd, 1913, Nelson Corinthians were beaten twelve goals to nil by Manchester United.

40

Samuel Grindlay — Ghost Writer

August 1920

THE AGEING SOLOMON GRINDLAY had not seen his nephew since sacking him as manager of the team some seven years earlier, but he was now busy with a scheme which once again required Samuel's assistance.

If all went to plan then Solomon's retirement nest egg would be considerably larger and Samuel would be enjoying a long stay in the big house, for a period determined by His Majesty the King.

*

One evening in the Rat and Cabbage on Carr Street, the unemployed ne'er-do-well nephew of Solomon was holding court for the benefit of all the regulars – or – he thought he was. . .

". . . Work for a livin'? *Work?!* Gaargh! What a waste of time! I tell you, lads, the difference between workin' and not workin' is so small, it just ain't worth it."

The rest of the bar just laughed and turned away from Sammy, but the barman had something to say on the matter.

"That's good to hear, then," said the burly barman who had tolerated Sammy due to an as yet unfulfilled promise that Sammy's Uncle Solomon would settle his considerable bar tab. But Jack Ferris on the orders of the landlord was not to extend credit any further. "If there's not much difference, then I take it you can now pay us what you owe us?"

"Uncle Sol will take care of that, no problem," said Sammy, who had been saying this ever since his estrangement a short while before from the person who had been his only means of support, no – not his uncle, but his mother, Mrs Elsie Grindlay – widower. "And while you're at it, I'll have another," cheekily added Sammy.

"Not on your life, Grindlay; boss's orders; pay up, or out."

"I've told you before, my name ain't Grindlay no more, it's Deedpole."

"You, my friend, are an idiot as well as a no good drunken layabout," said the barman. "You are supposed to change your name *BY* deed poll, not *TO IT!* But the fact is – *DEEDPOLE WITH AN E!* It's time to pay up or else!"

"Come on, Jack, just a nice glass of stout and a wee dram of the strong stuff," persisted Sammy, in a silly Scottish accent, "and I'll see Uncle Sol tomorrow," he added, which was an outright lie.

"Out!" insisted Jack. "Now!"

"You can't talk to me like that! I used to be the manager of Kelsononn Norinthianssss – hic!'

"Yeah, for five minutes, and a fat lot of use you were, too. Now – for the last time – *out!* Or I'll knock you out and dump you in the canal!' said the burly no nonsense barman.

"Oh yeah, you and whose–"

Samuel came round five minutes later, slumped against the entry wall down the side of the pub.

"I shall take my custom – *helse – where,"* said the pretentiously haughty Sammy as he got up, dusted himself down and began to walk off to the hostel for the homeless – he had lost his house some time before.

The hostel was on Carr Street which ran parallel with the Leeds-Liverpool Canal for about fifty yards.

Sammy, as he used to do when he was a child on the way to school or while out on errands for his mother, climbed up on the small sandstone wall, built with a rounded top to supposedly prevent access to the canal. He held his arms out wide as he inched along as if he was on a tight-rope while singing a song he had heard in the music hall.

***'While strolling through the park
one day, in the merry merry month of
Maayaarrrggghhhhhhh … !'***

Splash!
Gurgle!

Nothing. . .

The piss artist formerly known as Grindlay – was dead.

*

At his palatial home on the edge of town, Solomon Grindlay took out various documents and a cheque book from the bureau on the side wall of the lounge. He placed them on his desk, sat down, and then made out a cheque for £50,000. But he wrote this out in the simplistic style of his under-educated nephew, which wasn't difficult as he himself had taught him to write some years before but had then given it up as a bad job. He first of all wrote Samuel's name as being the payee; and in the space for the signatures he signed his own name as well as that of the club secretary, again in the style of his nephew. Solomon knew he may also have to sign his nephew's name on the back as some banks request this when paying in cheques, but he had also perfected this in the last week or so, copying from the documents from Samuel's short tenure as manager of Nelson Corinthians.

He then checked over the documents, muttering "U-hu, u-hu," every so often, which actually meant that all was in order, at least as far as Solomon's scheme was concerned.

"There, that should do it," said the gleefully devious Solomon Grindlay to himself. He went into his study, carefully placed the documents and the club's cheque book back in the bureau on the side wall and then sat down in a large leather armchair to read the evening newspaper.

"Not another one," sighed Solomon as he read the headlines.

'Drowned in the canal. Body identified as being local man.'

Solomon read on:

'. . . the body pulled out of the canal was identified as being one Samuel Deedpole. . .'

"Daft sod," he tutted as he turned to the business pages.

The next day Solomon took the 0500 train from Manchester to London, and called in at the first bank he came across, which was the Saint Dunstan's Savings Bank on Oxford Street.

Using forged documents, he opened an account in his nephew's name and then brazenly paid the cheque into the new account. Barring meeting anyone from the footballing world, Solomon knew that the odds of being recognised so far from home were very low. He then had afternoon tea in the Ritz, and then caught the train back home.

The next day, he got up, had breakfast and then whistled and sang as he jauntily walked across town to what he assumed was still Samuel's house.

Although it mattered little if Samuel was in or out, he knew it was best to assume he was in and duly knocked. After three very loud knocks and even a shout up to the bedroom window, it was clear Samuel was not in after all. Solomon then used a key he had had made many years earlier when he had actually given a damn about his nephew, and let himself in.

Although he was surprised at how clean and tidy and well furnished the place was now ("Some gullible widow, no doubt," thought Solomon), he placed the 'stolen' cheque book in the left-hand drawer of a sideboard against the separating wall and then left the house.

All Solomon had to do now was wait a further nine days for the cheque to clear, make another little trip to London, withdraw the cash, and in the highly unlikely event they found Samuel innocent and the fraud was traced back to him, the forward thinking Solomon had also made plans to vanish to a nice warm non-extradition country, and enjoy his ill-gotten gains. He had tired of football, bad weather and bland food. But the new tenants of Eighteen Garibaldi Street unwittingly put paid to Solomon's retirement plans.

"'Ere! Mavis! Are you seein' someone from the Corinthians?!" demanded Zak Lupton. "What'd I say last time I caught you at it?! Eh?" he added, as he perused the various bits of bumph he had found in the drawer, and which seemed to have something to do with Nelson Corinthians FC. But Zak and Mavis Lupton did not get divorced, instead, they handed in the incriminating evidence to the police.

A few days later. . .

"Solomon Grindlay. I am arresting you on suspicion of fraud. You do not have to say anything, but whatever you may say, will be taken down and used in evidence," said Chief Inspector Dixon.

"Knickers!" exclaimed the shocked Solomon. "I'm ruined!"

41

The late great Aunt Celie Comes to the Rescue

THREE MONTHS LATER Solomon was in court facing charges of fraud, and Samuel, rather unfairly thought Solomon, was still dead.

News might have filtered through to Solomon of his nephew's sad demise a lot sooner, but sometime before he came to a watery end, an outraged Samuel had opted to change his surname so as to disassociate himself from his mother; her perceived transgression had been to take up with a local Conservative councillor.

To be fair to Samuel, this news also shocked the whole town (many of whom knew his mother quite well), which was famed for its proud, strong socialistic character.

*

Sadly for the fans and even the whole town, Solomon's inept stewardship of the club from even before the attempted fraud, resulted in a dramatic downturn in the club's fortunes, on the pitch and off.

Not long into the 1920/1921 season, Nelson Corinthians were declared bankrupt and ceased functioning as a professional football club. It was all over.

*

In September 1939, Grindlay Park was demolished to help with the war effort; lorry loads of metal went to the smelters, and the plush fixtures and fittings from the inner stadium offices were removed intact for use in the various regimental army headquarters dotted around Great Britain.

*

February 2006

Nelson resident, fifty-three year old Ken Snoddie was the sports teacher at Nelson Comprehensive; he was also football crazy. Not only that, he was the only known descendent from his own generation of the old fraudster, Solomon Grindlay, via illegitimate issue in the form of his grandfather, Joseph Snoddie.

Joseph had been brought up by old Alfie Snoddie, who forgave his wife and had at least gained some satisfaction from knowing that the old lounge lizard had been confined to a prison cell.

Ken's dream of many years was to resurrect his great-grandfather's own football club – Nelson Corinthians; football is a great healer when it comes to family vendettas – sometimes.

Although Ken and his wife Eleanor and their son, Kyle, lived a perfectly happy, comfortable life, Ken always thought it lacked a bit of spark. One morning in the middle of a sports lesson on an icy windswept school field, Ken's mobile phone rang and he got far more of a spark than he could ever have imagined. . .

"Come home right now, Ken; don't bother changing; don't bother telling Grouty (the headmaster); just come home right now," implored his wife, Eleanor.

"Why, what's the matter?" replied Ken, worried that something terrible had happened. But the line went dead. Ken rang back but got the engaged tone.

A little while later. . .

"Sit down, Ken. . ." said his wife, who was sitting, rather girlishly on the edge of the sofa with her hands joined together and her legs dangling and swinging over the edge, as Ken dashed into the lounge of his semi-detached house.

"You're not. . ."

"Don't be silly, Ken, at fifty-two. . .?"

"What is it, then?" replied a very bemused Ken.

"Through an absolute freak, we are now billionaires!"

"What?! How?! How can that be?" demanded Ken.

"Well, we should be sad, really, but none of the family really know her. . ."

"Who . . . what on earth are you talking about?!" spluttered Ken.

"Great Aunt Celie, in Boston. Apparently she won the largest ever pay out on the Powerball Lottery in America, but there's more; she then sent out her nurse to buy some oil – she meant for the car but the nurse went and bought an oil company. By the time Celie realised this, most of America thought she was onto something big, shares rocketed, and she sold the company – for twenty-billion dollars! But, here's the sad bit . . well, sort of. . ."

"Her nurse spent the lot on the national grid?" suggested Ken.

"No, stupid, Celie died last month – but – she's left me – er – us – the lot! We are her only known relatives! Or I am, anyway. . ."

Ken bent down and gave his wife a big smacker of a kiss with squishy noises she thought would be heard next door.

Ken came up for air and shouted "Yeeesss! Stuff the school, the mortgage, the lot!"

"Er, Ken, I think I jumped the gun a bit there. Celie only died recently and it will take ages for it to all to be finalised and paid out."

At first this did not register with Ken, his mind felt like scrambled eggs, he just couldn't believe it.

"Ken?" said his wife. "Ken?"

"Eh? Oh, yes, see what you mean, but still . . . twenty-billion dollars!"

"That's another thing, it won't be that much in the end; there's duties, taxes and commissions, but it will still be a lot though. . ."

That was an understatement; although Ken and Eleanor had to plough on as they were right now for over another year, not just while things were sorted out but to allow the money to start accruing interest, they eventually received the sum of nine billion dollars, around five maybe six-billion pounds. . .

42

The Snoddie-Grindlay Stadium

ALTHOUGH THEIR NICE, comfortable semi-detached house was far from being a grubby shack high up on a mountain somewhere in the southern United States, Ken and Eleanor felt like the Beverly Hillbillies as they *'loaded up their truck and they moved to'* – a large manor house in its own grounds just over a mile from where they lived now.

Despite the whopping six-billion pounds legally belonging to Ken's wife, Eleanor nevertheless freed up half of what she received and allowed Ken to use this as he saw fit. If he went bonkers and tried to sell ice to the Eskimos, they at least still had the other half plus any interest accrued, which Ken was certainly not going to get for use on high risk projects.

Shortly after checking that far more zeros copiously punctuated his bank statements than could ever have been possible before the sad demise of a relation of his wife's he had never even met, Ken contacted the FA to enquire if, despite the insolvency many years before, they had retained the registration of former English League Division One club, Nelson Corinthians, and if so how could he make it rise from the ashes. . .

*

June 2008

Ken's dream of domestic and European glory for his team, his very own football team – Nelson Corinthians, had had to be put on hold, for a few years at least. He had indeed been able to resurrect the club and had had a new ground built thus saving the land from park and ride ignominy, and had signed up a good, strong squad made up of older but still very able players from the lower professional leagues and divisions. But Ken had overlooked one very important factor: neither the FA nor the English League authorities were going to allow Nelson Corinthians to simply return to carry on in either the top division of the Football League or the FA's comparatively recent and very own Premier League, as if the Corinthians had never been away – such a high honour had to be earned. But they were allowed to join the North West Counties Football League; this is a feeder league for the national professional leagues and it is possible although highly unlikely for a team from here to rise right up to the FA Premier League.

*

To mark the club's return to the game, Ken Snoddie decided to hold an opening ceremony for the new club and stadium, as well as hosting a curtain-raiser to the first season back in the game for Nelson Corinthians – this was the 2008/2009 season.

He first of all worked with club secretary, Tim Robinson, to put together a basic running order for the opening ceremony to be held the day before the curtain raiser; and then with the help of Mrs Snoddie (to the displeasure of Tim), put together invites for local dignitaries as well as the architects and builders, inviting them to the ceremony.

Tim Robinson then asked his counterpart at Nelson FC, a good solid semi-professional side from the same town and with similar origins, if they would like to play Nelson Corinthians at the Snoddie-Grindlay Stadium in a charity match. The secretary with great regret had had to decline, as his team had already pencilled in a preseason friendly against Blackburn Rovers that day, but he did put Tim onto another club secretary, none other than the secretary to Manchester United. . .

Less than a week later Ken could hardly contain himself. Manchester United's secretary had called to say that United would be delighted to play in the inaugural match for the new stadium and resurrected club.

Through a combination of naivety and his immense wealth, Ken had not built a local stadium purely for a few thousand die hard fans; to the amazement and delight of the entire town as well as the whole of the footballing world, Ken had commissioned the construction of an exact replica of the Bernabeu Stadium, the state of the art famed home of Spanish side, Real Madrid. He even went one better than Real and had asked for the addition of a retractable roof and had instructed the architect to ensure the design for the stadium reflected an all-seater capacity of at least one-hundred and twenty-five thousand, which is forty-five thousand more than the current Bernabeu Stadium.

The four-towered multi-tiered forty-five metre high Snoddie-Grindlay Stadium, with all seats duly tilted for a better viewing experience, was now the showpiece of the town.

*

August 2008

In the week leading up to the curtain-raiser, Ken received a telephone call. "Is that Mr Snoddie?" said the voice.

"Mr Snoddie speaking, how may I help you?"

"Ah, at last. Hello there, been trying to get you for days . . . still, a busy man I suppose. My name is Reginald Naismith, in fact, the Reverend Reginald Naismith. I am the Vicar of Saint Ogbert's. I am not sure if you know this already, but the stadium is just within the parish boundaries. . ."

The vicar stopped dead, forcing a stuttered reply from Ken.

"Er – oh, yes, I did know, actually. I recall reading about the local vicar years ago. He was a big fan apparently, and he used to bless the right boot of some fella called Ramsbottom, just before each home game."

"Good job Casanova or Rudolph Valentino weren't in the parish, then!" joked the Reverend Naismith, which highly amused Ken, more so because of whom his caller was rather than the smuttiness of the quip on its own.

"Good one that! Must tell the Mrs – well – maybe not," finally replied Ken after he forced himself to stop laughing.

"Oh, I don't know," said the vicar, "my good lady comes out with far worse, usually after she's emptied the sherry bottle. Now then, Mr Snoddie; I couldn't help noticing the feature in the paper and on the local radio, even on the telly. I believe you are having an opening ceremony and inviting the Mayor and so on. . . ?"

Again the vicar stopped dead, brazenly hoping his loaded question would indeed be perceived as such.

"Yes, that's right. I can get you and your good lady VIP tickets if you wish? You don't need one for most of it, that's all outside; but there's bubbly and stuff afterwards for the guests of honour," replied Ken, who also gulped at realizing he and Tim had, perhaps, made a faux pas.

"Ah, I am a tad embarrassed, Mr Snoddie; I was actually going to suggest to expand it to be more of a dedication ceremony. Usually with these affairs a few prayers are said and a blessing given; I just thought it might be nice to do this for you, but of course if that would disrupt your plans. . ."

"Oh – erm. . ."

"Call me Ishmael," said the Reverend.

"Er – Ishmael. . ." said Ken.

"No, no, sorry, I was just helping my daughter with her English Literature homework, but do call me Reg, by all means."

"Oh, I see, well – Reg – I am the one who should be embarrassed, I just didn't think, I am so sorry. Yes, of course, let's do this properly. I'll get the club secretary to call you to go over the running order," said Ken.

"Thank you, that will be fantastic," overstated the vicar. "Now one thing I'd best mention: these days we are and better for it I may add, a far more multicultural and multifaith community. Can I politely suggest we make some overtures to the leaders of other faiths to see if they would like to contribute. . . ?"

"Yes, yes of course we can do that; that is a very good idea, actually. . ." said Ken, and who meant it.

"Lovely jubbly!" enthused the vicar. "Now, help with the costs etc; shall we say, five-hundred?"

"Oh, that's OK, Rev–er–Reg, I think we can stretch the coffers to pay for pink gin for the mayor, no need to worry on that score," replied Ken, whose almost former perception that the clergy led sheltered lives made him think that perhaps the vicar was not aware that Nelson now boasted its very own billionaire.

"No, sorry, I meant for me," said the Reverend Naismith.

"Oh! Oh, yes, of course, how stupid of me. Yes, that's reasonable. The club secretary will sort that out with you as well; we can pay it in cash – in advance, if you like. . . ?"

"Ah, if only, Mr Snoddie, if only . . . the days of the little brown envelope surreptitiously handed over during a few scotch and sodas at the presbytery are well over. I will bill you in due course."

"Sounds fine. Well, Your – er – Reg. . ."

"Yes, that's right – Reg."

"No, no, I meant – erm – no matter, no matter. Is there anything else I can help you with today, only. . . ?"

"No, no, I'll hammer it all out with your secretary, although I may be in touch with you again before the big day. Nice speaking to you, and bye for now."

"Bye, Reg, thanks for the call, see you soon."

As Ken put the receiver back down, his wife came in to his office, scanning an itemised list on a sheet of paper with her finger.

"Outrageous! Do you know how much the phone bill has gone up?"

"Hmmm . . . let me guess . . . by about five-hundred pounds? And rising. . . ?" ruefully suggested Ken.

"Pardon?"

"Nothing, nothing. Just get a surreptitious little brown envelope and just pay the damn thing. . ."

43

Before the Munchies and Slurps

THE DEDICATION CEREMONY took place on Friday, the day before the match.

On the Victoria Road side of the stadium which was where the main players and staff entrance and club reception area were situated, a gazebo had been erected on the car park opposite the main doors. The invited guests were all sat underneath the canopy on small wooden (and for many, uncomfortable) chairs. But the gazebo was a welcome shelter from the baking temperatures.

Ken opened the proceedings with his own speech, which started with a warm welcome to all gathered and went on to include thanks to all but the plasterer's mother.

Ken then invited both the Mayor of Nelson and the CEO of the building firm to undo the rope-pull and draw back the little purple curtains, which revealed a white marble dedication stone set in among the red brickwork. The message was very simple, and just stated the official date of opening and named the major dignitaries present. ("Phew!" went Ken, due to all of those named actually having turned up.)

As a round of applause was given, the press who were gathered to the left of the main doors snapped away, with the odd hack directing one person to shake hands with another, then all of the VIPs together, then him with her, her with her, her with him and her and so on. It took firm intervention from Ken to bring the haphazard photo' shoot to an end.

As usual, the difference between speakers and guests, especially when one person is both, or at least a speaker who then rejoins the guests to supposedly become a patient listener, showed itself. Ken sat down and then found he was unfortunately bored stiff by whatever anyone else had to say.

While he secretly hoped they would soon get to the post-ceremony munchies and slurps, he nevertheless maintained dignity, stifled his yawns – and feigned appreciation of the words being uttered.

First up was the Mayor. He rather frustratingly provided a host of trivial details about the construction of the original stadium and gave a run down of the then Mayor and his staff in the Engineers Department, as well as relating, (His Worship thought), a funny anecdote about an argument between the private builders and the Borough Surveyor while perched on a narrow girder a hundred feet up. The punch line was, the surveyor fell off and next in line for his job was the builder's brother-in-law.

And then to the annoyance of Ken and to the dismay of the others, he repeated much of what Ken had had to say but padded it out far more than Ken had done so.

Finally the Mayor stopped, and retook his seat.

Thankfully the other guest speakers realised, with the very real snore from the Reverend Naismith, that things needed to be jollied along. Finally, it was the turn of the said reverend along with a small party of multi-faith clerics to bless the stadium and this would also mark the end of the proceedings.

"Reg," whispered Connie Naismith. Reg grunted and his head lolled further back in his seat with drool running down his black jacket. "Reg!" came a sharper whisper, accompanied by a gentle dig in the ribs.

"Not again!" muttered Reg. "Oh, very well, but you really should have married a younger man like your mother said," added Reg, with his eyes still closed but who then went to climb on top of his wife.

"Reg! You've got to give the blessing!" shrieked Connie, pushing away her hubby and with it being perfectly obvious that Reg, right at that moment did not think he was at a dedication ceremony as both one of the guests and the lead member of the spiritual delegation.

Although Ken and Connie Naismith had been married for over twenty years, people always thought how odd they looked as a couple when viewing them at close quarters. The reverend looked to be in his mid-fifties (but was only forty-eight); he was below average height and of a slight build, but he had a big belly. His shock of wavy ginger hair and full set ginger beard to match, gave him a look of someone looking through a well used toilet brush.

Connie was a lot younger than Reg, but was rather Olive-Oylish and gawky, but those who knew her well loved the bones of her, as she, like her beloved Reg, was a staunch champion of the poor and disadvantaged. The reverend's fee, perhaps obtained a tad forcefully, was all going on food for serving up at a homeless shelter.

A very red-faced Reverend Naismith stood up, rubbed his eyes, forewent the apology as he saw the sea of smirks (apart from Connie who looked like a cross between a rose-red gala apple and a beetroot), gestured for his fellow clerics to follow and walked over to the main doors where a little lectern had been placed to the right. From the lectern, he gave a brief introduction to himself, where he was from, and then gave a few words on what the parish did both in and for the community. He rather amusingly had overlooked the fact that most gathered there already knew him very well indeed. He then conferred a very short concise blessing on the club and all those present.

The reverend then invited each of the other clerics and ministers to bestow their own blessings and then stepped down off the little wooden box borrowed from Nelson High School, and stood to one side.

A Muslim Imam, a Hindu Brahmin, a Jewish Rabbi, a Siekh Granthi and a Buddhist Ennin all took turns to provide a blessing of their own faith, and sometimes in a foreign or ancient tongue.

There then followed a human microcosm showing what is best about modern day former cotton giants of the Lancashire moors, such as the former mill town of Nelson.

The clerics, with the Reverend Naismith now amongst them and representing all Christian denominations, became two groups of three as they lined up side by side, facing each other; this was to ensure they did not turn their backs on the guests of honour.

With a nod from the vicar, all six then read out the final prayer and blessing. This had been written by all the clerics together and all had agreed that its general nature was suitable for use, both jointly and severally.

Most of the guests, (which then prompted the remainder to follow), perhaps through being subconsciously reminded of the end of a church service, all stood as the final blessing was given.

"May the Heavens forever watch over this ground, this club, its players and management and training staff; all those who help in its day

to day administration, and its loyal supporters from both this town and from far away. . .

"May the club always remember to graciously receive its visitors, guests, opponents and their supporters before the contest, and may they offer a fond farewell at the end of the day, no matter the result. . .

"May all who serve in and for this great beacon of hope for our little town, be happy in their endeavours, and may the club be a gracious, shining example of sporting excellence; may we always remind ourselves that the club's very name represents the very spirit of the great gift that is sport. . .

"May the ground of olden days now give up any secrets, and may any troubled spirits rise and move on and up to that great stadium above where they belong and there find peace. . .

"May the Heavens forever cherish and protect the good name of this club, as we ourselves are honour bound to do so. . .

"We ask this, in the name of Heaven. So be it."

The clerics then turned fully, bowed towards the dedication stone, and then, purely to provide a ceremonial style ending, turned again, and walked single file in procession to the side of the gazebo and out of sight; once there they could then 'stand easy' and become as informal as the rest of the gathering.

At the same time as the gathering vacated the gazebo and walked in through the main doors and on upstairs to the hospitality suite – for the munchies and slurps – a little gust of wind blew around the penalty area at the Grindlay Road end of the Snoddie-Grindlay Stadium. . .

44

Trapped Wind

THE GREAT DAY FINALLY ARRIVED.

Ken Snoddie drove his wife mad as he was up at 5:00 am on the second Saturday in August 2008, wringing his hands in an emotional maelstrom of elation and anxiety. He then contacted the entire board and demanded that they be at the ground by 10:00 am to go over the arrangements. He also picked up his mobile phone and dialled the number for his team manager, then turned the phone off, put it back in his pocket, then took it out again and dialled again, then turned it off yet again. This went on for over an hour until his wife snatched the phone out of his hands, threw it onto the couch, and yelled at him.

"For God's sake, Ken, it is not the done thing for the owner and chairman to dictate playing strategy to the manager! Just leave him to do the job you've hired him for!"

As Ken blushed and went off to water the roses for the third time, his wife whispered, 'Usually. . .'

Ken was actually looking for someone and something to worry about, such was this strange happy tension, but everything had come together without a hitch. Ken's worries about filling a stadium which could hold the whole town's population four times over were unfounded. The new stadium combined with the fact that Manchester United were the visitors, saw thousands upon thousands of fans from all over Lancashire, including many who supported neither club as well as many more from around the rest of the country and even a few hundred overseas dignitaries and fans, snapping up the tickets as soon as they went on sale a week before the match.

The weather was glorious, but Ken wasn't sure if he was happy or sad as it meant that the retractable roof would not have to be used.

The stadium was packed to the rafters and was a sea of colour and a cauldron of noise well before kick-off.

Ken, in a moment of madness shortly after getting the nod from the Manchester United secretary, had booked Elton John and even the Coldstream Guards Band for prematch and halftime entertainment.

With Elton scheduled to bash the ivories and yodel away during the break, the Coldstream Guards' prematch session came to and end and they marched off back across the pitch and down the tunnel to the tune of *'Colonel Bogey'*.

It was time. . .

The noise was incredible as the two teams trotted out on to the pitch, led by two team mascots. For Nelson Corinthians this was Kyle Snoddie, Ken's twenty year old son (there were howls of laughter and some shouts of anger at seeing a mascot with fuzz on his face and a beer belly); and for United this was nine year old Alice Satterthwaite from Chorley, who had won a prize draw to lead her beloved United out onto the pitch. The mascots stood in the centre circle, first with their own teams and then both mascots and two teams together while the press and club photographers took their pictures.

Although nothing bar a telegram from the FA stating that the game was cancelled could possibly spoil the occasion, there was, however, one thing that would very soon irk Ken Snoddie.

DJ, Del Winters, usually of Radio Pendle and who had beaten off over five-hundred other applicants for the job of matchday presenter, announced the sides over the tannoy in a showbizzy fashion, giving each player's shirt number and then their name, starting with the visiting team.

"Number one — Graaaaham Steele!"

The clusters of red and white dotted around the ground cheered, the rest initially gave a sort of collective, "Eh?!"

It went on. . .

"Number two — Keiiiith Callaaaaghaaaaan!"

"Hooray!" yelled most of the visiting fans.
"Eh? Who's he?" came the home fans' reply.

"Number three — Niiiiiiiiiigel Cotton!"
"Yeaaaah!"
"Blimey – no-marks and kids!"

"Number four — Nicky Vaaaaan Breeman!"
"Good ole Dutchy!"
"Never heard of 'im!"

"Number five — Timmmmmy Tunstall!'

And so it continued. . .

" . . . John Cousins and Dave Hewitson complete the outfield substitutes, and reserve goalkeeper is Tony Wright. . ."

Del went on to do the same for the home team; this was to huge cheers from the home fans and even louder boos and hoots of derision from the United fans. . .

" . . . And our officials today. . ."

Ken looked at the United team, one by one, and shook his head. United had taken the opportunity to give a run out to a hotch-potch assembly of fringe players, reserves, and apprentices; Ken did not know one single player, nor did most of the home crowd. Despite the initial disappointment for all those who wanted to see the billion pound plus United first team, it didn't really matter to anyone – apart from Ken. (A few days after the game this still rankled with Ken and knew he would not rest until he had telephoned the United secretary to ask why; the reply was: "Perfectly normal, Mr Snoddie; check any big club's preseason friendlies; the sides are never what the manager thinks of as being his first choice starting eleven." When Ken said he knew this, but to his knowledge it was usually a mix of at least some of the established players as well as some try-outs, the line went dead).

The two team captains shook hands, the pitch was cleared of all non-combatants, the United captain went for heads in the toss of the coin, lost, and so Nelson Corinthians skipper Tony Waites opted to kick into the Solomon Lane End. The game was underway. . .

Phil Potsworth, Nelson Corinthians' lone striker, for this game anyway, felt unusually cold. This was despite the temperature on the pitch registering on the digital thermometer to the right of the electronic scoreboard, as being well over eighty degrees Fahrenheit.

The referee blew the whistle. The United skipper kicked the ball out to the left-sided midfielder, who was duly robbed by Phil Potsworth who had dashed from the centre and committed a terrible forward's foul into the bargain. He got away with this as the referee was at that moment, reminding one of the linesmen to let the wine breathe a short while before dinner later that evening – at the Snoddie Hotel attached to the stadium.

Phil, out on his own and seeing the mass of United players barring every possible route through, turned and kicked the ball back to the nearest Corinthians player, who then kicked it right back to the goalkeeper; although it seemed negative play this was in keeping with the game plan.

Nelson Corinthians' manager, Lol Woodbridge, had given the team much the same instructions as the tragic Eric and his team-mates had been given all those years ago, and against the same opponents; this was to pack the defence out and hope to get a break at some point in the play.

But on this occasion it all began to go disastrously wrong.

Within twenty minutes Nelson Corinthians were three goals down at home; their defence just could not withstand the relentless pressure exerted on them by all the United out-players; all ten swamped the Corinthians penalty area and on this occasion, made it tell. Reserves and boot boys with smiles on their faces they may have been, but you don't get to Old Trafford and polish Wayne Rooney's boots unless you have shown some promise yourself, and it showed.

The Corinthians skipper and central defender, Tony Waites, gave up trying to think his way out of trouble. Each time the ball fell loose during the seemingly never ending United attacks, he just punted the ball right upfield knowing full well it would soon be coming back his way, as the rest of his team-mates were right by his side. But then Tony had an idea. . .

He had often talked with his grandfather about the huge difference in the game now compared with Gramps' time. Although old Hughie Waits conceded the players were faster, fitter and more skilled nowadays, he maintained there was nothing as exciting as seeing the ball being blasted up the pitch and the team's forwards streaming after it hoping to latch on to the ball and either indulge in some fancy trickery on the wing before slipping it through to the other forwards waiting in the penalty area, or continue with the route 1 method and try and blast a hole in the net.

"Potsy!" shouted Tony. Phil turned to his team-mate and Tony gestured for him to get running up the field. Phil knew what he intended straight away and raced away as fast as he could. But the United team of 2009 were far more aware of every tactic ever thought up, including Route 1, than their 1913 counterparts; as Potsworth and company came at them like marauders of old, they duly marshalled their goalkeeper and defence accordingly. Luckily, the punt had been straight, which was not quite Tony's intention who had hoped to send the ball up to the far right; but before Phil Potsworth had streaked diagonally across the pitch he found the ball right at his feet. He deftly went round one player and let fly. The ball left his foot at about seventy miles per hour; however, the United defence were perfectly placed to stop the thunderbolt – until the ball stopped – then it went around both central defenders and then sped up again and flew straight past the goalkeeper into the far left-hand corner of the net.

The home supporters went wild with delight – *apart from one lady in the crowd who screamed.* Everyone else was simply stunned by what they had just seen.

As both teams lined up again for the restart, Nigel Cotton, the United captain asked Phil, "How on earth did you manage that?! Even Becks could never do that when he was with us!"

"I dunno;" admitted Phil, "my guess is it was a freak gust of wind; this stadium's so big and oddly designed it probably traps the wind in different parts and maybe the currents clash."

The United player, totally none the wiser, simply nodded. "S'pose so. . ."

With the boost of getting a goal back, Nelson Corinthians fought hard to keep United out, and perhaps even bag another goal themselves, but this was not to happen, although the score was still 3-1 to United when the referee blew his whistle for halftime.

As the home team trooped into the changing room for oranges and a breather, the manager came running in after them.

"Stay decent, lads, you have a lady visitor. Be back in a sec'."

While Tony very quickly pulled his shorts back up – he always had to adjust himself at halftime – and with the rest of the team looking bemused, the manager came back in with none other than the Reverend Naismith and his wife, Connie.

"Er – excuse us, fellas, my wife just wants a quick look around," said the vicar.

Connie Naismith, very red-faced both through the copious prematch sherry in the VIP lounge and now with embarrassment, scanned the entire room, but then her eyes focussed on the bench. For a second her face froze, but then she turned to her husband.

"There, right on the end of the bench, the left side. . ." said Connie Naismith, very nervously.

The vicar appeared to look at Tony, and then back to her wife, and said, 'That's the centre-back, dear, are you sure you saw—"

"Don't be stupid! Next to him – on the end!"

The vicar looked again, but still he saw nothing other than a red-faced Tony Waites sitting near the end of the bench.

"Right, OK, Con," the vicar whispered to his wife, "I'll need a quick word with the manager. . ."

45

The Spectre of Victory

THE FINAL REFRAIN OF, *'Saturday Night's All Right for Fightin''*, died away. Elton bowed, left the pitch to huge cheers (many of these were cheers because he'd finished), the piano was wheeled away and the makeshift stage and sound equipment was dismantled.

The call came through to the dressing room for the second half.

The vicar hung back while the lads trotted out again. He was lucky: although the manager turned out to be a dyed in the wool atheist who only had room in his mind for how to keep out the United marauders for the rest of the game – the vicar could do what he wanted as long as it didn't *'mess with the lads' 'eads and spoil their game'*.

The vicar fumbled in his jacket pocket for his accoutrements. . .

*

The whole ground erupted within a minute of the game resuming.

Tony Waites thought he may as well take advantage of the freak local weather conditions. Ironically he waited for the first Corinthians attack to break drown and for United to have possession on the wing. Tony raced out of position and over to the left side of the pitch; he then robbed the surprised United midfielder and simply hoofed the ball diagonally across the park. As the United defence ran back and as the goalkeeper ran forward to make what he thought would be an easy save, the ball landed just outside the penalty area, bounced once, stopped, then rolled to the right, and then it left the ground at great speed and whizzed right past the stunned goalkeeper. 3-2 to United.

While the home fans shouted and yelled with glee, this was not accompanied on this occasion by a scream from a lady in the main stand; Mrs Naismith had gone back to the VIP lounge.

Before the restart, Nigel Cotton signalled to the referee that he wanted a word; he also called Tony Waites up to the centre circle.

"This ain't fair, referee, they are taking advantage of some funny effect the design of the stadium has on the weather; we can't defend against a ball that stops and then gets sent off again at angles caused by trapped wind. . . (Tony smirked and sniggered) Can't you call this off?"

"Now look here!" spluttered a now angry Tony, but his protest was waved down by the referee.

"I will admit that there must be freak weather conditions affecting the play, at times. However – this is only a friendly, and after all, there's no such thing as weather which knows how to favour the home team, so—"

"But they've been practicing in it, we haven't!" retorted the United skipper.

"Enough! I was about to say . . . use it to your own advantage, the game will carry on. Now – play!" demanded the referee.

The referee blew his whistle and the game restarted. The United captain was still so angry that he was the cause of Nelson Corinthian's equalizer.

After an incoming punt from Tony, a still angry Nigel Cotton swiped at the ball, missed entirely, and Phil Potsworth nipped in, rolled the ball to the left which tempted the goalkeeper out of position and Phil slotted the ball into the net. 3-3.

"Glad to see you can do more than stoppy stoppy bendy bouncy," sneered the even angrier Nigel Cotton.

"Ian Rush Master Class, 1982 – get the DVD, you'll learn something," replied Tony Waites with a smile, as he passed the United captain and went back to his own position to be ready for the restart.

To their credit, United mounted a magnificent rearguard action to fight off the most unusual shots on goal they had ever encountered. The 'trapped wind' caused the ball, without being touched by a player, to jink around the defence, go off at the strangest of angles, sometimes towards the United goal, other times to another Nelson Corinthians player, and sometimes it flew right up in the air and then floated over to the middle of the penalty area. But with all the United team back in defence and covering every angle the ball could possibly travel along no matter if it defied the laws of physics or not, Nelson Corinthians were kept out – just, but to Nelson Corinthians' credit, so were United.

The full ninety minutes had passed but there had been a few delays in the second half to warrant three minutes of time added on. It was the dying seconds of the extra third minute; both sides thought the game would end in a draw, but. . .

Tony Waites hoofed the ball upfield, but on this occasion it was a lame punt which saw the ball fall in the centre circle where only two United midfielders could be found.

But then yet again the ball suddenly indulged in some silky trickery, seemingly all by itself. It veered to the left of one player, then to the right of another, then through the legs of a third; and on the ball went. One player had come up to try and control it only for the ball to bobble up and down a foot off the ground, bounce past, bobble again, and then it went round in a full circle, bouncing lightly on the ground as it did so, causing the United centre-back to fall down on the ground, dizzy. With the players of both teams closing in fast to either take advantage of the freak weather or to try and get the ball away, the ball was in the United penalty area with only the goalkeeper to beat. But then United midfielder, George Cummings, who had run back to help shore up the defence, made a long, lunging sliding tackle. His intention was to side hoof the ball away and out of danger, but the ball just chinked ahead of his outstretched leg, but George travelled on, still with his leg stretched out – and swept Phil Potsworth to the ground.

"Penalty!" roared half of the crowd.

Phil clutched his knee; he was in agony.

The referee first of all blew for help from the bench; he then went to Cummings and showed him the red card; he was sent off. After Phil had been stretchered off the pitch and as the linesman signalled to the referee to allow a Nelson Corinthians substitute to join the game, the referee then blew his whistle again and pointed to the spot. It was a penalty to the home team.

The trouble here was the only near-decent penalty taker was Phil Potwsorth; he had scored twenty-five out of thirty-five penalties in his career, but he was now out of the game. The next best but way below in terms of successful conversions was Tony Waites – he had scored eleven times from thirty-three penalties, but as he was the best available and as he was team skipper, Tony Waites did his duty and duly stepped up.

He kicked a little dent in the penalty spot for which he received an immediate reprimand.

"This ain't Twickers, Waites! Get on with it!" warned the referee as he tooted again to signify the kick should now be taken.

Tony just smiled, turned, trotted back ten steps, turned again, and ran up to the ball.

A split-second before his right boot would have made contact with it, the ball left the penalty spot and almost burst the net as it thundered past the left side of the stunned goalkeeper.

The referee blew his whistle once to signal the goal, then gave a combined two short blasts and a long blast to signal the end of the game – Nelson Corinthians had beaten Premiership giants Manchester United by four goals to three.

The crowd went wild as the rest of the team raced up to Tony and hugged him; all Tony could do in return was point at his boot and at the penalty spot and then at the United goal, totally bemused. Even if it was trapped wind – that was one belcher of a blast which he had had no part in whatsoever.

The home fans were euphoric.

The vicar's wife was very happy.

The vicar smiled.

A little gust of wind which could be felt by those still in the United penalty area, seemed to gently lap the players, spiralled around them, and then rose into the sky, "to rejoin the normal free wind", thought Tony.

46

Reg and the Conster

DUE TO BOTH THE VICAR'S AND HIS WIFE'S ANTICS at the dedication, as well as the superb ending to the ceremony which had been mainly put together by the Reverend Naismith, Ken and Eleanor Snoddie had taken to the couple and thought it would be nice to invite them to their house for dinner, both as a thank you gift and to get to know them better.

Although neither Ken nor Eleanor were church-goers as such, Ken had met the vicar many times at church services connected with the school, and both had seen the vicar and his wife at various local fundraising functions. But up until recently they had only ever seen a formally frocked vicar and a Stepford-like wife, and not the real couple as had been the case more recently, and refreshingly so, agreed Ken and Eleanor.

*

" . . . No need to ask Reg, he'll be round like a shot. Thank you very much; this is very kind of you. See you Thursday at seven, then. Bye-bye," said Connie Naismith on the telephone.

"It will be our pleasure; see you Thursday. Bye bye for now, Mrs Naismith." Eleanor put the receiver down and turned to her husband. "Well, that was less awkward than what I thought it would be."

Just before she rang to invite the couple to dinner, a doubt had crept into Eleanor's mind due to thinking that perhaps Connie Naismith may not want to leave the house for a while, but this was far from being the case.

"You know, they're only human after all, aren't they?" mused Ken but out loud.

"Yes, I was very surprised myself to find that Anglican vicars are not actually from Mars – unusual that," joked Eleanor with a sarcastic twist.

"You know what I mean," replied Ken with a smile. "Oh, don't forget the extra sherry. . ." he added.

*

On the Thursday evening, a nervous Ken and Eleanor Snoddie looked through the curtains of their front lounge every few minutes despite it being well before 7:00 pm. But bang on the hour the huge iron gates opened electronically and a taxi drove in through the gateway with lion-topped stone pillars on either side, and drove right up the long, winding gravelled path and pulled up by the main doors of the old manor house. Out got the reverend and his wife.

"Come in, come in! Great to see you again!" said Ken at the front door in welcome to their guests.

"Hello, Reverend; hello, Mrs Naismith, glad you could make it," added Eleanor.

"We'll put a stop to that one straight away!" said the vicar but with a big broad grin. "Reg and Connie to all who know us. And – of course . . . hello to you both. . ."

"Hello," said Connie, who seemed to follow this with a little burp, or it could have been a nervous gulp or cough.

Ken took their guests' coats and hung them on the coat-pegs along the wall on the right, just before the wide staircase

"Erm – well now . . . would you like to go into the lounge? Ken will sort some drinks out for us all. One thing I forgot to tell you, we're having lamb, should have asked really. Is that OK for you both. . . ?" asked Eleanor, fearing the worst and waiting for a lecture on cooking things with faces.

"Lovely," said Connie.

"I eat any old shite, me," said Reg, as he and his wife sat down on the sofa against the near wall.

The four laughed out loud at this. Connie and both of the Snoddies knew that Reg had only said it for devilment and that he was just hamming it up. Ever since Reg had heard the line on a TV comedy he had been dying for the moment when he could use it.

After the laughter had died down, Eleanor noticed a little more steam than should be the case drifting out of the kitchen and down the hallway. She looked around the door and into the kitchen and realised a pan was boiling over, but she also noticed that Ken, no doubt due to a distraction in the form of ribald banter coming from a man of the cloth, had not yet poured the drinks.

"Ken, the drinks, dear. Let me just sort the peas out and I will be right back."

"Sherry, anyone. . . ?" asked Ken with a smile.

"Lovely jubbly," replied Connie.

"Easy now, Con, there's the rest of the night to go. . ." said Reg.

Reg and Connie settled on or rather in the huge comfy sofa like a pair of old friends who came round for dinner every night.

The predinner drinks went down very well indeed.

With Eleanor drifting in and out in between pan checks, meat turns and a little chopping and dicing here and there, Reg and Connie told of their life together, their two teenage children, their work at Saint Ogbert's, previous parishes, and what their main interests were away from the church: for Reg this was football, although he owned up to being a Burnley fan, and for Connie this was gardening. In turn, Ken and Eleanor moaned about the exploits of Kyle, said one child was enough for them, and then explained about how they came to be owners of Nelson Corinthians and talked about moving out of their old home and into the huge manor house a mile out of town.

When dinner was ready and the party moved to the dining room, Connie looked through the French windows and noticed that outside in the garden were quite a few large crates. She had already noticed something odd on their arrival; the very long hall seemed to have been blocked off about halfway down with boxes and small items of furniture, as if barring access. It seemed to Connie as if the Snoddies did not utilise all that they now owned and were using only the front portion of the house.

"Erm . . . Eleanor," said Connie in between slurps of her onion soup, "hope you don't mind my asking, but are you still sorting things out, or don't you use all of this huge house?"

Ken just smiled at his wife while Reg was busy trying to clean up some soup slops on the table-cloth.

"I wondered if you would notice," said Eleanor. "We did try and live in the whole place but it's just too big, so we set the place up like our old house and just secured the rest. I think the money went to our heads, it was daft of us to come here. We even had staff but it didn't feel right so we let them all go. We paid them way over the usual in settlement; neither Ken nor I would have been happy just to shunt them back on to the dole without some sort of cushion. Also, I am not sure if you saw it, but there is a for-sale sign up in the garden; we're going to buy a nice house somewhere, but not a huge rambling place like this."

"I did," said Reg, "but I just thought it was from when you bought the place and no one had got round to taking the sign down. Going, eh? Can't say I blame you; no offence, Ken, but, stinkin' rich or not you don't seem to be the sort to stand in the garden wearing plus fours, tweeds and a Sherlock hat while digging your walking stick in the ground and surveying all that you own."

While Ken and Connie laughed, Eleanor said, "He's done that! The daft sod! I was hanging my knickers on the line when Ken came out dressed like an old toff and did just that as if it was the most natural thing in the world! He even went back into the house with his stick over his shoulder, with a pair of my drawers on the end of it!"

More laughter ensued and then Eleanor served the lamb.

"Ken, before you commit to sell to anyone, could I ask you to hang on until I have had a word with the Church Estates Commission?" asked Reg, over rhubarb pie and custard.

"I could do, yes, but, why, may I ask?

"Well, the diocese is hoping to open up a new centre for a sort of all-in-one how's your father; you know, spiritual advice, credit unions, mothers and pensioners clubs, a crèche or a nursery and other odds and sods, sort of all in the one place. They haven't found a suitable place yet and this would be ideal."

"A one-stop God-shop, eh?" said Ken with a grin. Although Eleanor Snoddie was uncertain if Ken should have said this, she need not have worried, Reg and Connie roared with laughter. "OK, well, tell you what: we'll pull the sign for now; just get back to us when you can, if they are not interested, that's fine, we'll just relist."

"That's very kind of you, thank you," said the vicar.

Neither Reg nor Connie noticed, but the thinnest of nods and smiles were then traded between Ken and Eleanor who had been looking for a worthy cause to give a leg up to; they had found it. (Within a month the deeds to the property had been signed over to the local diocese without a penny being charged; this was on the proviso it would be used only for the purposes as described to them by the Reverend Naismith.)

It was now Ken's turn to broach a particular subject but each time he went to speak he clammed up, but eventually, probably helped by a large brandy, he turned to Connie.

"So . . . er – you . . . saw our ghost, then. . . ?"

"Aha! Pay up, lass! The Conster loses again. Get that purse out, that's the girl!" suddenly exclaimed Reg.

Eleanor, who had initially decided to chastise Ken for mentioning what she had earlier insisted was not to be a topic of conversation over dinner, stopped at "Ke—!"

As a smiling Connie reached in her handbag and handed over a five pound note to her husband, Ken had also been stopped in his tracks. He was about to ask what Reg meant / what was going on, but the perceptive Ken quickly cottoned on.

" . . . Aaah, I see; you two bet each other we either would or would not mention our mega star of a spook? Sorry, Connie, I lost you a fiver there."

"She wouldn't have done if you had done as you're told, Kenneth Agincourt Snoddie!"

"It's OK, no problem at all," said Connie. "I don't mind talking about my being able to see ghosts, or even just sense them. But the embarrassing thing is, it's only when I'm, well . . . you know . . . when I've had a few. . ."

"And you saw him clear as day?" asked a stunned Ken.

"Yes, sat on the end of the bench; he was as clear to me then as you are to me right now. I am ashamed to say it, in a way, it's the sherry, well, any drink taken in excess. It is all about altered states, frequencies of the mind and so on. It's well-known that animals, some children, and – erm – drunks can perceive the presence of ghosts, even see them, much more than other people. I also saw him running around the pitch as if he belonged there, that's when I screamed."

"Well . . . I suppose he did belong, in a way. . ." said the vicar. "I've been doing a bit of reading up. I am sure it was the ghost of Eric Ramsbottom who collapsed and died as he was about to take a penalty in a match against Manchester United. It was obvious to me once Connie confirmed his presence, that the poor lad thought he was still playing in the same game from all those years ago, same opponents to boot, pardon the pun. Quite fitting really and it also shows why he did not rise when the final prayer was said at the dedication ceremony."

"Oh, why's that, then?" asked Ken.

"The prayer asked for troubled spirits to rise and leave, but – he was not troubled in the least. He was no doubt stuck in limbo due to the suddenness of his exit from this life; happens a lot I am led to believe (Connie nodded to no one in particular when she heard this). Although I know you may choose not to believe in that, but to me, nothing else can explain how he came back – and right now."

His wife screamed – again.

"Figuratively, Connie, figuratively. Dear Lord above, I thought you'd know that! I mean as in this era, and not a year later or ten years later, but, you know . . . now."

"Sorry," said Connie Naismith, while the rest of the dinner party rubbed their ears.

"So if you only asked for troubled spirits to rise, why did he come back at all?" asked a confused Ken.

"I, or rather we, also asked for the ground of olden days to give up its secrets; I am sorry to say that that was a bit of schmaltz I made up myself some time back. I use it if I feel the occasion can take it. It's not authorised by the Bishop but it sounds good; the other clerics had no problem with it and the odd thing is, it actually worked, fancy that. . ." said the refreshingly honest vicar. "But I said a special prayer for him at half time; not an exorcism in the usual sense – poor chap didn't deserve that – just sort of reset the celestial traffic lights to green. I hope you don't mind, but I – er – asked for a little delay of about forty-five minutes as he was playing a blinder. . ."

And once more hearty laughter punctuated the dinner party, and also marked the conclusion of all things spectral on the conversation front; and, as the coffee and mints had been drunk and eaten, it also marked the end of a very good meal. The ladies washed up and the chauvinists retired to the lounge where they moved on to the port.

All too soon it was time for the Naismiths to leave. The taxi arrived and as Reg and Connie tottered out, a slurred return invitation was uttered, something along the lines of, "And fon't d-d-d-dorget, thinner next Dursday . . . eigh-eightyeightyeight – aargh shite on it! By-uurrpp-Hic!–Bye!" said Connie.

"Bye-bye, Eleanor; bye-bye Agincourt!" said the Reverend Naismith with a wink.

47

The Great Big Boot-Room in the Sky

ERIC RAMSBOTTOM, many years late in doing so, finally ascended the golden escalator. When he reached the top, a familiar gathering of radiant smiling faces were there to greet him. His sister Mary Arkwright-nee-Ramsbottom, who had shkaen off her mortal coil at a tragically young age, ran forward and flung her arms around him. His parents and other relatives, some of whom had left a tearful Eric behind when he was very young, waited patiently for Mary to stop strangling her brother – when she had, Eric rushed forward to hug them all.

A little further back in between the shame-faced Weber and Carruthers, stood the Reverend Heath Harrop. The understanding cleric kept the two of them a diplomatic distance from the family reunion, patiently waiting for the right moment to allow the two now enlightened former enemies to offer their sincere apologies. Heath was also biding his time until he could have a little chat with Eric about being the oldest player ever to play in a professional football match – and score a penalty in the dying seconds of the game. . .

Then. . .

"I'll punt 'em. . ." said an old friend with a smile.

"I'll blast 'em. . ." replied Eric.

www.ingramcontent.com/pod-product-compliance
Lightning Source LLC
LaVergne TN
LVHW012049160826
845678LV00014B/2758

* 9 7 9 8 6 6 3 1 8 2 7 2 0 *